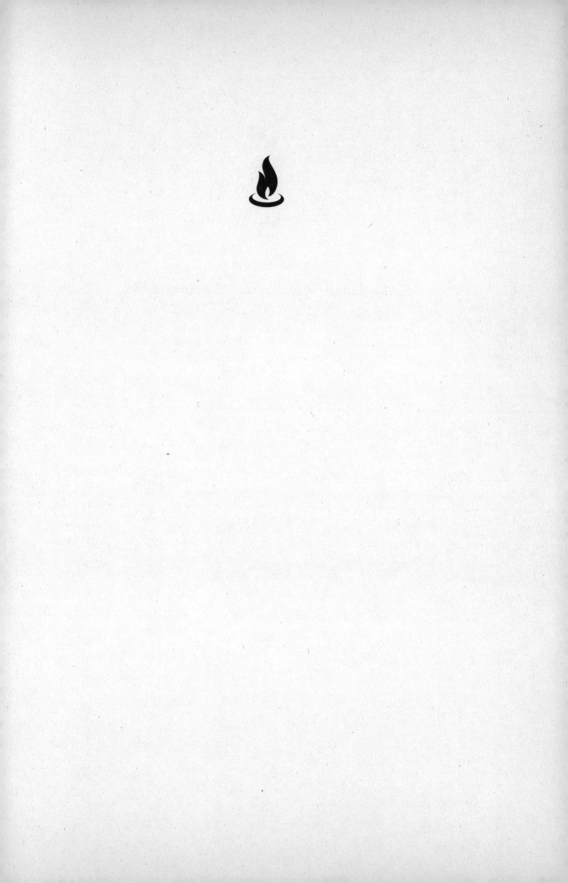

Also by Kate Wenner

Setting Fires

Shamba Letu: An American Girl's Adventure in Africa

Dancing with *Einstein*

A NOVEL

Kate Wenner

SCRIBNER
New York London Toronto Sydney

SCRIBNER
1230 Avenue of the Americas
New York, NY 10020

This book is a work of fiction. Any reference to historical events, real people, or real locales is used fictitiously. Other names, characters, places, and incidents are products of the author's imagination, and any resemblance to actual events or locales or persons, living or dead, is entirely coincidental.

For information about special discounts for bulk purchases, please contact Simon & Schuster Special Sales:
1-800-456-6798 or business@simonandschuster.com

DESIGNED BY ERICH HOBBING

Text set in Adobe Jenson

Manufactured in the United States of America

1 3 5 7 9 10 8 6 4 2

Library of Congress Cataloging-in-Publication Data is available.

Wenner, Kate.
Dancing with Einstein: a novel/Kate Wenner.
p. cm.
1. Nuclear warfare—Psychological aspects—Fiction.
2. Scientists—Family relationships—Fiction. 3. Fathers and daughters—Fiction.
4. Atomic bomb—Fiction. 5. Girls—Fiction. 6. Women—Fiction.
I. Title.
PS3573.E55D36 2004
813'.54—dc22
2003065681
ISBN 0-7432-5164-4

For Gil, Jake, and Sophie,
the treasures of my life

The Peace of Wild Things

When despair for the world grows in me
and I wake in the middle of the night at the least sound
in fear of what my life and my children's lives may be,
I go and lie down where the wood drake
rests his beauty on the water, and the great heron feeds.
I come into the peace of wild things
who do not tax their lives with forethought
of grief. I come into the presence of still water.
And I feel above me the day-blind stars
waiting for their light. For a time
I rest in the grace of the world, and am free.

—Wendell Berry

Dancing with *Einstein*

1

It begins between the thoughts of Marea. Marea, named for the dark seas of the moon. It begins with the token it takes to enter the subway station beneath Union Square, where a solitary woman stands by the tracks, waiting for the trains to cross in front of her. She is waiting for the moment when two passing trains line up so perfectly that she can see through their windows to the other side. It doesn't always happen. It depends on coincidence, timing, and luck. It depends on one train traveling north and another traveling south, crossing at the platform at just the right speed. Sometimes there is so much screeching and banging of metal wheels that it can be difficult to discern the direction from which the trains are actually coming. Marea is keyed up, but patient. Hope rises in her chest when a second train appears. She smiles as the north- and southbound trains begin to cross, their windows shuffling like a deck of cards. Heads blur, gestures drift, and the row of opened newspapers flows into a radiant ribbon of white light.

When the northbound train comes to a stop in the station, Marea steps in to take a seat and opens her subway map to check her destination. She traces the Lexington line and then runs her finger along the other routes, the Broadway local, the A, B, and D, the L traversing Fourteenth Street, the RR, the NN, all weaving over and around each other like brightly colored neon piping, the urban arteries. Marea is happy to enter the map, to enter the world of the subway. She learned very early as a child at a school desk that maps can replace the territories for which they stand. Maps can substitute for places, as travel can substitute for life.

The subway car swaying north rocks Marea into a childhood memory of maps. The immense and imperious Miss Pearl wielded her wooden yardstick like a scepter, whacking it against her huge palm, the slap of flesh curdling the stomachs of the children who sat before her waiting for the promised land of morning recess. The day's lesson was about Pharaohs inbreeding to make morons, Chinese babies preposterously crowned as emperors, Indian children of a caste so vile they could not be touched. Miss Pearl hauled her massive body around the classroom, her chin melting into her neck, her neck sloping into the Matterhorn of her undulating flesh. Sweat made moons below her armpits, and the odor curled nostrils as she handed out tracing paper and boxes of crayons—emerald green to color in the Fertile Crescent, cerulean blue for the Mediterranean Sea, burnt umber for the deserts of Egypt. When Miss Pearl's fleshy hip saddlebagged over the Formica of Marea's desktop, Marea withdrew into the safe territory where her crayoned map replaced the living world.

The lesson in maps, the lesson of one thing standing for another, came in handy on the day Miss Pearl ushered in "our very important visitor from the department of civilian emergencies." A short beetle man with a black pompadour, dark blue suit, and shoes planted like duck feet had brought his own map and climbed up onto a chair to hang it from the hooks above the blackboard. He climbed back down and borrowed Miss Pearl's yardstick to give the third-grade class its instructions for survival. Marea saw that he was uncomfortable with his task of confronting children, and she smiled at him to help ease his pain.

The beetle man settled down to his responsibilities. On his map of the United States he stuck large black plastic dots over each of the major cities from Washington, D.C., to San Francisco. He used Miss Pearl's yardstick to count them off in the order the Russians would destroy them. Then he took a black crayon and drew five concentric circles around each of the targeted East Coast cities. The concentric circles around New York and Washington, D.C., intersected at Princeton, New Jersey, where Marea and her classmates listened silently to the man's grim prediction.

Concentric Circle One would be a huge crater into which all of New York City would disappear before a bird had time to flap its wings. In Concentric Circle Two bodies would melt like ice cream left in the summer sun. In Concentric Circle Three gases would fill lungs with death-breath and people would collapse like rag dolls without bones, and the only hope for life would be to flee in station wagons to Concentric Circles Four and Five. Cars would line up outside Abraham Lincoln Elementary, and good children would be brave and never cry or think about melting mothers and fathers. One by one the station wagons would fill and begin the drive into the western mountains, where children would be given shelter and new parents and, God willing, be saved.

During air-raid drills Miss Pearl stood at the front of the room with her arms folded across her vast breasts. "When we go outside, you will line up nicely, children, even if there is an atomic bomb."

At home Marea kept the lesson of the concentric circles to herself. Her parents fought. Did all parents fight? Maybe, but not all fathers made bombs big enough to blow up the world. Each time her father left to work with Dr. Teller in New Mexico, Marea could hear her mother's crying through the walls at night. Marea wanted to tell her mother how lonely it felt when she got under her school desk to practice for nuclear war, but she knew her mother would blame her father. Her parents argued so much that Marea worried that one day her father might leave forever.

Marea examines the woman seated opposite her in the subway

car, a dreadlock-weighted West Indian who cradles her work shoes wrapped in newspaper in her lap. Through force of will, the woman holds herself erect against tiredness, her eyes glazed and her mind set on dollars to send to children left behind, children with distended tummies, flies feasting on crusted skin sores, a grandmother shaving coconut flesh to feed them while she tells stories of the cold land where white ice drops from heaven and their mother rides on trains that pass beneath the earth. Marea studies this exhausted woman, someone's maid, and cannot keep the woman's sorrow outside her own heart. That is Marea's problem and her life: she feels her way into other people's skin, and her own skin is as thin as moth wings.

Marea's eyes travel to a pair of lovers pressed together against the door between the cars. Teenage girl, mouse-face, shagged hair, pregnant belly pushing at the buttons of her satiny shirt. Her lover, with a dagger tattoo on his cheek, strokes the pale flesh of her neck, hearing his music, not hers. Marea sees the fetus tucked inside a cavity of fluids, eyes protected by unseparated lids, still God's creature, the ropy umbilical cord winding around the cells dividing and redividing with the propulsive force of new life. The pregnant girl cups a hand below her stomach, feeling the weight of this growing thing that will rely on her, a child like herself. When the girl notices the odd woman who is staring at her, she quickly drops her hand to her side.

Marea regrets that she has made the pregnant girl ashamed of what is growing inside her. Marea is her own growing thing. In her jeans pocket she has a folded piece of paper with a name written on it, a name she found in the address book of a man she met in a bar, a man who has generously shared his bed with her for five nights without expecting sex. The name was listed under *S* for shrink. Dr. Angela Iris. Marea called, left a message, got a call back: "Why don't we see what's on your mind?" East Ninety-first Street, between Park and Lex, second floor, Tuesday morning at eleven, ring up.

In the palm of her hand Marea cups the token she bought for

the return trip. It is small enough to lose. Small things—the morning, perspective—can be lost in the bowels of the earth, in tunnels where trains convey bodies, human beings with purposes, human beings surviving. Marea wishes to survive, but she doesn't know if she has the skin for it.

At her stop on the platform at East Eighty-sixth Street Marea hears the sound of a second train coming into the station, and turns back to face the tracks and watch the trains cross. She stands still, traveling only in her heart, until the cars hit the perfect speed and the windows line up and open the way to see through. For those seconds she has no body of her own, no subway platform, no appointment, and then the speeds change again, the crossing windows break up the space, the fog of daily living floats in. But those stilled moments, the moments of seeing through, are the grace she needs to carry on.

Up the stairs and outside Marea breathes in the newness of the sweet summer morning. A street vendor roasting candy-coated peanuts catches her in her pleasure and smiles. Marea weaves into the sidewalk traffic of pale Irish nannies and dark Jamaican maids who navigate baby strollers, their infant charges in a stupor of warmth and movement. On East Ninety-first Street the sidewalks are being hosed down by doormen in uniform. They turn their hoses toward the street to let Marea pass. All around her the June morning has unleashed the city: lives are being lived, money is being made, and Marea is setting forth on the last leg of her journey to retrieve the real thing from the crayoned map of the gossamer world.

Dr. Angela Iris stands at the top of a stairway in a narrow brownstone that is sandwiched between tall buildings. This is her home and office, a place much darker and cooler than the outside street. Dr. Iris's eyes are in shadow, but the light from within her room brightens one side of her face.

"Yes, you've found the right address, Marea Hoffman. Come ahead."

Dr. Iris has settled back into her chair by the time Marea comes through the door at the top of the stairs.

"Please close the door behind you and have a seat," Dr. Iris directs.

Marea stands inside and considers her choices: An upholstered chair on a swivel base, a match to the one into which tiny Dr. Iris is tucked. A wooden chair with a thatched seat and a ladder back, pushed up against a floor-to-ceiling wall of books. A low couch, covered in nubby gray wool with a blanket folded at one end and a tapestry pillow at the other. Marea knows that once you enter a therapist's domain, no choice goes unobserved.

A heavy old-world perfume hangs in the air. The summer is not present in this room that has no season. Dark red velvet curtains keep out light. Thick Persian carpets dull sound. Marea sees that Dr. Iris does not rush people or decisions. She waits as Marea tries to imagine where she would be comfortable, and nods when Marea finally alights as tentatively as a butterfly on the ladder-back chair by the wall.

Dr. Angela Iris, the age of grandmothers, wears a plum-colored blouse and matching calf-length skirt. Her knees are angled to one side, her elbow is on the armrest of her chair, and her bony chin is pressed against her palm. She has fine-penciled eyebrows, high cheeks, gray hair twisted into a bun. Her extravagance is jewelry—long silver earrings, a heavy silver necklace with a jeweled pendant that rests in the small valley between her breasts. Every finger has a silver ring, some black with tarnish. It is clear that she was once beautiful. It is also clear that she has outlived all her men. Wearing blue jeans, a striped T-shirt, and red sneakers, Marea feels as if she comes from a different world.

A standing lamp casts a pool of light over the table beside Dr. Iris's chair, a table that holds a mug, a leather-bound datebook, a collection of ceramic turtles of different sizes and colors. When Dr. Iris sees that Marea's eyes have settled on the turtles, she explains, "Sometimes we need to slow down enough to arrive at our destination."

"I found your name under *S* for shrink."

"Can you tell me why you were looking under *S* for shrink?"

"I came back to the United States a week ago after being away for seven years. I traveled through twenty countries, three continents—seven years of wandering. I'm turning thirty next month. I was afraid if I didn't stop now, I might keep traveling forever."

Dr. Iris cocks her head as if determining something. "But you didn't want to stop."

"I think that's right." Marea's small shoulders round forward, and her thick black hair falls like curtains across her pale cheeks. She had anticipated a different kind of response, more like the judgments her own mother delivered in her letters, always ascribing them to friends. "Is your daughter ever going to settle down?" "Do you suppose she's got some problem she's afraid to tell you?" "How on earth does she support herself? I hesitate to think." "Is she ever going to find a man to marry, have a career of her own—such intelligence, from such a brilliant family—what a pity to let all that promise go to waste."

"My father is a scientist, a nuclear physicist."

"Is he the one who chose your name?"

"You know what it means?"

"The way you pronounce it, I'd guess that it's 'mar,' for sea. If I recall correctly, the marea are the dark seas on the far side of the moon."

"Even when I say my name, people usually still call me Maria."

"It's an unusual name."

"But you knew it."

"My husband was an astronomer. I can tell you more about the skies than you'd want to hear. I got to be quite an amateur astronomer myself."

"I thought therapists never told you about themselves."

"Oh, I've never been very good at rules like that. I don't find them very helpful. You were saying that your father's a scientist."

"I should have said 'was.' My father's dead."

Dr. Iris considers this a moment, such a crucial piece of information misspoken. "Did his death have something to do with why you decided to stop traveling?"

"Is this what therapists do?" Marea challenges from the ladder-back chair. "Keep the conversation on track?"

"Sometimes."

"Maybe his death is why I started traveling."

"So he died when you were in your early twenties."

"Earlier."

"Oh?"

"I was twelve."

Marea had watched him curl his fingers around the bottom of the leather-covered steering wheel. He seemed confused. He should have been in a hurry to be on his way, and yet he didn't move. He was dropping her off at school on his way to the airport, going back again to work with Dr. Edward Teller, the invisible man who stood like a ghost between her parents. Dr. Teller was building bigger and bigger bombs, and Marea's father was helping him.

Marea stole a look into her father's eyes, dark under heavy lids. Through the walls, the night before, she'd heard her parents fight. They had thought she was asleep, but it was hard for her to sleep when she knew her father was leaving in the morning. Her father had been standing outside the door to her mother's bedroom, the room her parents once shared. How long ago had her mother folded his clothes into the bureau in the spare bedroom across the hall and put a lock on the door of her own room? Marea couldn't recall, but maybe her father's banishment was her fault. Her mother blamed her father for frightening their only child with "this wretched work" of his. But Marea had never been frightened of the gentle father who showed her how nature lived in the forest. Whenever he was home, they walked through the Institute Woods to gather specimens for their collections. Butterflies were their specialty, and by now Marea could identify nearly every one they saw. He laughed when they walked outside, but when they came back into the house, he grew silent again. Marea had wanted to explain to her mother that it wasn't her father's fault that Dr. Teller was making bombs. Marea had wanted to tell her mother that she shouldn't be angry if Dr. Teller made her father help him.

Her father's shirt collar was unbuttoned, collar points askew, his red hair barely combed. It was early morning, and the low sun was stuck behind gray clouds. There was activity all around their car, children hopping out of the back seats of station wagons in front of them, swinging metal lunch boxes and meeting up with friends. Inside, behind their windshield, it was quiet. He took her hand and kissed it gently, then turned away. Marea waited for him to turn back to her. Did he know it would be the last time, her last memory to hold?

"My father was part of the Manhattan Project during World War II. He helped design the mechanism that fired the bomb's detonators. When the war was over, they wanted him to stay and work on the development of the hydrogen bomb, but he said no. I don't know how it happened, because my mother was dead set against it, but at some point Edward Teller got my father to change his mind and come back to work for him. At first he went back to Los Alamos to work with Teller, and when Teller moved to California, my father traveled out there on a regular basis. My parents were friendly with Albert Einstein at that time because my father's office at the Institute for Advanced Studies was on the same floor as Einstein's. Einstein and my mother both tried to convince my father that he was making a terrible mistake working on the development of the hydrogen bomb."

"Your family knew Albert Einstein?"

"I called him Grandpa Albert. He would come to our house for Sunday dinner a lot. Since my real grandparents were all gone, when I called him grandpa one day, it just stuck."

"Do you remember much about him?"

"Of course. We used to play together. He liked to do puzzles and play with toys. And he was nuts for the professor character on *Your Show of Shows*. Sometimes he would come over on Saturday night, and I got to stay up late so we could watch together. We used to sit on the couch watching Sid Caesar and howling."

"Tell me what you thought about your father's work. As a child were you aware of what he did? Did it upset you as it upset them?"

Marea feels a flash of anger toward this prim woman seated so calmly in front of her.

"You don't have to answer me, Marea. Many questions are asked without needing answers."

"I found your name in an address book. How do I know I can trust you?"

"You don't. Certainly not yet."

"Then what's the point?"

"I assume you came here for a reason."

"I thought you could help me."

"What would you like help with?"

"Once when I was quite young Einstein gave me a compass as a present. He told me about his first compass and how it started him thinking about the magic of the universe. When he gave me my compass, he explained that what it did was make an invisible force of nature apparent to the human eye. And then he told me that I also had a compass inside my heart, and if I could learn to feel it, it would help me know what direction to go. If that's true, I haven't learned to feel the force of it. I don't understand how people know what direction to go in, when to stay where they are, when to move on, when to stay for good. I don't know the answers to any of that. I can turn myself in any direction and walk on, because it doesn't seem to matter."

"I imagine it must feel frightening at times to be so adrift."

"I'm not sure how I'm going to pay you."

"I don't suppose you're working yet."

"No, but yesterday I called about a job making bread in a health food bakery in Greenwich Village. I'm going for an interview this afternoon."

"Why don't we talk about what you're going to pay me once you find out your salary for making bread?"

"Do therapists do that?"

"Do what?"

"Let people come even if they have no money?"

"Sometimes, when they're intrigued. We'll meet again next Tuesday at eleven."

Marea gets up to leave, but finds that standing feels like swaying in a wind, while Dr. Iris sits securely anchored. Marea wraps her hand around her wrist, and the feel of her woven bracelets beneath her fingers reminds her of the Incan woman who tied them on for her in a street market in Quito. Even though she has come home, she can still touch her travels.

Bread dough, Marea is advised, must be treated as lovingly as babies' bums. Andrew Martin, baker and owner of Dawn's Early Rising, has a body as tall and thin as a cornstalk, and straight, corn-silk hair. His eyes are bright blue, and his smile is easy and uncomplicated. A man in his late twenties, Marea guesses, who takes his time with his words.

Andrew and Marea are perched on stools on opposite sides of the work counter in the middle of the kitchen. The bakery is a small storefront on Greenwich Avenue, on a block that runs diagonally between Tenth and Charles Streets. The kitchen's back door is propped open to an alley with ceramic pots holding gangly geraniums and overgrown herbs. The alley wall has a mural of the Milky Way, the sun and the planets—Saturn and its rings, Jupiter and its moons.

As master of his own universe, Andrew bakes only whole grain breads with only the very best organic molasses and honey, and never uses refined sugar or bleached flour. Marea listens to these details as Andrew shares his love of bread baking. In the late afternoon his ovens are cold, and Andrew sits with his limbs folded like a stork's, one long leg bent back under the other, as he sips cold mint tea.

He offers Marea his personal history before asking hers. He was most recently a two-year resident of a utopian experiment in Tennessee, and before that he had been a gardening apprentice at a self-sustaining spiritual community called Findhorn in Scotland.

"By the way, I'm gay, in case that bothers you."

Marea shakes her head. "In my limited experience, gay men are a lot more fun than straight men and usually nicer than straight women."

"I'll try not to disappoint."

"So how did you learn to bake?"

"My first assignment on the farm in Tennessee was making soy milk, but I kept letting it turn to yogurt. I think I identify with things that need to go through a process of fermentation. When I found yeast and bread, I found my true happiness. I'm a ruminator. Things take time to grow in me. You see, you can't be in a hurry with bread. I've never managed to hurry anything. Probably I got dropped on my head when I was a baby. Something like that, for sure."

They both laugh, and Andrew gets up to fill their glasses with more tea from the gallon jar where he keeps it brewing.

"How come you left your communal farm if you were happy baking bread there?"

Andrew settles back on his stool and flips his long blond hair away from his shoulders.

"I got tired of being stoned all the time. Smoking dope was a sacrament there, morning, noon, and night. It definitely cut down on the arguments, but my mind started to feel like pumice. Anyway, I'm from Ohio. I wanted to be a real American, start a business, build something of my own and contribute to the world. I like the pronoun 'I.' On the farm there was only 'we.' I wanted to speak in the first-person singular and not worry that I had offended someone."

Marea shakes her head. "You're funny."

"Funny funny or funny weird?"

"Oh, definitely funny weird. I have to confess something. I know absolutely nothing about baking."

"Are you in a hurry?"

"Wish I was."

"And do you have a ruminating mind?"

"Afraid so."

"Sounds like we're a match. No yin and yang in a bakery. It doesn't work."

"I'm going to have some appointments during the days. Can I work nights?"

"Nights are when I need you." He points through the kitchen door to the storefront window where the name of his bakery can be read in reverse. "Bread makes its entrance with the dawn. Can you be back here at eight tonight? Wear shorts. It gets brutal when the stoves are fired up."

"You don't need to know anything else about me?"

"I know that you laugh, and I can tell that you're honest. That's enough for me."

Marea feels light as she walks down Christopher Street. At the newsstand in Sheridan Square she purchases a copy of the *Village Voice,* and then settles down on a bench in the shade of Christopher Park to scan the classified ads for a place to live. That morning as she was leaving for her appointment with Dr. Iris, the man who had shared his bed with her for the previous five nights had called after her, "What time should I expect you back?"

With half a dozen possibilities circled in the newspaper, Marea changes a dollar for dimes and closes herself into a telephone booth on Seventh Avenue. This is the first time she's looked for a home of her own in seven years. The last time she paid rent was for the apartment she shared with three roommates in her senior year at Barnard. One by one they had all left before the end of school. One roommate followed her boyfriend to Canada, where he'd gone to escape the draft. Another roommate had taken a midnight bus to San Francisco, leaving a note on the kitchen table saying that anything anybody wanted from her room they should take since she wouldn't be needing possessions anymore. The third roommate was ordered back to Utah by her Mormon parents after she'd been arrested for taking her shirt off in an antiwar demonstration in Central Park. Marea was the last one to go and had no one to say good-bye to on the afternoon she bought a backpack, filled it with a few essentials and her passport, withdrew all her money from her bank account, and set off by bus to Mexico. Her only plan consisted of a direction—south. She informed Barnard that she would not be attending graduation, and she made no arrangement to pick up her diploma. At a bus station in St. Louis, she telephoned her mother to say she had decided to go traveling, though she didn't say where she was planning to go or when she would be coming back.

On East Second Street, on a block where a row of discarded sofas is home to a crew of strung-out hippies and bottle-sack bums, Marea knocks at the basement door of a nondescript three-story apartment building. The super leads her up the stairs to the top floor and unlocks a studio apartment, one narrow room with a grime-covered window looking out onto courtyards shared by surrounding tenements. There is a bare mattress on the floor, a single gooseneck lamp, a hot plate, tin shower stall, sink, toilet. The apartment walls have been newly painted with a thin whitewash. Marea is drawn into the whiteness of the room, a place to be in the world but not of it.

She pockets her new key and goes to retrieve her backpack from the locker at the YMCA on Fourteenth Street. She had stashed it there the previous Thursday after arriving by Greyhound from Montreal. Flying to Montreal had been the cheapest way to cross the Atlantic from London, where she had been holed up in a squatters' flat in Stoke Newington, sharing cold cereal, blankets, and joints with an ever-changing group of ageless, wordless types. Some lived there to make a political statement. Others were drug casualties. A few were certifiably insane. Marea came and went from the squat for eight months as she made forays into the north and to Scotland, Ireland, and Wales.

When she lifts the heavy backpack out of the YMCA locker, hefts it onto her back, and fits one arm and then the other through the worn shoulder straps, she feels an acute relief at reclaiming a part of her physical self. Inside her backpack are the seashells, chunks of coral, tufts of coconut hair, bits of quartz, dried flowers, and stones she has collected in her years of traveling. It is her store of evidence that the physical world is organized by reliable principles. Molecular structures determine the patterns of crystalline growth. All animals, even those in the sea, require protective housing. The reproductive urge at the center of life can be seen even in the stem and stamen of plant anatomy. These were the rules her father taught her as he showed her nature in its exquisite particularity. Even now she can recall the feel of his soft hand around hers, and how his step and voice grew quiet to avoid frightening away a bird or animal with the presence of a human intruder. The memories of being with him in the Institute Woods, of standing at his side, are still her greatest happiness.

On the way back to East Second Street, Marea stops at a discount store and buys a set of sheets, and soap and a sponge to scrub the grimy window. Inside her new white room she strips down and takes a cold shower in the tin stall. Dripping wet and still nude, she unpacks her traveling treasures and lays them out on the wooden floor. She spaces out the items, a trained naturalist with reverence for plant and animal life. With her collection laid out, her bed made up, and the clean window letting in the afternoon sun, she feels the pride of ownership. This will be her home for as long as she can manage it.

Later that night, at Dawn's Early Rising, the long hours pass quietly, Andrew and Marea each at work at their separate tasks. Marea sifts buckets of flour, cracks dozens of eggs, greases rows of blackened bread pans. Andrew patiently demonstrates each new assignment and then assumes Marea will continue on her own. At last, when the long night's work is done, Marea steps out into the purple-blue dawn and enjoys an unaccustomed sense of purpose. Trudging back through quiet streets, she examines this new sense of purpose, as she has been in the habit, as long as she can recall, of examining everything.

As she crosses Washington Square Park on the diagonal path,

she hears a violin playing into the quiet morning and recognizes Mozart. Marea has no particular aptitude for music, has never studied an instrument, but has a deep regard for anyone who does. It was one of Grandpa Albert's most adamant lessons, that music is a source of happiness. He would unpack his violin, tuck it under his chin, and his eyes would drift closed with the pleasure of being reunited with his true love. Afterward they would sit in the small living room in the brick house on Blossom Street, Marea, her father, and her Grandpa Albert, while her mother worked in the kitchen finishing up the last preparations for their Sunday supper. Marea would crouch on the rug and try to solve the riddle of a new wooden puzzle her grandpa had brought her, while above her head the two men spoke in their peculiar language of time and light and a bending universe. In these early years of their friendship, there were no arguments, and it was only when they all sat down at the table that the conversation turned to world events. That was another language Marea had to try to understand. Without knowing the meaning of all the words, she listened to the melody of it. The room filled with the talk and laughter that was missing when she had her meals alone with her parents. When Marea climbed into her Grandpa Albert's lap, it was because she hoped that with her arms anchored around his waist, he wouldn't be able to leave. But then she would wake up in her bed in the dark and know she had failed her watch, and that she and her parents were alone again.

In the late afternoon, Marea wakes into her white room. It takes some moments to know what city she is in, where she slept, how she got there. She is accustomed to this process of waking and getting her bearings, accustomed to getting up in the night and not knowing the direction of the bathroom, accustomed to searching for the sounds and smells that will situate her. Once she realizes that it is June, that she has returned to America and has a job as a baker's assistant, that this room is paid for and hers, she relaxes between her new sheets and luxuriates in the warm summer air coming through the window. From someone else's open window she can hear the plaintive tune of "Eleanor Rigby." The song penetrates Marea's skin, and she rolls onto her side, pulling her knees to her chest. She is used to sadness coming like that, like a breath.

Into sadness and out of sadness. The ache in the arches of her feet brings back the pleasures of her night's work, the rows of loaves resting in their pans like a nursery ward of babies sleeping in their bassinets.

Dropping her head over the edge of the mattress, Marea checks the classified listings in the *Village Voice* that lies open on the floor. The night before she found a page with the heading "Getting Better All the Time." Now she reads through the alphabetized listings: *A* for Arica, *E* for EST, *F* for Feminist and Freudian, G for Gestalt and Group. Hydro, Jungian, Transactional, Yogic. Has she made a mistake, committing to Dr. Angela Iris, a name from a stranger's address book?

For seven years Marea has made decisions on the slightest whim, but lately she has begun to feel anxious about the passage of time. Her thirtieth birthday is only weeks away, and she has the notion that whoever she is and wherever she is on that date will determine her fate. Will she continue to drift—or will she finally find some mooring to call home?

Every year of her travels Marea has dutifully telephoned home on her birthday. The calls have been an effort to be considerate of her mother. Their relationship has never been easy. Marea didn't blame her mother for her father's death, but on the day he died something between them came apart and was never repaired.

In each of these annual birthday calls Marea's mother has grown more insistent on her recommendation that Marea go into therapy. This is not because Virginia particularly believes in therapy, but because it is what experts and other mothers have advised her is the best way to help such an aimless child. Marea knows that in her heart her mother believes in willpower, not therapy. After all, it was willpower that got her through the dark days after her husband's fatal car crash. She had no time to mourn, as she told

Marea many times, a point of pride or perhaps resentment. To supplement her husband's pension and support her daughter and herself, Virginia chose to tutor the children of her middle-class friends and neighbors. Her dining room table was stacked high with every textbook used in the Princeton public schools, and Marea shared long afternoons with the students her mother triumphantly saved from failure.

Marea tears out a listing from the *Village Voice,* though she knows her mother would never consider the *Village Voice* an appropriate place to find a therapist, no more appropriate than the address book of a man picked up in a bar. According to the advertisement, as part of its training program the New York Psychoanalytic Institute is offering psychoanalysis free of charge to qualified candidates. Interviews required, minimum commitment of one year.

It was the word "institute" that caught Marea's eye. An institute suggests permanence, a place that predates its present members and will outlive them. The Princeton Institute for Advanced Study had predated its star, Albert Einstein, and had long outlived both Einstein and Marea's father.

Marea remembers one spring afternoon when she slipped out of her father's office and went quietly down the thick-carpeted corridors to the office where Grandpa Albert worked, often with nothing but a pencil and a pad. Whenever she came to visit, he would be staring out the window, or gazing off into space, or at the wall. Was he lonely sitting there all by himself? He never seemed to mind when she appeared alongside his desk, waiting for him to pat his thigh, the invitation for her to climb into his lap. Even though she was almost six years old now, his lap was still one of her favorite places to be.

"My young professor, what is it you have to report of your fine observations of human nature?" His words smelled of pipe tobacco as she leaned back against the scratchy wool of his sweater.

"A boy at my school says scientists can't believe in God."

"What a very big subject for a Friday afternoon."

"He's wrong, because if God didn't make the world, scientists wouldn't have anything to study."

"Perhaps this young fellow is imagining a God who sits on a throne and has a long white beard. I do not know if such a gentleman had so much to do with the creation of the universe. When scientists imagine God, they think of a mystery, something very special that cannot be explained."

Her father was at the door. He knew where to look for her whenever she slipped out of his office. He would scold her for bothering Professor Einstein while he was working, but Marea knew her father liked the excuse to come down the hall himself. Then Marea got to listen to their funny conversations. Once Grandpa Albert insisted that if a spacecraft could travel fast enough, the man inside wouldn't have to shave because he'd return from his voyage before he left.

"Marea, why are you disturbing Professor Einstein?"

"Marea has brought us a question to discuss."

"We're talking about God," Marea said importantly.

Jonas Hoffman leaned against the doorjamb. "God?"

"Marea wants to know if you can be a scientist and still believe in God."

"I know you can," Marea said. "It was stupid Alfie Martin. He says his father is an atheist, that smart people *have* to be atheists. I think Alfie wanted to show off that he could say a big word."

"What do you say, Jonas? Can a scientist believe in God?"

Marea saw her father drift away to his sadness, and she felt bad, as she always did when his mouth tightened and his eyes looked far away. "Alfie Martin is stupid," she declared.

Einstein put his finger to Marea's cheek. "A scientist sees the proof of God in every squirrel and rose." He turned to Jonas. "But God's existence is more difficult to believe when we examine the affairs of man."

The following Sunday when Grandpa Albert came for supper, he brought Marea a puzzle to work out, an assortment of colored blocks that had to be arranged into a perfect cube. They worked on the puzzle together alone in the living room while her mother finished cooking supper. Her father had driven off early that morning to a faraway place called New Mexico, where he would work for the rest of the summer. Before he left he had spread out the map to show Marea exactly where he would be, and he promised to send picture postcards of cactuses as tall as three-story buildings. Marea had stood at the end of the driveway long after her mother had gone back inside the house. When Marea had asked why they weren't all going together, her parents had looked at each other and waited to see which one would explain.

The smells of roasting chicken and baking pie wafted from the kitchen as Marea leaned against her Grandpa Albert and watched him contemplate the colored blocks. Marea didn't want to be doing a puzzle. She wanted to be with her father, driving to a magical place with giant cactuses and Indian mothers with papooses on their backs. Marea went to the piano and lifted the keyboard lid. With her index finger she tapped on the highest notes, pleasing herself with the tinkling sound they made and looking out of the corner of her eye to see if her grandpa was watching. When he continued moving the colored blocks around, trying out one combination and another, she used both her fists to pound the keyboard until Einstein threw up his hands and barked at her, "You must stop that awful sound!"

"Play me a song," Marea demanded.

"I will play something my ears can stand!"

Triumphantly, Marea flopped down on the piano bench, leaving room for her grandpa to sit beside her. He was a stomping bear at the piano, not soft as he was with his violin beneath his chin. Now he threw his whole body into the oompah-pah of the "Merry Widow Waltz," and his sandals slapped the pedals. "Get up, get up!" he ordered Marea off the piano bench. "Go dancing!"

Obediently, Marea marched around the room, swinging her arms like the leader of a band.

"This is not dancing!" Einstein exclaimed, and pushed back the piano bench. "Like this, my silly princess." He held out his hands to her. "Oompah-pah, oompah-pah," he sang as he swung her hands in his, and then he set out spinning her around the room. They sang together, louder and louder, and as they raised their feet high and pounded the floor, Marea forgot all about her father's car disappearing into the silent Sunday morning. But then Einstein stopped and flattened his hand against his heart. Breathing heavily, he told Marea that he had to sit down. He dropped onto the living room couch, tipped back his head, closed his eyes, and in a little while he was snoring.

Marea stepped in close to examine the dark creases in his long face and the sunken wells around his eyes that were as deep and dark as pitted plums. She studied the shape of his nose with its small round bulb at the end, the hair that curled around his long ears. Though she knew people called him the father of the atomic bomb, she had never told him about her nightmare of atomic bombs dropping out of an airplane like a mother cat giving birth to black kittens. She never told him about the dream that came back again and again and made her cry, her dream of waking up after an atomic bomb and being the only person left alive. Marea loved her Grandpa Albert, and she knew it was wrong to make people feel bad about their mistakes.

With her first week's wages as a baker's assistant Marea purchases a tailored skirt, blouse, and leather flats, an outfit she hopes will make the right impression at the New York Psychoanalytic Institute. She has interviewed for jobs all over the world—for work as a typist, nanny, store clerk, fish scaler, English tutor, and a hundred different jobs that earned her money to reach her next destination—but she has never before interviewed to tell the story of her short life.

On a couch huddled between arching ficus trees, using a pen attached by a string, Marea fills out an application on a clipboard. She knows how to exaggerate her typing speed and previous experience, how to construct the picture of herself that will land the job. But this application to be a candidate for psychoanalysis asks for something more mystifying—the description of a self worthy of examination and repair.

"State your reasons for seeking psychoanalytic treatment at this time."

In careful script, Marea writes, "My father died in a car accident when I was twelve. He was an unhappy man, and I've always wondered if he might have killed himself. I have never known how to find out the truth. My mother would never discuss his death with me or with anyone else, as far as I know. I am an only child. I have no one else to ask, and no one to share my speculation. My father helped make the first atomic bomb. He worked with men like Robert Oppenheimer and Edward Teller. I was born the day they tested the bomb for the first time. My father saw the birth of the bomb in 1945, but he didn't see my birth. I'm not sure how to describe my problem. I have not been able to form lasting attachments to other people or to work—even to a place. I know there is something wrong, but I don't know what name to give it. I guess if I did I wouldn't need psychoanalysis."

In answer to the question "Have you ever had any form of psychotherapy before or are you currently engaged in treatment?" Marea reflects for a moment and then writes, "No."

The woman at the reception desk disappears behind a closed door with Marea's application, comes back empty-handed, and replaces the earpiece attached to her dictating machine. Marea surmises that it is her job to transcribe the notes from the psychoanalysts' sessions with their patients. Marea sees her pleasure in judging their troubled lives. Her brown polyester pantsuit is too tight for her fleshy body, and the platform she constructs for herself above humanity is too high. When she falls off, she will shatter into a million polyester pieces.

Marea skims through the cover story of *Time* magazine, "The Poisoning of America." Modern-day alchemists are brewing a thousand new chemical compounds each year, fifty thousand currently on the market, thirty-five thousand of them classified by the Environmental Protection Agency as hazardous to human health.

She studies the photograph of dairy farmer Emmett Johnson, his frightened family squeezed together on their living room couch. The smallest child holds a framed photograph of their missing member, his younger sister, recently dead of kidney cancer. The rest of them have failing kidneys, too. They have drunk well-water laced with poisons leaching from a corporate dump a mile from their farm. Their eyes are all similarly stunned by the photographer's flash. What they share there on the sofa, besides their riddled livers, is the knowledge that they will all be departing soon. They are all waiting for the same train, at the same stop.

When Marea looks up, she sees a man holding a door open, looking for the woman he is to interview. He is short and slight and has the curly hair of Verrocchio's *Boy with Fish*. He looks uncertain, but earnest. He wears the young professional's uniform of the day—a yellow button-down Oxford cloth shirt, pressed blue jeans, flowered tie. He could be older than Marea or younger, it's hard for her to tell. He is carrying a manila file under his arm, her application.

Seeing Marea, he makes his smile friendly but official, practicing what he's been taught. He doesn't want to make mistakes, and to the three of them involved in this encounter—the candidate for psychoanalysis, the psychoanalyst-in-training, and the middle-aged receptionist with the wire in her ear—the territory of possible mistakes is obvious. Marea is a beautiful woman, slender, with sleek dark hair and jade green eyes. There is a tentativeness about her, and almost nothing in the way of protective armor. The psychoanalyst-in-training is shy, not the sort who has ever known how to be casual with women.

"Marea? Have I pronounced it correctly?"

"Yes, that's right. Are you my doctor?"

"I'm Colin Ross. Dr. Ross. Would you please come in?"

"Am I accepted?"

"We're going to take a few minutes to talk first."

As Marea's new skirt rustles past, the receptionist barely suppresses a smirk.

Marea follows Colin Ross down a hallway of heavy wooden doors and imagines lives being unraveled behind each one of them. The walls are hung with portraits in gilt frames, a gallery of Freud's men, the pioneers of the psyche. Near the end of the corridor, Dr. Ross opens a door and waits for Marea to pass by him into the room.

There is nothing personal here, not a photograph or memo pad or eyeglass case. The shelves are filled with leather-bound books. There is a large, ornate desk, and behind it a high-backed throne of a chair. Once again Marea faces a choice: the small armless chair in front of the desk, or the long couch pressed up against the wall, leather with carved wooden arms that curve inward to enclose anyone bold enough to lie there.

They look at one another, momentarily stalled, until Colin Ross points Marea to the small chair in front of the desk and makes his own way to the throne behind it.

"I thought I was supposed to lie down," Marea says to help her psychoanalyst-in-training.

"First we'll talk a little here," he says, pointing toward the desk.

She looks around the room, then back at him. "This feels like a blind date. Are we supposed to figure out if we're compatible?"

"I'd like to ask you a few questions."

Marea adjusts herself, fitting one knee over the other, taking the pose of a woman interviewing for a job.

"I can type, but I can't spell very well, and I'm fairly pleasant to have around. Actually I can be quite funny at times. I bet it's pretty boring being a psychoanalyst if the patient never makes any jokes."

Dr. Ross looks down at the manila file he's spread open on the desk. "I read through your application. I was impressed with your honesty. I need to ask you, though, is psychoanalysis a commitment you feel prepared to make?"

"Am I being too sarcastic?"

"It's important that you understand the nature of the commitment you're undertaking."

"How could I? I've never done this before."

"Sometimes psychoanalysis can feel meaningless. There isn't always a steady sense of progress."

"As a matter of fact, I'm quite used to meaninglessness."

He waits for her to say more.

"That's why I came here."

"There's another issue I need to go over with you. I want to be sure you realize that your analysis will be part of my training."

"They made that clear in the advertisement."

"I understand, but what are your feelings about it?"

"It's not surgery, right? You can't exactly leave a sponge inside me."

He smiles, the first spontaneous response Marea has elicited from him. "That's true," he agrees, "we won't be performing surgery."

"Will that woman be transcribing what I tell you?"

"Only a summary."

"I got the feeling she's collecting characters for her screenplay, 'The Dark and Dangerous Psyche.'"

Colin stiffens. "I hope you understand that my being a student doesn't make this any less important."

"Sure, of course," Marea agrees.

"There's one last question I'd like to ask you. What do you think you'd like to take away from here after the year is over?"

The reminder that he expects a one-year commitment torpedoes her. She looks past him, to the large framed mirror that tilts slightly off the wall behind the desk.

"Is something wrong?"

She shakes her head.

"You look troubled about something."

"It's just that a year seems like a long time to do this."

"Some psychoanalysis takes five years, even ten."

"When people are really screwed up."

"Not necessarily. Psychoanalysis is like making a painting or writing a novel. Only the artist or the writer can say for sure when the work is done."

"Who's the artist, you or me?"

"Back to my question, if you don't mind. Do you have an idea of what you'd like to take away from here?"

"This probably isn't the sort of thing you have in mind, but I'd like to feel a force like gravity pulling me toward some kind of desire or other. I'm sorry I can't come up with anything more specific than that. Listen, it's okay if you don't think you can work with me."

"I don't feel that way at all," he answers quickly.

"Will you get your degree or whatever it is you need to get even if I'm a failure at psychoanalysis?"

He smiles once again. "You can't be a failure at psychoanalysis, not in that way."

"I wouldn't want to think your future depended on me."

"Why don't we let my future be my responsibility?"

"What's next, then?"

"We set up a regular schedule of appointments, a minimum of two sessions a week, preferably three if your time allows." He points toward the couch. "Next session you lie down. We'll get started and see where things go."

"Do they observe us?" Marea points to the mirror behind him. She can imagine his teachers on the other side, old men dissecting his performance.

"Can you manage ten o'clock, Mondays, Wednesdays, and Fridays?"

"I can manage Mondays and Wednesdays," she says, gently mocking his determination to stick to his script.

"Then I'll look forward to seeing you next Monday."

"I'm sorry if—"

"Don't worry. We're going to do fine."

As soon as she's out the door, down the hall, past the receptionist, and back out on Sixty-sixth Street, Marea is overcome with the childish hope that Dr. Colin Ross liked her.

Instead of riding back downtown on the Lexington line to return to her white room until baking time, Marea crosses over to the northbound side of the platform and takes her subway map from her shoulder bag to see if it's possible to follow the contour of Manhattan and make a full circle underground. If she takes the Number 6 to 161st Street, she can cross over to the B or D going south, and then get off at West Fourth for a short walk back to East Second Street. The idea intrigues her, and there is nothing else she has to do right now. If she completes the circle, following the neon piping of the map, she will hold the whole island of Manhattan in her imagination.

At five-thirty the northbound IRT coming into the East Eighty-sixth Street station is packed with commuters. Marea steps aside as they pour out from the open doors, and then watches as people waiting on the platform press ahead without any doubt that the dense crowd still left inside will take them in. Marea cannot will herself forward and she remains standing alone as the doors close and the train departs. The platform is empty for a few moments, until new commuters course through the turnstiles. At the end of the platform a clarinetist plugs her instrument into a portable amplifier. The soothing melody of Randy Newman's "Sail Away" fills the tunnels. People lift their heads to the sound, as if tracking the scent of sweeter air. When the next train arrives, metal wheels screeching, Marea steps ahead to join the herd.

The humid summer heat has passengers in a languid stupor, bare limbs everywhere, jutting at angles like a Cubist painting. Since the train is traveling north into Harlem, most of the limbs are black, and Marea's thoughts drift to the black man with silken thighs she made love with in the Moshi Business Traveler's Hotel, as clouds fell in rings around the broad base of Mount Kilimanjaro. In the morning, twisted in sheets, their slight bodies were beautiful in their stark difference, hers pale white, his the darkest umber. They had laid eyes on each other the afternoon before at a volleyball game organized by Peace Corps volunteers teaching at Moshi Region Secondary School. After the game Marea and the school's slim-hipped mathematics teacher drifted toward each another. "My wife has gone into the bush to see her mother." For three nights and three days they were together in a room, and they could not exist together beyond it. When it was time to part—his wife had returned—Marea took away from her sweet teacher of mathematics one of the best gifts she had ever been given. She had no more fear of black skin. Her fear had evaporated with their sweat.

The door slams open between the cars. A beggar who is a stump on a board with roller-skate wheels pushes his way through, and sleigh bells attached to the four corners of his board herald his arrival. He has no legs; his buttocks are the end and root of him. He uses his large hands as paddles to pull himself forward. There is a sign hanging around his neck on a string: "Don't ask me details. I don't need your compassion. I need food." The crowd parts to make a path—there but for the grace of God go I—and the beggar rolls along, accepting coins dropped into his paper cup, without requiring eye contact. Marea digs out the remainder of her first week of bread-making money and stuffs it into his cup. Startled by her generosity, the beggar brakes in front of her. She smells his greasy hair matted with sweat, his body stinking of urine. The sleeves of his army fatigue jacket are torn off, revealing biceps that are huge from the work they do to move him. A bronze medal hangs from a red-white-and-blue ribbon pinned to his breast pocket.

"Vietnam," he tells her, looking up from the level of her knees.

His eyes are dull, and Marea sees that his life took a wrong turn. He was supposed to become a biologist or a playwright. He was supposed to have children, not stumps.

"Doesn't the government help you?"

"Only if I stay in their home for vets. And then I have to listen to the screaming all night long. I have enough nightmares of my own."

"But you wouldn't have to beg."

"I don't mind begging. It's a job, like any other. Riding the trains all day rattles my bones, but no one runs away here."

"They run away from a vet?"

"They ran away from Vietnam."

The train slows into the 125th Street station. The beggar knows his stops. "Got to cross over," he explains. "No money uptown." He drops his head to get momentum, and wheels out.

At midnight the bakery is peaceful, an island unto itself, lights aglow and full of the luscious smell of baking bread. Andrew is busy sifting pounds of rye flour while yeast dissolves and grows in a ceramic crock. Marea is perched on a tall stool, hunched over a project of cleaning caraway seeds. It satisfies her to ferret out tiny stones and bits of dry hull. She is pleasing herself and also pleasing Andrew, who wants every ingredient he puts into his breads to be blessed with loving attention. Each new task he assigns Marea comes with a lesson in its true purpose. He tells Marea to think of the preparation of caraway seeds as prayer, to recognize that food is a link in the chain of creation that unites God and man.

Andrew is often taciturn as he works, ruminating, as he first explained to her, over each choice he makes. In the quiet Marea has hours to follow the tributaries of her own thoughts.

"You don't measure?" Marea asks when Andrew pours molasses from a square tin into a large bowl of beaten eggs. The metal sides of the tin contract, making the sound of a distant gong as the yellow sea of foamy eggs takes in the cataract of black molasses.

"I measure. I just don't count."

"But if there are no set amounts, how can I learn the recipes?"

"Marea, all recipes are God's. God will guide your hand."

She shakes her head in mock despair. She has encountered spacey New Age types all over the world and knows their maddening self-containment.

"Maybe God will publish a cookbook."

"All right, all right. Come over here."

Marea pushes back from her caraway seeds and walks over to the bench where Andrew has lined up his ingredients. She has known him only a week, but since they have spent hours working through long nights, they are already comfortable friends. He puts his arm around her shoulder to show her the mixture, his warm hand on her bare skin.

"See that?"

"See what?"

"See the world in there, the world becoming?"

"Honestly, Andrew, I see eggs, oil, and molasses."

"Come on. You don't see the hope, the expectation? Go on, look deeper."

"What did they do to you at Findhorn? Lend your brain to extraterrestrial visitors for experiments?"

Andrew shakes his head at her. "I don't know why I bother."

"Because I'm charming, and if you weren't gay, you'd want to marry me."

Andrew points to a spot at the end of his bench. "How about you sit down and watch." He opens his hand, palm and fingers flat like a stop sign. "Don't do anything, don't say anything, don't *think* anything. Don't let your busy little mind go clickity-clack."

"Yes, my swami." Marea sinks down where she's been told.

The radio is playing John Coltrane. Before continuing with his mixture, Andrew presses a fist into the small of his back and arches his body to relieve an ache. He flips aside his ponytail so he can rub the tendons of his neck, and then he bends toward the dish towel tucked into his cotton pants to wipe his face. As always, he works with no shirt, and his skin glistens from the heat of the ovens. Marea has met Andrew's lover, Tim, a high school English teacher with doe-eyes and a flat Kentucky drawl. She likes the way they are together, the way they rest their hands on each other's shoulders, hips touching. Marea has watched them, studying their happiness.

Andrew slides a wooden paddle into the bowl of ingredients to mix the liquids together. Marea is silent as she observes the molasses folding into the eggs. She gathers herself up in a ball on the bench, and pulls her knees to her chest.

"Can I ask you something?"

"Will the answer help you become a better baker?"

"Have you ever seen a shrink?"

"Once, when my parents wanted to see if I could be cured of my homosexuality."

"Oh? What happened?"

"The guy was gay. My parents didn't know. Or maybe they did know. Who knows what parents know? Anyway, he didn't cure me of being gay. He cured me of caring what my parents thought about it."

"So it was a good thing."

"Sure. Talking helps."

Andrew crosses to check on the yeast growing in a blue-and-white crock. He nods with satisfaction and carries the crock back, careful not to disturb its surface, and shows Marea the smooth gray mountains bubbling up. The yeast is always the main event of the night. In Marea's first lesson, Andrew taught her that yeast has no self-discipline, that if it gets too much sugar it will feast and collapse. If it gets too little sugar, or water that is too cool, it will sink back into a useless stupor.

He returns the yeast crock to the shelf, leans back against the counter, and folds his arms. "So you're planning on seeing a head stretcher?"

"Maybe."

"If I went that route again, I'd find myself a Jungian."

"Why a Jungian?"

"Because they've figured out that the universe has its own dreams. Not all that Freudian sex and repression junk. The Jungians say you've got to discover where you fit into the world's memories, not only your own. I read a book about it. Jung believed that an individual consciousness is the flower of a particular season—and there's the whole history of seasons, the myths of man from all time. Ever heard the word 'rhizome'? According to Jung we're all connected by this rhizome thing—underground roots that go everywhere and send us up as little shoots, plants, flowers"—he points to the crock of bubbling yeast—"all the living things."

"Huh?"

Andrew shrugs. "Hard to explain, I guess."

"I think I'm going to try it—the head stretching, that is."

"Good luck," Andrew says. "Therapy is pretty much a crap shoot."

The smell of freshly baked bread fills Dr. Iris's room, making it smaller. If Marea cannot afford to pay Dr. Iris's full fee, she will bring her bread—a gift of loaves from the bakery, carried in a basket covered with a gingham cloth. Dr. Iris lifts the cloth and breathes in deeply to enjoy the smell. Marea decides not to tell Dr. Iris about her interview at the New York Psychoanalytic Institute. She will have to make a choice eventually, but for now she doesn't know how she'd do it.

"Are you a Freudian or a Jungian—or what exactly are you?"

"Are you asking if I have a theory I subscribe to in my work?"

"Don't therapists need some idea of what they think is normal behavior so they can tell if their patients are getting better?"

"I don't see it quite that way, Marea. I don't see my job as 'helping you get better.' I'm more interested in your freedom."

"Freedom?" Marea scoffs. "Maybe I've had too much freedom. Isn't that what they say about the sixties generation? My mother always told me I'd be much better off if I learned to accept the rules other people live by—if I made commitments and stuck to them."

"For some people that is freedom. Not for you, perhaps."

"So the freedom you're talking about is one of those movable things?"

"The freedom I'm referring to is an internal knowledge—an internal knowing."

Marea is tired from her night of baking. She lets her eyes drift closed. She considers Andrew's advice about finding a Jungian, and imagines that a Jungian would wear orange robes like a Tibetan monk. When she opens her eyes again, Dr. Iris is waiting to speak to her.

"Marea, I'd like to try to answer your question as clearly as I can.

What I mean by freedom is when you find what cannot be taken from you, your truest self. Unfortunately this is not something we can define in advance. There are things you only know once you find yourself acting in new ways. The process of coming to that place—where one day you see that you're acting from your truest self—that is the work we do here."

"So your brand of therapy is an act of faith."

Dr. Iris smiles. "You're a very bright young woman, aren't you?"

Folding her arms across her chest, Marea tosses off, "Step right up for the ride to freedom."

"What do you say we agree to mutual respect?"

Chastised, Marea admits, "This is new to me, putting myself in someone's hands."

"Is that how you see it? That you're putting yourself in my hands?"

"I have to put my trust in you. Isn't that the point?"

"May I make a suggestion? Trust is a marvelous accomplishment that often takes quite a bit of time. Why don't you wait and allow me to earn your trust."

Marea examines Dr. Iris, who seems to have so little need to mold or manage the world.

"Where do you want me to start? Should I tell you about my childhood, my parents, that kind of thing?"

Dr. Iris takes a sip of her coffee, deciding. "Can you tell me more about your travels?"

"My travels?"

"Seven years is a long time to be traveling. You must have had some extraordinary experiences."

Marea settles back, pleased. Her memories are her one accomplishment.

"I could tell you about when I hiked the Inca Trail."

"Where is that?"

"In Peru—in the Andes—fifteen thousand feet above sea level. The air was so thin, you could almost float. The old Inca path went along the mountain ridges from Cuzco to Machu Picchu. It was supposed to take five days to hike it."

"You weren't frightened climbing up into those mountains?"

Marea shakes her head. "Not of the mountains, but of something else I'll try to explain. We hiked through meadows full of lupines and poppies, past the most beautiful lakes. Sometimes we pushed through high grass for so long, I didn't think we were still following any kind of trail at all. Then the stones of the Inca path would appear again. It was amazing to think of them walking there five hundred years before us.

"On our second day of hiking we spotted the first ancient city along the path. It was completely covered in moss, but the water system was still working, so we bathed below a clay pipe where the freezing water came pouring out. Two days later, when we were light-headed from the altitude and barely eating, we found the next ancient Inca city built onto the side of a mountain. The way the sunlight hit, it looked like the prow of a ship draped in jewels."

"That sounds beautiful."

"Nobody was there but us."

"And you became frightened."

"How did you know?"

"You said that something had frightened you."

"It was after we climbed the stone stairs that led up into the city, and we took off our backpacks to start exploring. Fog was covering the jungle below, and so I went to the prow of the city to watch the fog roll up the mountainside. I stood there thinking about Inca men and women with gold jewelry around their wrists and necks, and how Pizarro came to trick them, steal their gold and murder them. The fog filled the sky all around me—that's when I got frightened."

"Marea, are you all right?"

Marea has her arms wrapped tightly around her chest.

"The fog stood still, and the city began to move, and I lost track of the earth beneath my feet, the mountain behind me. My chest tightened, and I began to panic—do you know the kind of panic I mean? I was afraid there would be no way to go forward or back. I was terrified that I had lost my connection to life, terrified that there was no reason or meaning in anything. I knew I had to find a vine or something fixed to earth, so I crawled back from the prow of the city until I found green grass. I looked up and saw a patch of sky, and I lay against the grass waiting for the fog to lift and my panic to go away. A month later I was traveling in the jungle in another part of Peru, and I lay down on a sandy riverbank to take a nap. When I woke, hundreds of butterflies had surrounded me. They were everywhere—on the sand, on my arms, my legs, their wings opening and closing silently. It was the opposite of the panic I felt in the fog. With the butterflies surrounding me I felt connected to everything."

Hearing footsteps on the stairs, Marea becomes agitated.

"Someone's coming."

"My next client."

"What did you think of my story?"

"I'd like to hear more."

"Is that what I do here? Tell you stories?"

"Telling stories is one way to discover your freedom."

"Can you say what you remember about him?"

"I remember his eyes."

"What about his eyes?"

"Their loneliness."

Marea is trying to get used to hearing Colin's voice without seeing him. Her view is of the bookshelves that rise up around her, leather spines divided and subdivided by dark wood, pushing her back into herself. Colin's voice floats behind her. She pictures him hunched over the yellow pad in his lap.

"Can you say more?"

"If a man makes bombs, how can he be anything but lonely?"

"Maybe you should tell me a little more about his work."

"I don't know that much about it. I know that during the Manhattan Project he worked on the timing of the detonators for the bomb that was dropped on Hiroshima. I asked him once, and he explained that hundreds of detonations had to go off in exactly the right order and at exactly the right millisecond or the explosion would fail. My father was a math genius. That's why they asked him to go to Los Alamos in the first place. They needed people trained in physics who could also handle the complicated formulas they used to map out a nuclear explosion."

"It's very impressive, your father's work."

"I suppose. He didn't talk about it much. There was so much he wouldn't talk about. The Nazis killed his parents, and he refused to talk about them at all. The only reason my father survived the Nazis was because his parents made him leave Austria and come to America to study. After the war all the family he had left in the world was me and my mother. I don't think he loved her very much. Maybe he loved her. I don't know. She was from a long line of Quaker pacifists. She hated him working on nuclear weapons, and she never stopped lecturing him about it. I think his work made her ashamed in front of her peacenik friends."

Marea is silent for a few moments, trying to bring back memories of her childhood.

"The arguments got worse when my parents became friendly with Albert Einstein because then my mother had an ally. My father got to know Einstein at the Institute for Advanced Studies, and Einstein started coming over for dinner a lot. I've often thought that since my father lost his own father when he was young, he was looking for a father figure in Albert Einstein. And the funny thing is that I started calling him grandpa. I think my parents liked that because it made us feel like family. My mother and Einstein were both against my father's decision to work on the H-bomb. The three of them argued about it endlessly. One night, after a terrible fight between my father and Einstein, Einstein left our house and never came back again. That's when things went downhill with my parents. I was probably around nine at the time. They never mentioned Einstein again until the day he died. I missed him. He was the only grandfather I ever knew. We used to dance together. Can you imagine? I was a little girl, and Albert Einstein would take me in his arms and waltz me around our living room."

"It's extraordinary that you had that kind of relationship. Were you close to your father, too?"

"Oh, yes, very close. Sundays were our day. Every Sunday afternoon we'd explore the woods behind our house. He wanted to show me everything about nature, to teach me all of it—how to identify different species of mushrooms, butterflies, insects—and he insisted we keep careful notes of all our observations. He taught me to examine things and then write down everything I saw. Those are my best memories from my childhood—walking hand in hand with my father in the woods, filling our observation notebooks, spending hours in his basement office tagging and sorting our collections. For my fifth birthday, he gave me the most beautiful cherry-wood specimen box you can imagine."

"At that age you would have been in your Oedipal phase."

"My what?"

"Girls go through a stage of development when they fall in love with their fathers and imagine they'd be better wives to them than their mothers have been."

Marea recalls kneeling by his side as they tracked the ant tunnels in search of the queen's throne. She recalls parting the leaves of skunk cabbages to find their chartreuse hearts, unhooding the purple cap of a jack-in-the-pulpit to examine its dark spadix.

"I suppose I should try to tell you about the day he died."

"If you feel ready."

"I've gone over it so many times in my mind."

"Of course. It's an unfinished time."

An unfinished time. Marea has an impulse to turn and look at the man who has perceived her so acutely, but she doesn't.

"He was leaving for California—he'd been going out for a few days every month or so to work with Teller. He'd always drop me off at school on his way to the airport. It was our special moment for saying good-bye. That morning he held my hand and asked me to sit with him for a while longer before I went into school. I was worried about being late, so I only stayed a few minutes."

Marea remembers getting out of the car, running into school, feeling guilty that she didn't want to stay with her father when he was acting so strangely.

"Go on," Colin coaxes.

"They got me from school. A neighbor came for me—the police brought her in their car. We rode in the back seat to the hospital. She told me it was my job to help my mother now. She said I was pretty, and not to forget that I had my mother to thank for that. When we got to the hospital they wouldn't let me see him. I tried to find him, but they held me back. At the funeral they wouldn't let me look in the coffin. I never saw him again after we said good-bye that morning, after he kissed me and told me to take care of my mother. For years I wondered if they wouldn't let me look inside the coffin because he wasn't in there. I thought maybe it was a trick and he was alive someplace—that he'd run away to become a new person so he wouldn't have to work for Dr. Teller and make bombs anymore. There were times when I was traveling that I'd get a glimpse of a man I thought might be my father—in a crowded market, or across a busy street—and I'd run to catch up with him. The man would turn when I touched his shoulder, see the disappointment in my eyes, and look at me with pity. I knew it was ridiculous, but sometimes I wondered if what drove me to keep traveling was that I actually expected to find him. In the years after the accident, I waited for a message from him. Maybe I'm still waiting."

Marea feels heat building, tears that refuse to come. She is curled up on the couch, the sailing ship that has carried her too far out into the open sea.

"You wrote on your application that you wondered whether he'd committed suicide."

She isn't alone, and she isn't safe. He is a detective asking questions. He will figure out the truth before she does, and spill it out to her before she's prepared to hear it.

After a silence, Colin says gently, "I'm afraid our time is up for today."

She rights herself, but does not look at him.

"I'll see you Wednesday at ten," Dr. Ross reminds the movement that darts past him out the door.

Marea's eyes alight in turn on each passenger in the row of seats opposite her. Each passenger is a mutable world, as she is a mutable world. She settles on the idea of tectonic plates, the subtle shifting of overlapping crusts of earth, each moving according to changes in the unseen transfer of heat miles below. Dr. Angela Iris has begun to discover the contours of one plate by asking to hear stories of her travels. Dr. Colin Ross, with his "unfinished time," has named another hidden structure. But there must be other structures that slip under and over each other, pressing together and pulling apart.

That night, near dawn, as she and Andrew work side by side at the kitchen sink rubbing the remaining bits of glutinous flour off their arms and hands, Marea asks, "So where would I find a Jungian?"

"You're serious about this therapy business."

"It didn't hurt *you*."

Andrew reaches for the dirty yeast crock to rinse it out, and contemplates it for a long moment.

Marea shakes her head ruefully. "I think I'm about to get a lesson."

Andrew shrugs. "I'm that predictable?"

"Go ahead—tell me what you were thinking about yeast as a metaphor for life."

"Actually I was thinking of yeast as a metaphor for therapy."

"Let me guess. Therapy can be the yeast for life, but sometimes people mistake therapy for life itself."

"Bingo."

Marea dries her hands on the dish towel hanging from Andrew's drawstring pants. "Seriously. How do I go about finding a Jungian?"

"You could try the Village Church on East Twelfth. They've

got a community bulletin board with all kinds of therapists. I checked out the board once when Tim wanted us to go into couples therapy. We had to find someone who was comfortable working with gay men."

"Any luck?"

"Oh, yeah—a sort of Auntie Mame type out in Brooklyn. She was wonderful. We got to be friends with her. She still invites us for Sunday tea from time to time."

"Can I ask why you went to see her?"

Andrew folds his arms. "You're pretty nosy, aren't you?" He flips his T-shirt off the hook by the back door and pulls it over his head. "Tim wanted us to have a child. A college friend of his had offered to do it for us. I was pretty shaky about the whole thing, but Tim was determined to go through with it, so we went to therapy to talk about it. His friend backed out, and that was the end of it. Too bad, I guess."

At the front door, Andrew turns his sign to "Open," and Marea steps out to head home. She yawns and stretches her arms into the cool morning air, feeling satisfied with the night's work and with her second week's wages in her pocket. As she walks along the empty streets, she thinks back on the first money she ever earned, the wintry afternoon she spent helping Albert Einstein compose his replies to the latest stack of letters that had come to him from children around the world.

She had never gone on her own to Grandpa Albert's house before, but she knew the way. Her father had pointed out the pretty house with the big front porch and the black shutters where his world-famous friend lived with his assistant Miss Dukas, his cat named Tiger, and Chico the dog. Marea was eight, old enough to make the trip alone. She was brimming with purpose as she marched along to her destination, her mittened hands swinging at her sides, her boots kicking up the dry snow like feathers. Grandpa Albert had promised that Miss Dukas would serve them hot cocoa and scones.

"I'm Marea," she said, when Miss Dukas opened the door.

"Yes, I know that."

"I've come to work for Professor Einstein."

"So I understand. Stamp your feet before coming in."

The house was quiet, and the air was sweet with baking smells. Marea didn't know what she was supposed to say to this stern woman in a long black skirt and polka-dot blouse who didn't have any children.

"Take off your boots and give me your coat. Professor Einstein is waiting for you upstairs in his study."

The narrow stairs creaked, and Marea took them carefully, one at a time. She knew Miss Dukas was watching her. The door at the end of the dark hall was open, the light from inside a beacon that called her. Grandpa Albert was relaxing in his chair, sucking his unlit pipe, and he laughed when he saw her. "Look at you. You have white hair like me." Marea put her fingers to her hair and touched the melting snow.

"Come in. Sit, sit. You've had an adventure walking all this way in a blizzard."

"It is not a blizzard," Marea said seriously. She knew he was making fun of her.

"Even so, you deserve a cup of hot cocoa."

"You've got silly slippers," Marea observed.

Einstein looked down at his furry feet. "Don't you like them? Don't you think they make my feet look like two big cats? Tiger always hides under the sofa when I put them on. Do you think she could be jealous?"

The room was stuffed with books and papers, and Einstein sat beside a low, round table, not at his desk. There were two other chairs near the table, and Marea sat in the one that let her watch the snowflakes grow fat outside the window. It would be dark soon. Her father would come later to pick her up in the car. Marea heard a rattling of dishes, and the slow footsteps of Miss Dukas on the stairs.

"It's good you're here." Einstein leaned toward Marea conspiratorially. "Otherwise I'd get nothing but tea and bread."

Marea sat back, newly confident of the importance of her visit, as Miss Dukas came through the door holding a silver tray by its handles.

They had their party, hot scones with orange marmalade and cocoa topped with cream.

"Time for work," he informed Marea, putting down his cup and reaching for a stack of unopened letters on his desk. "I'll read each one aloud and you will give me suggestions for what to answer."

He settled down and crossed his feet so that his furry slippers looked like two cats sitting on their haunches. "Miss Dukas and I have a special file for the letters that make us laugh, our 'curiosity file.' You must tell me if you think any of the letters we read today qualify for that special honor. Will you do that?" He perused the first letter.

"This young fellow's name is Robert. He seems to have an interesting question. 'Dear Dr. Einstein, can you please tell me, if nobody is around when a tree falls in the forest, would there be a sound, and why?' What do you think, Marea? What shall we tell him?"

"Of course there would be a sound," Marea declared. "It's only that there would be no way to prove it."

"Should we tell our young man that he has to take sound on faith?"

"I think you should tell him that sound is like gravity. Even when you can't see or hear it, it's still there."

"I like that answer," Einstein said, folding the letter back into the envelope and reaching for the next. "You have earned your first nickel."

He scanned the next letter and laughed. "I think this may be one for the curiosity file. 'Dear Dr. Einstein, my brothers and I were having a discussion. We were talking about you being a genius. The world knows you are a genius, but how about you? Do you think you are a genius? Sincerely yours, Jonathan Etoile.'" Einstein shook his head. "I don't think I need help answering this one. Any man who thinks of himself as a genius would have to be a very stupid man."

"But you *are* a genius," Marea protested. "My parents say you are."

"A genius to some, a fool to others."

"What will you tell him?"

He put the letter aside and wove his hands together over his belly. "What if I tell him that what the world likes to call a genius is only a person who isn't afraid to hear what his imagination is telling him."

"I don't think that's an answer to his question," Marea advised.

"I suppose you're right."

"What if you say that a genius has other things to think about besides whether or not he's a genius?"

Einstein laughed. "You've earned another nickel."

They continued at their work, and dusk had fallen by the time Miss Dukas returned to remove the tray and inform them that Marea's father had telephoned and would be coming soon to get her. Einstein counted up the letters they had discussed, ten in all. He removed a crumpled dollar bill from his pocket.

"That's twice as much as I earned," Marea informed him.

"You get a bonus for keeping your grandpa company on a cold afternoon."

Marea stood up to take her dollar, and she looked around the room, preparing herself for the moment when she would have to leave it.

"Can I ask the question I would write in a letter?"

"Perhaps I can earn back my dollar." Einstein smiled.

"Why is my father helping Dr. Teller make a bigger bomb?"

Marea watched her grandpa run his thumbnail along his lower lip. She had never had the courage to ask this question before. She had barely had the courage to think it.

"This makes you sad."

Marea didn't want him to see her cry, but her tears were already dropping to the rug.

"Come here, my princess."

She could have sunk all the way into his chest, into the warmth of him. She felt the weight of his chin on her head, and the smell, as always, of his forbidden pipe tobacco. Her father would be downstairs soon. The car would be in the street, lights on, motor running. He would meet her at the door and put his hand on her shoulder as he reclaimed her.

"Don't tell him," Marea murmured into her grandpa's sweater.

They were as quiet as the snow still falling outside the window. "You know, my little one, when I feel sad, I play my violin. When you feel sad, I think you should dance. You dance our oompah-pah, oompah-pah. Play the music in your own mind and dance around the room."

Marea sleeps soundly in the soothing emptiness of her white walls. When she wakes in the afternoon she climbs out onto the fire escape to eat a bowl of cereal and sliced peaches. In the dirt courtyard below, two young Puerto Rican boys dig for worms they're collecting in a jar. On the other side of a chain-link fence a man wearing only boxer shorts and leather shoes is hanging his wet laundry to dry, methodically pinning socks together in pairs. On the adjacent fire escape a girl with wavy red hair down to her buttocks picks out "Stoned Soul Picnic" on an acoustic guitar. Her boyfriend, oiled from head to toe, lies spread-eagled toward the sun at a perfect roasting angle, his penis curled against his thigh. Marea's fire escape is her doorstep. People wave to her or nod acknowledgement, but ask nothing in return.

At the Village Church Marea presents herself to a matronly volunteer who sits behind a desk, ready to offer Christian kindness and a host of services—referrals to free medical care, restaurant vouchers for healthy meals, the use of the telephone for long-distance calls home to parents who have given up hope for the return of their wandering children.

"The community bulletin board?" Marea asks. "I'm looking for a therapist."

"We've checked out each and every one of them. No one is allowed to put his card up on our community bulletin board until he's been through our screening process."

The ten-foot-long bulletin board is a collage of multicolored announcements of meetings, events, and reminders of the need for every kind of medical test from screening for sexually transmitted diseases to eye examinations. Under colored construction paper letters that spell out "Self-Help" are support groups for every variety of intemperance—overeating, alcoholism, gambling, cocaine use. Under "Spiritual Paths" the listings range from Jews for Jesus to Ram Dass. The "Professional Help" corner has business cards arranged in neat rows. Some have been annotated with consumer comments: "a self-important twit," "hard of hearing," "lesbians beware."

Marea scans the cards until she locates a Jungian: Dr. Eric Silas, "compassionate Jungian analyst—individuals and groups." She writes down his information and continues reading the cards until she comes to one that has a poem taped to it.

Our whole life a translation
the permissible fibs

and now a knot of lies
eating at itself to get undone

Words bitten thru words

meanings burnt-off like paint
under the blowtorch

All those dead letters
rendered into the oppressor's language

Trying to tell the doctor where it hurts
like the Algerian
who has walked from his village, burning

his whole body a cloud of pain
and there are no words for this

except himself
—Adrienne Rich

Marea writes down the name and number of Nina Wolf, who has used a poem to explain herself.

Back home with hours still remaining before baking time, Marea lies on her unmade bed. She has the phone numbers of the two therapists in her pocket, but she will wait until morning to telephone and leave them messages, since she'll have to find a public phone booth where she can camp out and wait for them to return her call.

Marea thinks back on her one early experience with therapy. After her father died, she would go down to the basement and sit alone for hours in front of the specimen boxes, studying the dead butterflies, willing them to fly. Her mother had tried to woo her out of the basement with what should have appealed to a twelve-year-old girl—shopping trips, ice cream, the movies. Marea hadn't wanted any of it, especially with her mother. Somehow—certainly at her mother's insistence—Marea was required to go to the school psychologist who came on Friday mornings to Princeton Junior High. The psychologist was young and nice enough when she encouraged Marea to write a letter to her father to say good-bye. But Marea had still gone silently to the basement every afternoon, until her mother had finally screamed at Marea, accusing her of selfishness and meanness. The school psychologist advised, Your mother is grieving, too. Marea surrendered, deciding she didn't have to go to the basement to keep him alive. She made a truce with her mother and learned to parrot the words "I love you" while keeping her fingers crossed beneath the kitchen table.

As Marea drums her fingers on the mattress, an edginess moves through her. When she tries to track it down, her uneasiness redoubles, dark cumulus clouds rising. It's the standing still, the decision to stop traveling. She feels it building at the back of her neck, crawling across her skin, making her breath short—symptoms of withdrawal. She has given up traveling too abruptly, a compulsive gambler sick with regret for throwing her dice into the sea. She gets up and leaves her apartment.

The F train passes in and out of Manhattan, a skittish visitor, in from Brooklyn, back out again to Queens, moving below the city's main arteries of commerce. When Marea moves with the crowd into the car, she is relieved at the discovery that all she needs to be traveling again is a subway token. The end of the line is Coney Island, and Marea walks out across the sand as the summer day is folding up, mothers and grandmothers carrying chairs tucked under arms, children straggling after them, nut-brown and black, a tinny honky-tonk tune playing from a faraway merry-go-round. Marea rolls her jeans to her calves, removes her sneakers, ties their laces together, and hangs them over her shoulder. The bellies of the clouds are etched in silver, and Marea's edginess evaporates as the ocean water laps over her bare feet and the leftover laughter of children slips through her porous skin.

When Marea arrives at the bakery door, Andrew is waiting with an apron held out for her. He loops the strap over her head, then spins her around to tie a bow in back.

"What's this about?"

"Time for you to learn to bake your own loaves. Plain wheat bread for starters. You have to earn your way up."

Marea salutes with two fingers to her forehead. "Aye, aye, *mon capitaine.*"

"Success is not guaranteed," Andrew warns.

"Would it be of any value if it were guaranteed?"

"Ahh, you are the perfect pupil."

Andrew moves a stool to the end of the counter and settles onto it with a glass of tea.

"I'm going to give you directions, but I'm not going to do anything for you. That's the only way to gain confidence."

"I went out to Coney Island this afternoon."

"Why?"

"I wanted to see the sea. I'm getting so domestic here, I'm feeling like a landlocked sailor."

"Did it help?"

"I'll last a little longer onshore, I suppose."

"That's good. I wouldn't want to give away my secrets to someone who was shipping out."

Andrew has prepared the kitchen surfaces, and they gleam with readiness for the night's work. The centerpiece of his kitchen is the marble slab that rests on a platform constructed of two-by-fours. That's where the kneading is done. Andrew does not believe in kneading machines. The dough requires human touch. Andrew's biceps are the size of bowling pins.

"Get out your ingredients and line them up. I want to see what you have learned."

Very smartly, eager to impress Andrew, Marea pulls down the cans of corn oil and blackstrap molasses, the canister of sea salt, the box of organic powdered milk, the block of yeast from the refrigerator. She drags the wooden barrel of wheat flour across the tile floor. With everything assembled, she awaits his verdict.

"And what's the final ingredient?"

Marea shakes her head, unable to imagine what she could have forgotten.

"You, my sweet Marea. You are the final ingredient—what you bring of yourself to the bread."

She sighs. "You're such a weirdo."

"You'll see," he says confidently, and folds his arms. "All right. Now, first the yeast."

Imitating what she's seen Andrew do, Marea uses a cleaver to chip a piece of yeast off the waxy ocher block. She goes to the sink, chooses one of the clean ceramic crocks, turns on the faucet, and runs water over the inside of her wrist to adjust it to the right temperature.

"Very good," Andrew acknowledges. "I see you've been watching."

"How hot should it be?"

"They say it should be the temperature you'd make milk for a baby's bottle."

"That helps," Marea says sarcastically.

"Not hot, not cold. Something the yeast would like."

"Will you check it?"

Andrew shakes his head. "The yeast will know if you don't trust yourself."

Marea fills the crock halfway and drops the chunk of yeast into it.

Step by step, Andrew guides her through the preparation of the dry and wet ingredients. Marea's confidence grows as she listens to the tinny rhythm of the sifter, watches the flour form dunes in the bowl, feels the silky flour dust coat her hands. She cracks the eggs, and without Andrew's prompting, adds the oil and the molasses. But as she stirs, and the ingredients lose themselves and blend together, she backs away. An unexpected sadness has come over her. She bites her lips to hold back tears. What has undone her? A feeling for eggs, oil, molasses? That they give themselves up for bread?

"What's wrong?"

Marea's arms hang at her sides, white to the elbows.

Andrew cocks his head. "Are you all right?"

He climbs down from his stool, goes over to Marea, and pulls her close so that her head rests against his bare chest. In the warmth between them Marea is comforted by not-being, and by not being separate.

"Was it too soon to teach you?" he asks. "Am I expecting too much?"

"No, no. I want to learn."

"Good, then. It's all about the wanting. You'll see, Marea. You're going to make a very good baker."

Dr. Eric Silas's office is on Prince Street in SoHo, close enough for Marea to walk from her apartment through the cannabis-soaked air of Washington Square Park, past the Loeb Student Center at NYU where a sheet drapes down from the second-floor windows, painted with the words: GET THE SHAH THE HELL OUT OF IRAN.

The black asphalt of Houston Street sends up waves of summer heat. A line of cars is backed up waiting to get into the drive-through car wash. July Fourth has come and gone, leaving a detritus of exploded firecrackers hanging from spindly trees. Marea spots a single black loafer propped up against a city trash can and considers its history. Did a one-legged man need only one shoe? Or did a trash scavenger looking for useful items come up with this one shoe and, after vainly searching for its mate, leave it propped up outside the can to warn or tempt others?

Sitting on the sidewalk with knees splayed and feet spread wide in the gutter, two urchins share a cigarette, inhaling with grave determination to make themselves bigger and their world smaller. One of the boys has a yo-yo balanced on the knob of his knee, the unwound string hanging down. The other boy stares frankly and blankly at Marea's breasts. Marea imagines the boy's little penis, all hope.

Crossing Houston Street into SoHo, she enters a neighborhood that's been reinvented in her years away. Walking along Prince Street, she sees a knot of people spill out of a doorway—cigarettes, champagne glasses, women wearing diaphanous blouses and throwing their heads back for men with slick ponytails and shirts unbuttoned to their waists. Marea crosses to the opposite side of the street to look. As they huddle to share a joint, she looks past them through the storefront window to the event inside, a gallery opening. Each wall holds a single large painting, all variations on the same theme, disconnected body parts lying in fields of primary colors. People hold their chins, paying homage to the violent images that confront them. Then they crowd around the painter, dressed all in black, his head shaved, serene in his chosen purpose.

Marea thinks about her days as a painter on the Algarve coast of Portugal. She spent nearly a month on the beach painting chalky seashells with watercolors from a child's paint box. The set she had purchased in the town came with a fine brush, made for a child's hand. Marea painted one white shell after the next, working feverishly. During the days she painted, and at night she slept on a blanket laid over stones in a churchyard where a Portuguese priest allowed traveling hippies to camp out. The waves off the Algarve coast pounded the rock caves relentlessly. Marea had no idea how long she would need to stay and paint her shells, but for several weeks she could not imagine doing anything else. She became a tourist attraction on the beach, a young American woman decorating seashells with embryonic swirls of color. Tourists stopped to watch her paint, and some offered money for her work. When they carried her painted shells away, holding them carefully, she felt a burning loss. Though she needed money, she hadn't been ready to part with something so newly found.

Dr. Eric Silas's office is on the fourth floor of a converted industrial building where immigrant girls once sewed buttonholes twelve hours a day. The words "Button Holes and Collars" are faded but still visible in the stone façade. The elevator is operated by a hand lever, and instructions for its use are taped to the wall alongside the schedule of each resident's co-op responsibilities. There is also a notice from a massage therapist in the building, offering a weekly massage in exchange for someone to take her turn collecting the building trash.

The elevator opens directly into Dr. Silas's loft, a modern and sleek interior with a wall of glass bricks, and pine floors refinished to a yellow gleam. A tall and bulky man, perhaps in his early forties, is standing at the elevator, hands folded together in front of his groin, a meditative posture, waiting for Marea to take in her surroundings before acknowledging her arrival. Japanese flute music plays through unseen speakers, and in the entrance to the loft artifacts are displayed on ebony shelves—museum-quality specimens of carved idols, bronze Buddhas, and Tibetan prayer bowls. The loft exudes spare elegance, and Marea guesses that Dr. Silas comes from a background of privilege.

He is wearing a red-and-black African dashiki, muslin pants, and socks, and he is so much taller than Marea that she has to step back and lift her head to meet his eyes. She sees that he is evaluating her, a newcomer to his consciously assembled world. He nods to her in a sort of welcome as he pulls his fingers through the wispy Ho Chi Minh beard that reaches halfway down his chest.

"Dr. Silas, I spoke with you on the phone. I'm Marea Hoffman. You said to come today at five."

"Eric. The doctor thing will only get in the way."

From where Marea is, she can see into the front area of the loft—chairs and couches, a circle of large pillows on the floor, a sheepskin rug, some drums and tambourines. Windows look out at the façades of other expensively converted buildings.

"Take off your shoes and come in," Eric instructs.

Marea sets her sneakers down on the mat beside the elevator alongside a pair of leather sandals and then follows him into the room.

"Where should I sit?"

"Wherever you'd feel most comfortable."

Marea considers this choice for the third time in two weeks. She knows where he would like her to sit, the choice that would be evidence of her enlightenment, the pillows on the floor. And that is where he'd be most comfortable. But Marea chooses one of the upright chairs. He watches her and then takes a matching chair.

He studies her frankly, and Marea is desperately uncomfortable. She sees a toad, breathing through its mouth, examining its prey. She considers getting up, hurrying back to the elevator, explaining nothing. After she's gone, he will dismiss her—unready for "the work," still too caught up in "self" to hear the deepest voices within. On the telephone he had warned her, "Jungian therapy requires more life experience than other therapies. It may not be the time."

"Can you tell me why you've come to see me?" he asks when she makes no move to start their conversation.

Despite her impulse to bolt, Marea says, "A friend suggested I see a Jungian therapist. He said Jung believed the world has its own memories."

"Yes, but why are you here?"

She owes him something now, an explanation. She telephoned to make an appointment. She presumed upon his time. She cannot leave.

"My friend told me that Jung believed we're all connected through our collective memory. For the most part, I don't feel connected to anything, but from the few times I've felt connected, I know it's better than being adrift."

"Explain what you mean by that."

Marea thinks about what she told Dr. Iris about the butterflies in the jungle. "When you feel connected to things, you see how beautiful they are."

"Yes, that's true."

"And you feel less afraid."

"Do you feel afraid?"

"Sometimes."

"Can you tell me how it is when you feel connected to things?"

"There was one time on the island of Iona—off the coast of Scotland."

"St. Columba established a monastery there in the sixth century."

"You know about Iona?"

"Of course. It was the earliest outpost of Christianity in the British Isles. You see, I studied early Christianity while I was living in a silent religious order in Switzerland—quite a long time ago. I was all set to become a monk until I discovered I wasn't suited to silence. As it turned out, I met Carl Jung then and stayed on in Switzerland to work with him until he died. I was one of his last students. There's quite a bit of similarity between the spiritual path and the work of a Jungian therapist—both require you to put faith in what you can't necessarily see or comprehend."

"Should I tell you about my time on Iona?"

Without planning it or even quite realizing what she's doing,

Marea moves off her chair to the pillows on the floor. Once she's made the move, Eric slides off his own chair onto the pillows nearest him.

"Last year I was staying on the Isle of Skye and someone told me that Iona was famous for ghosts and apparitions. It was near the end of October, so I thought it would be fun to go there for Halloween. I hitchhiked as far as Oban. When I told the driver where I was headed, he warned me that Iona could play tricks on your eyes. At Oban I took a ferry across to Mull. It was raining hard, but finally I found someone who was willing to row me across from Mull to Iona."

Marea checks Eric Silas for his interest in her story, and he waves his hand for her to go on.

"On Iona I found a pub where I could wait out the weather. When the rain stopped, I stored my backpack there and went exploring. I hiked from one end of the island to the other, climbed around the old monastery until I got tired, and headed back to the pub. A bunch of people were hanging out. It turned out I wasn't the only one who thought it would be cool to spend Halloween on Iona. We had some beers, and then one guy, who actually lived on the island with his parents, invited us all home for supper. His mother was really nice and fed us meat pie. She told us stories she'd heard from the local people, who swore they saw ghost ships full of Norsemen exactly like the Norsemen who crossed the North Sea hundreds of years ago to conquer Iona. Apparently they insisted they'd witnessed reenactments of the very battles that took place in the ninth and tenth centuries."

Eric has hunched over, cross-legged, his elbows on his knees, his Ho Chi Minh beard hanging down to his ankles.

"Go on," he instructs. "I'm very interested."

"After sunset, we went to the beach and built a huge bonfire. I don't know how it got started, but we took turns running through the flames. Then someone got the idea to climb to the top of the island and look for the Norsemen coming across the sea. There were about a dozen of us, I guess. We stretched out in a line, holding hands as we hiked. Then we huddled together on the crown of the hill to wait for ghosts."

"A perfect Halloween adventure," Eric comments.

"Eventually the moon came out from behind the clouds, and the wind picked up, so the clouds began to move fast in the sky. Then the strangest thing happened. The clouds formed into two columns—and then one column drifted around until it cut across the other so that together they formed a crucifix that hovered above us. It was an amazing sight. Here we were at one of the most sacred places in Christianity, and it's All Saints' Eve, and the clouds form into a crucifix. Of course, it had to be from a magnetic field or something from the storm that had passed, but even so, it was an extraordinary sight. And that's when I had the sensation of being connected to everything. For those moments there was nothing that separated me from my experience, nothing at all."

"I want you to come back and work with me."

"I don't have much money."

"I'm not worried about that."

He is staring at her, and her skin tightens as she slides back.

"I had my appointment with the Jungian."

It's two in the morning, and Marea is kneading dough at the work island while Andrew is sitting astride the wooden bench, cracking eggs into a large ceramic bowl, two at a time.

"What'd you think?"

"He was pretty weird, but it was hard to tell—I did all the talking."

"Isn't that what you're supposed to do with a therapist?"

"So why the big deal about seeing a Jungian? Honestly, I don't see the big difference between him and someone else I'd jabber on to."

"Maybe it's not how you see him, but how he sees you."

"But if every therapist is going to see me differently, how am I supposed to know what's real?"

"I think it's the relationship between you that's supposed to be real."

"But what if I only show him the version of myself that fits with what I think he believes in?"

"That would be natural to some degree."

"So I guess it's a good thing I'm seeing three therapists—to fill out the whole picture."

Andrew stops cracking eggs. "Excuse me, what did you say?"

"I've got three shrinks, now that I've added the Jungian."

Andrew shakes his head in disbelief. "This is a bit strange."

"I didn't exactly plan it. I saw one, and then I saw another thinking he might be a better choice, and then the third—the Jungian—*your* suggestion. I meant to choose. I thought I would. But now I don't know how I could. It's what you said—each one sees a different version of who I am—or maybe I'm a different person with each of them. I'm going to meet another one later this morning. Her card was right below the Jungian."

"Do your therapists know about one another?" Andrew asks doubtfully.

"I'm not sure that would be such a good idea." Marea grins. "You know how shrinks are—they like to think they're the only one."

"Very cute, Marea."

As she turns to a new project of cracking walnuts, Marea wonders why she has chosen not to tell her three therapists about each other. Maybe she wants to keep the three relationships separate, like the separate relationships of her childhood—her mother, her father, her Grandpa Albert.

Marea had been unhappy when her mother began to require her help in the kitchen preparing Sunday supper. She didn't like having to cut short her Sunday hikes with her father, and she was sorry to miss her time before supper in the living room with her father and Grandpa Albert. She worked at her chores, counting silverware and folding napkins, with the awareness of her mother's needs clamping down on her.

"Grandpa Albert brought over a model airplane for us to put together," Marea informed her mother one Sunday evening. Marea was sitting on a stool with her legs astride a metal waste can, trying to skin each Cortland apple in a single, curling peel.

"You must finish your chores first. You can work on the model after supper."

"He'll be too tired to stay for long after supper."

"Yes, Marea. He has to take care of his heart."

Not before dinner and not after. Her mother wouldn't even look her way as she tightened the knot around her.

"But this is the last apple," Marea insisted.

"You can't always do just whatever pleases you." Virginia's tone was steely, and Marea wondered if anything ever pleased her mother.

"He brought it so we could build it together," Marea said with agitation. She got down from the stool and defiantly began to untie her apron.

"Marea," Virginia said, "you are not to contradict me."

Marea tightened her mouth, unable either to concede or rebel. When her father appeared at the kitchen door and crossed to the sink to fill a glass with water for Professor Einstein, Marea pleaded, "I've finished my chores. I want to work on the new model."

Jonas and Virginia exchanged looks, the one imploring, the other cold. Marea watched them, her apron untied but still hanging around her neck. Her parents had long since ceased being a united front.

"Come along, Marea." Jonas extended his hand. "You can get a start on the model before we sit down to dinner."

As Marea took her father's hand and left the kitchen with him, she felt a moment of shame that she had triumphed over her mother, but once she was settled into the living room with the plastic pieces of the model laid out in front of her, she felt proud of her escape.

At the dinner table she watched the three adults in her life, saying one thing to each other and thinking another. She was old enough now to notice the meanings pooling beneath the words. She knew she sat among volcanoes that could erupt at any moment.

Dr. Nina Wolf is a founding member of the West Side Center for Self in Society, with offices in a defunct synagogue on West Ninetieth Street, off Central Park West. There are gilt-edged Hebrew letters on the painted walls of the room where Marea waits for her appointment.

When Marea spoke to Nina Wolf on the telephone, she was told that at the Center for Self in Society they practiced alternative therapy, "therapy," Nina Wolf explained, "that takes into account that society is often inhospitable to the growth of the individual."

"We're political," she summed up.

"I understood that from your poem."

"I don't want to waste your time or mine if this doesn't suit you."

"That's why I called."

"Our fees are fair, but we're not free. We have rent, expenses—you understand."

"I have a job. I don't make much money, but I can pay something."

"We'll require a letter from your employer. We have a sliding scale."

"Who's this we?" Marea finally asked with mild irritation.

"Our collective. We share expenses and fees. We believe that politics is personal. We're nothing if we don't live what we believe."

Marea sits alone in the waiting room. For this first consultation Nina Wolf's only free hour was nine A.M., and Marea has come straight from the bakery. There are no magazines to keep her entertained while she waits, only a sagging couch, so she drops her head back, closes her eyes, and is asleep before she knows it. She sleeps soundly until someone enters her dream but is not of it.

"Are you my nine o'clock?"

Marea opens her eyes. The woman is too close. Marea sees

only a stretch of tight black jersey that covers a torso from flat chest to sharp hipbones.

Sitting up abruptly, Marea's quick movement causes Nina Wolf to step back. With the full view, Marea imagines that Nina Wolf could be a women's basketball star, long and lanky, with barely any female curves, shoulders broader than her hips. With her lips slightly parted and her widely spaced eyes, she has the look of an attentive fish. Her hair is clipped back with two barrettes, a short crop of bangs on her forehead. Even though it's July, she wears boots that meet the hem of her black dress. She offers her hand for Marea to shake, her fingers pointing down like a divining rod seeking water. "Nina Wolf. Sorry to keep you waiting."

Marea follows her from the drab waiting room to her office, a nest of comfort—potted plants, linen drapes, kilim rugs, a gallery of black-and-white photographs in metal frames—pictures of peasants from all over the world. Nina Wolf's armchair is at the center of the room. On a nearby stool sits a pastel blue Princess telephone. A small table holds a spiral-bound date book, a pad and fountain pen, a folding travel clock, its face positioned to be visible to Nina Wolf but not to her client. Every one of these props seems weighted with purpose, and Marea feels as if she's walked onto a stage set in the middle of a performance. The star of the play, Nina Wolf, settles back into her armchair. The only other seat is a smaller armchair, a little too far from Nina's, outfitted with a pillow and a folded blanket. More props. Marea imagines curling up in the empty chair and going back to sleep. Her arms and feet ache. Breadmaking is hard work, and now that she works side by side with Andrew preparing dough of her own, she emerges at each dawn thoroughly spent.

"Is it so hot out already?" Nina asks, taking note of Marea's T-shirt and shorts.

"I came straight from work," Marea explains. "These are my work clothes. I work nights in a bakery. The ovens heat up the place."

"Will you be chilled if I leave on the air-conditioning? It helps block out the street noise."

Marea pulls the blanket off the back of the chair. "It's okay. I'll cover up."

Once Marea is seated, Nina Wolf flattens her palms on the tops of her thighs.

"How about telling me a little bit about yourself, Maria?"

"It's Marea."

"Not Maria?"

"It's spelled with an *e*, not an *i*."

"Oh? That's new to me."

"What would you like to know?"

"Something of your background, your issues."

"I grew up in Princeton. My father was a research scientist, and my mother was a homemaker."

"Brothers and sisters?"

"No, just me."

"Anything special about your childhood?"

"My father died in a car crash when I was twelve."

"That's a difficult thing."

"My mother supported us by tutoring children. I guess that's why I always imagined I'd become a teacher. I went to Barnard with the idea that I'd go on to Columbia Teacher's College. But after I graduated—actually before I graduated—I left the country and started traveling. I needed to get away from everything. I'd been having nightmares, horrible dreams about Vietnam."

"Do you remember any of them?"

"There was one where I was walking along a path in the jungle and a woman came toward me pushing a cart. When she got close, rifles poked out of the straw in her cart and riddled me with bullets. I wasn't surprised. It made sense that she'd want to kill me. The dream felt real. I thought I was dead."

Nina reaches for the pad and pen from her table. "Do you mind if I take notes?"

"I've had nightmares about nuclear war since I was young. There's one I'll never forget from that same time in college. I was in a line of cars trying to escape a burning city. The cars went on forever. Behind us the city was melting like candle wax. Even though everyone was trying to get away, we knew we wouldn't survive. When I woke up, I couldn't shake the sadness of it, the futility of our effort to survive. I made a drawing and called it 'The Dream of the Melting City,' and I took the drawing with me when I left the country."

"Where did you go?"

"Mexico, then all through South America. That took almost three years because I had to find work to support myself along the way. I went by freighter across to Africa and up the east coast—Zimbabwe, Kenya, Egypt—across to Greece, then back through Turkey and Israel—all through Europe, England, Scotland, Ireland—seven years altogether."

"Wow."

Marea looks down at her hands, folded together over the blanket that covers her lap and legs like a passenger on an ocean liner.

"I'm not sure why I came back. I knew I couldn't keep going forever. I knew I had to face things."

"You mean your fears."

"My fears?"

"Isn't that what you've described in your dreams—your fear of war and violence?"

"I don't know if it's so much fear as a morbid preoccupation. Ever since I was a child, I've waited for nuclear war. I've always believed it was inevitable."

"Even now you believe that?"

"I don't know if I still think it, or if in a way, I am it—I've become it. Do you know what I mean?"

"I'm not sure."

"Maybe if I tell you about something that happened when I was in London."

Nina checks her clock. "Go ahead. We have about twenty minutes."

"Last November the IRA set off a bomb in Harrods department store. No one was killed, but the papers had photographs of the arms and legs of store mannequins blasted out into the street. It was a bizarre sight, and frightening, because it showed what could happen to real people. Then the IRA bombed two pubs in Liverpool, and this time people were killed. Not long after, I was in the London Underground changing from one line to another when there was a huge bang that sounded like a bomb. Everybody froze in place there in the tunnel. I'm sure we all had the same thought—that other explosions would follow, that we were trapped. It was an incredibly long moment. Then we heard another bang, but this one was clearly recognizable as the sound of a train banging on the tracks, and so we realized we had all jumped to the wrong conclusion. Everyone went on about their business, but for those moments what united us was that we expected to be dead."

Marea looks at Nina, who appears puzzled.

"I'm not sure what you're getting at."

"I'll tell you about some people I met in Israel. Maybe it will make more sense. I was walking around the sculpture garden at the University of Jerusalem, and I stopped in front of a sculpture of a family seated at a dinner table—the father reading his newspaper, the mother serving food, two children—they were all made out of weapon parts. Their legs were machine gun tripods, the mother's breasts were empty mortar shells. A man was standing near me, and we got talking. He was a professor of semiotics, and he explained that the sculpture showed that all objects are symbols. He invited me home to have supper with his family. Israelis do that—they invite you home. At dinner we discussed the sculpture again, and their oldest son—he was fifteen, I think—wanted to show me his room. It was a cave of military paraphernalia—gas masks, camouflage jackets, grenades. The only empty spot was the bed. When I asked his parents whether they thought Israel's identity had become dependent on being at war, they answered by suggesting we take a trip to see the Golan Heights."

Marea points to the clock. "Do I still have time?"

"Yes, a little bit."

"The next day we all drove north so they could show me the way the Israeli government had preserved the Golan Heights exactly as they found it after it was captured in the Six Day War. We took the elevators the Syrians had installed for carrying ammunition to the top of the heights, and then we crawled along the cement halls and climbed the ladders to gun turrets. That's where the Syrians had aimed howitzers at the Israeli villages below. You could put a coin in a telescope and look out at their targets—the gardens and schools and women hanging out the morning laundry. The son with the weapons collection was my tour guide since he was the expert on concussion shells, phosphorus shells—which ones targeted buildings, which were meant to murder or maim people. This was the family's way of answering my question—and it's my way of telling you what I mean when I say that fear of annihilation can be something that people become."

Nina leans forward, locking Marea down with her fish eyes. "As I explained on the telephone, I don't do traditional therapy. I think Freud had it exactly backward when he said that the women he treated were hysterical and needed to be cured. How about the rape and abuse they suffered at the hands of their fathers and husbands? I'm not interested in helping you adjust to oppression, Marea. I want to help you get strong enough to fight it."

"I don't think anyone is oppressing me."

Nina flips her hair back. "We've been trained our entire lives to make excuses for our oppressors."

"Who is my oppressor?"

Crossing one leg tightly over the other, and folding her arms, Nina says, "That's what you're here to discover."

Sitting on the floor of her white room, Marea folds a single piece of paper into four squares, creases the folds, and then neatly tears the squares apart. Afternoon sun is streaming through the window, and the white sheet that had covered her in sleep lies twisted on the floor, fallen away as she moved toward the project that had come with her out of a dream. She writes the name of each of her four therapists on one of the four paper squares: Ross, Iris, Silas, and Wolf. Below Ross she writes the word "psychological." Below Silas she writes "spiritual." Below Wolf she writes "political." Then she considers the square with "Iris" written on it. She sits up Indian-style, with her fists pressed beneath her chin. What should she write on Dr. Iris's square? Freedom? But freedom is her goal, not her belief. Marea pushes the four squares together again, fitting their edges, studying them until she gets it. She scribbles "existential" underneath Dr. Iris's name and pulls the four pieces apart.

It's her birthday, July 16, 1975, and she must telephone her mother. The last address she gave her was London, weeks ago. How many of the letters her mother sent have been returned to her, addressee unknown?

The birthday calls are never easy. Marea strains to come up with things to say. Virginia tries to keep herself from saying too much. Politeness carries them a little way, but the tension is there, and inevitably Virginia's neediness and anger spill out.

Marea always calls from a public phone so that when her money runs out, there is no time for extended good-byes. Always, soon after the birthday phone call, a lengthy letter arrives at whatever American Express address Marea has last provided, a stream-of-consciousness report of Princeton news, and then always, the same final paragraph, pleading with Marea to explain why she has turned away from the woman who rowed her to safety after the death of her father. That had been Virginia Hoffman's repeated refrain for years, that the two of them had been left at sea in a lifeboat and had to rely on one another to survive.

Marea often speculated that her mother felt more alone after the departure of Albert Einstein from their lives, and then his death, than she had after her own husband died. Einstein had been the one Virginia dressed up for. It was only when he visited that her cheeks flushed and she smiled. Virginia reacted to Einstein's death with a strange and unexplained silence, to her husband's death with a flurry of household activity and public displays of resolve and strength. It was clear to Marea that her father had disappointed her mother in ways Marea couldn't begin to understand.

Virginia invoked her lifeboat image of survival whenever Marea tried to pull away, and so Marea had had to struggle against that image and against her mother throughout her high school years. Marea never walked out of the house, or went out with friends, or met a date without guilt. What sort of callous daughter could have fun when her widowed mother was left all alone? What kind of mean-spirited girl could no longer make herself utter the words "I love you"—even as a lie—to a mother who waited morning and night to hear them?

Finally, to try to break free of her mother's hold on her and to assert her independence, Marea stayed out all night with the editor of the school newspaper, who, Marea knew, only wanted to get information for an article he was writing about Albert Einstein. They drank Mateus wine and smoked Marlboro cigarettes and made out with an urgency that surprised them both. It wasn't the alcohol or the sexual stimulation but the guilt of leaving her mother alone that finally overwhelmed Marea like a fever and caused her to throw up all over the back seat of the boy's parents' car. With Lysol and paper towels they worked until sunup to get the smell out of the upholstery.

Virginia ran to the front door as soon as Marea opened it. "Where have you *been?*" Virginia shouted.

"With friends."

"With *friends?*"

"I'm seventeen. I have a life of my own."

Her mother stiffened. "Of course you do."

That night Marea stayed out again until dawn. This time she and the newspaper editor could barely hold back as they hurried into the darkness of the Institute Woods. It was the first time for both of them, and it happened so quickly that at first Marea wasn't sure he had entered her. The next night was different. Her body heated like a furnace and she pulled at him, digging her fingers into his skin. Her passion must have frightened him, because he didn't call again. She didn't care. She was relieved to be rid of her virginity, something she didn't want to take with her to college in the fall. And after three nights away from home, it was as if a spell had at last been broken—she had swum away from her mother's lifeboat and was floating on her own in a warm summer sea.

Marea knows where her mother takes her telephone calls. The black telephone has sat on the top of the mahogany rolltop desk in the dark downstairs hall as long as Marea can remember. The desk is where her mother methodically separates her mail into bills to pay, invitations to accept or decline, letters to answer. She sits on the straight-back chair in front of the triptych of photographs that have also been there as long as Marea can recall, photographs that document Virginia's wedding, the birth of her daughter, her friendship with Albert Einstein.

Marea knows her mother's habits. She knows her mother will wait until the fifth ring before answering the phone. It is not that Virginia Hoffman wishes to make callers wait on her, but, as she explained to Marea long ago, she prefers to let them think that she is busy in order to spare them any worry about her lonely life.

Inside a glass telephone booth near the subway entrance at Union Square, Marea listens through the rings and wanders the house in her mind, follows her mother to the telephone, watches her wait to pick up the receiver. Perhaps she is fortifying herself for her conversation with her estranged daughter, or perhaps after these weeks of returned letters, she has given up hope that there will be a call from her daughter this July 16 at all. Perhaps she is only expecting the chairwoman of the Ladies' Auxiliary, who promised to confirm the arrangements for Virginia's lecture on "Ten Tips for Helping Children Become Lifelong Readers."

"Hello?" The voice is as dry as the desert.

"It's me, Marea."

Silence.

"Hello? Mother? Is something wrong?"

Tears?

"I've been so frightened. All my letters have come back."

"I didn't have a new address."

"I can't tell you how relieved I am you called."

"I always call on my birthday."

Silence again.

"Yes, of course."

"I'm thirty."

"You've grown up, haven't you."

"I have some news."

Is she afraid to hear?

"I hope you'll write me all about it."

"I'm back."

"I don't understand."

"I'm in New York."

"New York City?"

Ambivalence. No more tears.

"I'm back here working."

"Are you coming home, then? Or I'll come there. I'll take the train. We could celebrate your birthday. How long since we've done that?"

Virginia is excited, breathless. Marea shrinks.

"I'll call again as soon as I can."

"Please, Marea—please don't hang up." Then, catching herself, "Tell me what you'd like for your birthday."

"There's a question I've been wanting to ask you. I'd like the answer for my birthday."

"I want to buy you something special. A wonderful piece of jewelry, something to keep your whole life. Especially now that you're thirty, a grown woman. It's been so long since you've let me buy you a gift."

"Would you answer my question? That's the only present I want for my birthday."

"Then why don't I come up to New York to see you? We can discuss what's on your mind."

"It wasn't an accident, was it? He didn't want to work for

Teller anymore. He hated himself for breaking with Einstein. So he killed himself. Isn't that right?"

Marea hears the phone click off. She stands utterly still and weightless, as weightless as she was on the morning she was told of her Grandpa Albert's death, as weightless as touching her fingertips to her father's black coffin, as weightless as floating out from the prow of the Inca city, unmoored.

She returns in her mind's eye to the brick house on Blossom Street, where she imagines her mother, also weightless, hovering by the telephone, willing it to ring. Virginia Hoffman has no way to call her daughter back or find her, even though she now knows that Marea is only a short distance away.

Marea pushes out of the phone booth and walks quickly and purposefully toward a destination she has already envisioned, a place where her weightlessness will float easily. She already sees the subway train windows crossing, the tumbling kaleidoscope of passengers, the whistling ribbon of white light.

2

Twice a week for nearly four weeks now, Marea has walked across Colin Ross's line of sight to slide into the bow-armed couch where she recalls her childhood. She likes it when she manages to make him laugh—when she told him that her earliest notion of sex was what happened under the bedcovers when a man and a woman hooked a garden hose between their belly buttons. She was sheepish when she told him about peeking up the leg of a boy's swimsuit to see his penis, a boy at summer camp who wanted to marry her and imitated Donald Duck's rubbery voice to make her smile. And she had to shut her eyes to tell him about the camp director who stood her up on a camp bunk and rolled his thick tongue around the inside of her mouth as his "thing" hardened against her leg. Forever after, the sweet smell of summer pine was ruined by the stink of Aqua Velva and her shame that she did not run away from this adult who was in charge of her.

Through all her childhood memories, what she returns to again and again, like returning to cool water, are the Sunday afternoons she spent outdoors with her father exploring the beautiful Institute Woods. Those memories are the melody, the sweet part of childhood that played against the strident chords inside their dark house.

Sunday afternoons, on returning from Quaker Meeting, Marea and her father changed out of their fancy clothes while her mother got busy in the kitchen with her most serious cooking of the week. Sunday dinner, the meal they sometimes shared with Albert Einstein, took all of her mother's energy. With pots and pans clanging in the kitchen above them, Marea and her father busied themselves in the basement below, outfitting themselves for their adventure. They laid out their gear along the workbench where they would later catalog the new specimens. Into her father's leather satchel went magnifying lenses, mayonnaise jars with air holes punctured in their metal tops, reference guides, pencils, and notebooks. When the ground was still sodden in early spring, they wore tall rubber boots. In summer they wore the hats Jonas had fashioned for them with mosquito netting that unfurled from the brims and covered their exposed skin. Before they climbed up the basement steps, Marea stood straight-backed and called off "check" to each essential piece of equipment her father named from a mental list.

At the top of the stairs on their way out the back door, Marea pressed close to her father's longs legs while he waited through his wife's last-minute instructions. Virginia wore her Sunday apron over her Meeting clothes, her favorite one with red roses, a gathered ruffle around the hem, a large bow at the back. Watch out for poison ivy, in spring it's still green, Virginia admonished. Or, Albert is coming early this evening because he's off to Washington tomorrow—you must be back with enough time to wash up and change your clothes. Marea could see her father's effort to listen and be agreeable. In later years he ushered her straight from the basement to the back porch, and her mother was forced to come after them to deliver her parting instructions. In the months before the accident, Virginia no longer even turned away from the stove to see them go.

Marea tried on all kinds of adjectives to explain to Colin Ross exactly how she felt when she and her father explored the woods together. At last she settled on *safe*. She felt safe with her hand in his. She felt certain in his presence. The darkness of her nights, her terrifying dreams, the agony of imagining an end to all she knew—all that went away in the hours they spent together studying the natural world.

For her fifth birthday her mother gave her a daily desk calendar with quotations from history's great pacifists: Gandhi, Tolstoy, Jane Addams, William Jennings Bryan. Her father gave her a new net and a glass-topped specimen box. With her new equipment he taught her how to preserve a butterfly, slipping the pin carefully through the thorax, taking pains not to disturb the stiffening wings. But no matter how carefully she handled each new butterfly, a fine film from its wings would leave a shine on her fingers, and when she and her father pressed their fingers together, their touch was satin.

Jonas required Marea to learn the names of things, making up rhymes to help her. "Though butterflies are fairer, and moths are not rarer, both groups together make up the Lepidoptera." They searched everywhere to find the amazing Papilionoidea, the one butterfly that never wraps itself in a dark cocoon but hangs by threads while it slowly pumps hemolymph into its crumpled wings to get them ready for its first flight. The afternoon they finally found a Papilionoidea, her father was momentarily overcome and had to brush away his tears. Seeing him cry brought tears to her own eyes, though she didn't know why.

"You were attuned to his deepest feelings, weren't you?" Colin Ross remarks one Wednesday near the end of July. "It's remarkable how close you were."

"Isn't that the way it is between fathers and daughters at that age? Your famous 'Oedipal phase.'"

"But you seemed almost to share a skin with him. Do you know what I mean?"

Marea is lying on her side on the couch. She can't see Colin, but she can see where he's hung his sports jacket off the back of the chair in front of the desk. With the midsummer heat in this stuffy room, he no longer wears a jacket and tie as he did in their first sessions together. He's allowed himself to be less formal with her in other ways as well. After all, though he's never admitted it, they are close in age and certainly of the same generation. They call each other by their first names—there's never been a time when she had an impulse to call him Dr. Ross. They could be friends, if the rules allowed it.

"Truthfully, Marea, your relationship with your father seems to go beyond the Oedipal complex. He seems almost mythic in your mind. It's odd, because Albert Einstein, who is mythic to so many people—almost the definition of a mythic man—was an ordinary person to you. For you, your father is the mythic one. With this important a relationship still unresolved with your father, it's understandable that you haven't been able to make lasting commitments in your relationships with other men. It would be difficult for any man to compete with your memories of him. And since he died when you were young, you never got the chance to grow out of your idealization of him and see him as an ordinary man with ordinary human faults."

This is more of an analysis than Colin is in the habit of giving, and Marea doesn't like hearing him speak in this detached and intellectual way about her father.

"I guess you've had a session with your supervisor."

Colin is quiet a few moments, then asks, "Does it make you uncomfortable to imagine that your father had faults?"

"How could I possibly think he had no faults? My mother never shut up about them."

"Perhaps her criticism made you idealize him all the more. You do seem to have taken on the role of his defender."

"I see you decided to earn your money today," Marea snaps.

"And since you felt you had to be his defender, you were never allowed to get angry with him either."

"So I'm angry at you. Transference, right? You can make a note there on your pad."

"Marea, I think we've hit a nerve here."

"Congratulations. You get an A-plus for the lesson on the advanced Oedipal complex. Go to the head of the class."

Colin doesn't respond to her sarcasm, and they wait out a silence.

Marea tosses off, "I guess I should be more polite since I get my psychoanalysis for free."

"I'm not concerned with politeness, but it might help if you saw your sarcasm for what it is."

"And what is that, Herr Dr. Freud?"

"What do you think it is?"

"Such a cliché, answering a question with a question."

"Would you like me to do your work for *you*?"

"Fine. Sarcasm is my defense. First prize for me. The refrigerator—no, better yet, the trip to Hawaii."

"Marea, we have to talk about something. How much of your anger has to do with our pause over the month of August?"

"Our *pause*?"

"Okay, my vacation. Monday is our last session together until September. Can I ask how you're feeling about that?"

"Oh, didn't I tell you? I can't come on Monday. I have something else I have to do."

"I thought you'd set aside these times for our work together."

Marea jerks herself upright on the couch and whips around to face him. "Who teaches you phrases like that? 'Our work together.' Do they give you a phrase book—a hundred and one ways of expressing yourself to maintain your precious detachment? I'm dying to hear something that's actually your own idea, your own words. Or will Doctor Freud reach out from the grave and grab you by the throat if you have a thought of your own?"

"Marea, what's wrong?"

"What? Because I sat up? I'm not allowed to sit up?"

Face-to-face with her, Colin is noticeably ill at ease. Weeks of his building self-confidence are being undone.

"Too bad I screwed up your lesson plan."

He is gripping his pencil, fighting an impulse to strike back. Seeing this, Marea looks away from him. If he succumbs and says something he'll regret, that will be the end of their work together, and she doesn't want to lose him.

Hopping off the couch, she says cheerfully, "I'll see you in September, then."

"Not on Monday?"

"No." She shakes her head. "Not on Monday."

There is no subway that crosses from the Upper East Side to the Upper West Side of Manhattan, so on Wednesdays Marea is in the habit of taking the crosstown bus from the Psychoanalytic Institute on East Eighty-second Street to the Center for Self in Society on West Ninetieth, where she has her weekly appointment with Nina Wolf an hour after she leaves her morning session with Colin.

One thing Marea has learned over the last weeks is that practitioners of the mind are rigid about their schedules, the one controllable part of their peculiarly uncontrollable days. Nina Wolf is unbending about the time she sets aside each week for Marea. Time is the bartered commodity. Even when Marea is quiet, the clock is not. Each Wednesday at exactly ten minutes to one, Nina uncrosses her legs, slaps her thighs with her open palms, and announces, "Until next week." The awkward moment for Marea is getting up while Nina withdraws in her chair, no more words to be exchanged between them, the gates closed. Marea knows she can't possibly get out of the room fast enough, that any dawdling will be noted, eroding Nina's goodwill.

As a mode of transportation, compared to the subway that Marea has begun to cherish in her weeks in New York, the bus is tediously grounded in the temporal world. Well-dressed women clutch department store shopping bags with boots to be resoled, lamps to be rewired, husbands' shirts to be exchanged for larger neck sizes. On the last Wednesday of July the crosstown bus moves slowly along the Central Park transverse, proceeding through dappled sunlight, past joggers who flit by on the dirt path around the reservoir. A soccer ball arcs in air.

Unlike on the subway, where people leave one another alone, bus riders scrutinize the other passengers. They judge the girl with a safety pin through her eyebrow who is biting her cuticles raw, pity the palsied man clinging to the chrome pole in a moment of private terror, recoil from the black nanny kissing her young charge's pink ear. Marea does not feel comfortable among the bus people, who know nothing of the release of sinking into earth. Whenever Marea rides the bus, she longs for the world underground.

Though Marea carries the same body, heart, and mind from Colin's couch to Nina's armchair, she is a different person. "Why does everything have to be reduced to sex?" she demands as soon as she sits down.

"Can you say more?"

"Freud," Marea sneers. "Penis envy, Oedipus complex—all that *crap*."

"Not here, not in my practice," Nina says, both reassuring and defensive.

Marea has learned not to be distracted when Nina compulsively squeezes her lower lip between her forefinger and thumb as she listens, playing with the flesh. Marea's guess that Nina's sexual preference is for women was confirmed two weeks ago when Marea arrived early one Wednesday and caught sight of Nina on the steps of the old synagogue bending toward a short and stocky woman. They didn't kiss, but the way they touched confirmed their intimacy. Marea has caught herself flirting with Nina in their sessions, not because she finds her attractive, but because in Marea's mind it helps level the playing field between them.

Marea scowls. "You say that, but think about it. When you get right down to it, what is your feminism but the same old business of sexual power? You make it into politics, but really, what's the difference?"

"You seem quite angry today."

"I thought that was the point. Didn't you tell me right at the beginning that I had to learn to get angry at my oppressors?"

"That's a bit abstract. Do you suppose your anger could have something to do with anticipating my absence in August?"

At the end of their last session Nina had informed Marea that she would be out of the country for the month and unreachable by telephone, and she made a point of explaining that her policy was not to tell her clients where she was going.

"What is it with you therapists and your precious Augusts, anyway? Maybe I'd feel better if it wasn't shrouded in such secrecy. It's not like I want you to pack me in your suitcase."

"I can understand your feelings."

"And I should be able to understand yours?"

"Do you think it's unreasonable to ask you to respect my privacy?"

"It's not a matter of whether it's reasonable or not—it just seems unnecessary and a little weird to make it such a secret. It's as if you're always finding new ways to remind me that I'm the client and you're the therapist. You talk about power all the time—how about the imbalance of power in *this* relationship?"

"Ours is a professional relationship. We have different roles. I don't believe you came here looking for a friend."

"But you make all the rules."

"Yes, that's true. I do make the rules here, because in my professional judgment certain rules are helpful. We aren't equals here, but that doesn't make it a coercive relationship. There's no exploitation—it's simply an issue of difference. The bottom line is that you've come here by your own choice, and you always have the option to leave."

"I'm wondering why that sounds like bullshit."

Nina smiles coolly. "And *I'm* wondering why this conversation seems like an avoidance. You're working very hard to keep me at bay here. You do that, you know. You put up barriers. I'm beginning to suspect why those barriers exist—what you're so afraid to let us look at. Last week you described that recurring nightmare you had as a child—of nuclear bombs dropping out of airplanes? Do you happen to recall that you used an image of giving birth?"

"I said that the bombs dropping out of the airplanes looked like litters of kittens being born."

Nina picks up the stenographer's pad from the table to check her notes. "I believe your exact words were that the airplane was like a mother's belly that had been cut open, so the kittens could drop down."

"That's right," Marea agrees impatiently.

"It's curious, considering how you began today's session by complaining that people reduce everything to sex." Nina closes her eyes, getting hold of the idea she's putting together. "I'm thinking about your image of bombs dropping. It's striking the way it puts violence together with sex, since birth is most certainly connected to sex." Nina's eyes fix on Marea. "I'm going to jump out on a limb here—I'm following a hunch—tell me, was there an episode of sexual abuse in your childhood?"

Marea scoffs. "That's a leap."

"It's not uncommon for a child to take one kind of fear and transform it into something more manageable."

"Fear of nuclear war is more manageable than fear of sex?"

"I'm not talking about sex, Marea. I'm talking about someone who may have taken advantage of you when you were too young to protect yourself, too frightened to say no."

"I've told you—what frightened me was the idea of waking up and seeing everyone dead."

Nina sits back, regroups. "Marea, sometimes when you talk like this, it seems as if you're describing an abstract idea—maybe something you think you're meant to feel as part of your generation. I'm left wondering if it's something you actually believe."

"Of course I turn it into an abstract idea. Who can actually grasp the reality of total nuclear annihilation?"

"My point is—is it real to *you*? Or is it some intellectual way of defining yourself as a member of a generation in order to avoid other more personal issues?"

"If someone sexually abused me, that would be real, even if I didn't remember it, but if the human race is bent on destroying itself, that can't possibly be real to me as an individual?"

Nina flips her hair back, as she always does when she has an agenda item she wants to complete. "Marea, would you consider coming for an additional session before I go away? I'd like to work a little further before we take our break."

"*Our* break?"

"Yes," Nina says impatiently, "I'm the one taking the break." She reaches for her datebook. "I think it could be important to push ahead right now. What do you say to scheduling an extra session on Friday? I'm pretty sure I have a cancellation." She studies her schedule book as if studying tea leaves. "Yes, I have a free slot at two."

Nina leans toward Marea to encourage her agreement, and Marea sees the flesh of Nina's pale breasts. She wonders about sex between women. Do they use fingers and tongues, and is it enough?

"I'm not sure I can afford another session."

Nina leans closer. "I think it's important. We're getting close to something here. At the very least it would give us a bit more time to develop trust before the separation."

"Do you know that when you insist on saying 'we' and 'us' when what you mean is me, it comes off as incredibly condescending?"

Nina cups her hands over her knees and hesitates a moment, heightening the drama of what she feels compelled to speak.

"Marea, you've been coming here less than a month, and building trust certainly takes much more time than that. But, even so, you seem deeply ambivalent about even *beginning* to trust me. It's so clear to me that someone betrayed your trust, once upon a time, long ago. We don't know who yet—we don't know how. But when someone's trust is so badly abused in childhood, putting trust in *anyone* can feel dangerous—even terrifying—a complete betrayal of self."

Marea feels tired, beaten down. She senses that Nina means well. Marea even imagines that Nina sees things about her that she cannot see for herself.

"I don't know," Marea says softly.

"What don't you know?"

"I've had so many questions about my childhood. I have so many questions that were never answered. Like whether he killed himself or not."

Nina sits up abruptly. "But you told me it was an accident."

"I've had my doubts. It's probably only stupid speculation on my part."

"Are you aware of anything he may have felt guilty about?"

"Building bombs."

"That doesn't sound like a reason for killing himself. Was there anything else?"

"Building an H-bomb that can kill a hundred million people at a pop isn't enough?"

"I think you know what I'm asking, Marea," Nina says firmly.

"I was twelve when my father died."

"Age has nothing to do with it."

"What you're proposing is absurd." Marea looks toward the clock. "It must be time."

"Will you come for the extra session on Friday? At two."

Marea is folding the blanket. She shrugs. "If you think it will help."

At the door Marea stops a moment, her hand on the knob. "My one consolation when I think about the inevitability of nuclear war is that I'll see my father in heaven."

"I'm not sure if I'm nuts or they're nuts."

Marea and Andrew are seated on stools on opposite sides of the work island, drinking iced tea and waiting while the last breads bake. Around them the cooling racks that line the shelves are full of warm and crusty loaves. The smell is luscious, almost overwhelming. The mixing bowls are overturned to dry in the sinks. Even the bakers themselves are cleaned up, their forearms pink from scrubbing.

"Therapists who don't know they're being cuckolded, or a woman who sees four therapists at once? I think it's all pretty nuts."

"You're the one who suggested the Jungian."

Andrew shakes his head. "I had no idea it would be part of a smorgasbord."

"It's interesting, though," Marea says seriously.

Andrew sets his glass on the work island, folds his arms across his chest, and sits back with his blue eyes on her. "Tell me how. I'm curious."

"You said that their different beliefs would influence who I was with each of them."

"Did I say that?"

"Something like it. I think you're right. Each one wants to hear different things from me—or maybe *sees* different things in me. Or maybe I'm a chameleon changing colors to please each one of them and it has nothing to do with them at all."

"Okay, but a chameleon actually has all those colors within it. It reacts to its environment as a protective mechanism—but the colors are all its own."

"It's an analogy, Andrew, not a biology lesson."

"It's an important distinction. Are the colors you become determined by your shrinks, or are they yours?" He takes a long drink of tea, then sets the glass back down on the wet ring on the counter exactly where it was before. "If you want me to understand this bizarre enterprise you're involved in, you have to be more precise."

"All right. How about a kaleidoscope? I'm all these fragments, but it keeps turning. The configuration changes with each one of them."

"Tell me something, if you don't mind. How do you manage to pay for all this shrinking? Certainly not on the salary I give you."

"They cut me deals. You don't know this, but you wrote a letter to one of them about my salary. You told a little white lie. I didn't think you'd mind. At the psychoanalytic institute, it's free because I'm a guinea pig for someone who's still training. The Jungian still hasn't gotten around to telling me what I should pay—

that worries me a bit. And my other one, my grandmother type on the Upper East Side—well, those three loaves I take home in a basket on Tuesday mornings, they're actually for her, not me. I pay her some in cash, and the rest she accepts in bread."

"You're a piece of work."

Marea is quiet a moment, her eyes cast down. "I make it sound like a joke, but there's got to be a reason I'm trying to get all these people to help me. It's not like I've had a whole lot of success so far with getting my life together."

"You're showing promise as a baker."

Andrew gets up to check the loaves in the oven, and Marea watches him pull down the door three or four inches to peek inside. These breads, his daily gift to the world, have their own needs, their own rights. He reaches in and lightly raps his knuckles on a few of the crusts. "I'd say ten more minutes for these guys. Why don't we get started putting everything else out front?"

Marea retrieves the wide basket they use for carrying the loaves from the cooling racks to the shelves in the store. They've developed a method of doing this project efficiently each dawn, the final stage of their night's work. Marea braces the large basket against her abdomen as Andrew sets in one loaf after the other, cradling each in two hands.

"I think Tim's right," Marea comments. "The two of you should have a baby. You'd be a wonderful father. Look at the way you hold each loaf of bread."

Andrew laughs.

"I'm serious. Any baby would be lucky to have a father half as tender as you."

"It's not in the cards, my dear."

"Why not?" Marea announces impulsively. "I could help you have a baby. I've got the equipment."

"That's a lovely offer, but what do you think your four therapists would think of it?"

"That is a lot of therapists, isn't it?"

"More than average."

The lapis light of dawn has brightened the bakery window by the time the breads are all in place. The morning outside is still quiet, only the occasional whoosh of a boy going by on a bicycle, and the groan of delivery trucks. Andrew is up on the stepstool erasing the list of yesterday's breads and prices from the blackboard and writing up the new ones. His prices are too low—they barely cover his expenses—but Marea's suggestion that he charge more has fallen on deaf ears. She is in awe of his pureness of heart. Marea, who is accustomed to feeling through people's skin to their doubts and worries, feels only a sense of peace when she works near Andrew. In their long nights together she has begun to love his lanky body, his iridescent eyes, his innocently cocked hip.

Once all the loaves are out of the ovens and neatly arranged on the shelves, Andrew turns his sign to "Open" and unlocks the front door for business. Marea is reluctant to leave, and as Andrew steps outside to breathe in the morning, she pauses in the doorway.

"What's brewing?" he asks.

"It's not impossible, you know. I could give the two of you a baby."

Andrew smiles. "You said you wanted to get your life together. Maybe that ought to come first."

"Or maybe a baby would help."

He reaches out, takes her hand, and brings it to his lips.

It's Thursday afternoon, July 24, and Eric Silas is not waiting until the first of the month to start his August break. In their last session he explained to Marea that he needs a few extra days to make the trip to Tibet and back. When he meets her at the elevator he is barefoot and shirtless, drying his wet hair and beard with a towel.

"Marea," he says aloud, jogging his memory.

"Did I mix up the time?"

"No, no. I'm sorry. I'm the one who screwed up. I'm a little frazzled trying to get ready to fly out tomorrow."

Marea is also feeling frazzled, having been woken by a midday thunderstorm from a nightmarish dream in which endless rows of loaves of bread became babies crying out in fright. In the dream Marea dashed back and forth among them, but could not calm their fears.

"We can skip today. I'll wait until you get back."

"No, absolutely not. You're here. Give me a minute to catch up."

He disappears back down the hallway to his living quarters, while Marea takes off her sneakers and goes to wait for him in the front of the loft. She settles onto the pillows to do what he's taught her, to begin each week's session with a series of deep-breathing exercises. Eric always sits close. Their proximity, the "physicality" of it, he explained, is part of the work. "We create a world. Energy passes between us." He has instructed her to inhale to a count of six, hold on seven, exhale to a count of six again, holding her lungs empty again on seven. This was the pattern established at the Creation—six days of work, a seventh day of rest. Breathing lines up one's soul with the Divinity, the all-being. They remain silent, the silence before creation. In each week's session the opening silence has grown longer. Eric has assured her that this is a good thing, and has guided her to look into his eyes without flinching, to experience the nakedness of receptivity. Receptivity and surrender are the true beginnings of change. Marea has imagined a stranger observing them in this bizarre scene, and once, when she giggled, Eric took her hand and ordered her sternly to "stay present" with him.

Last Thursday Marea told Eric about a morning some years back when she watched the sun come up over the red dunes of the Western Sahara. She climbed to the top of the dune in the dark hour before dawn, digging in one heel after the other, as sand closed up behind each step like flowing water. Men wrapped in black muslin, coal eyes peering, offering camel rides to the top of the dunes for exorbitant prices, called after her, negotiating against her wordlessness. She pressed on, as mulish as their ugly camels, who waited below with downtrodden, lip-lidded eyes. At the top, her legs aching, Marea sat on the sand to wait for the appearance of the sun. At last it peeked over the black horizon, a tip of a fingernail aglow, and then rose quickly, transforming into a fiery orange ball that broke for sky and swept away the darkness. Marea looked out on the shimmering gold landscape, undulating softly as far as the eye could see. The suffocating heat of the day was instantaneous, but she was immune. She wrapped her arms around her shins and stared, pinned by the wonder of it all. Even when the heat became unbearable, she could not make herself get up and go. Another sunrise watcher had to climb up to her, tap her on the shoulder, and point her back down the dune where the bus was waiting to return them to Erfoud.

Marea told Eric this story because it was another time she lost herself into the wonder of the natural world.

"That's how some people define God, isn't it?" she asked.

"You mean the connection you felt?"

"The way I lost track of my separateness."

"It's true that people who reject the teleological view of God often describe what you've described, an inner God they recognize when they lose their sense of a separate self."

"How do they know when it's God?"

"Have you ever thrown a pot?"

"You mean on a wheel?"

"Yes."

"A few times, at summer camp."

"Then you know that you have to have the clay perfectly centered on the wheel before you can open it up and begin to make your pot. The problem is that looking at the clay won't tell you if it's centered or not. You have to sense it through your fingers, through touch. If the clay stays centered when you press down to open the pot, that confirms it. I think it's something like that when you apprehend the presence of God. You sense it, but you can't be sure until you push down with your thumbs and begin the opening."

Of her four therapists, Eric Silas is the only one who intimidates her. In part it's his towering height—he's a full foot taller than she—but it's also the mix of his spiritual beliefs and his wealth, a double dose of self-assurance. Marea can imagine him as a young boy dressed in jacket and tie at Exeter, or making the Atlantic crossing alongside his mother on deck, or in his twenties as a visitor to his father's study, waiting to receive his father's blessing on his decision to make a career of the human psyche, an appropriate calling for a son of a son of wealth.

As her first words out of the silence on this dark July afternoon of clouds and thunderstorms, Marea asks, "It's five weeks in all that you'll be gone?"

"I know the timing's difficult, considering we've just begun."

"I've rarely stayed put in one place for five weeks in seven years."

"So it's possible you won't be here when I return?"

"I'm not saying that. It's only that it seems far away—your return, my return."

Eric extends his hand toward her. "For some people touch helps give things more substance."

Marea takes his hand, still warm from bathing. What are the rules here?

"For some people it's helpful," he says, answering her unspoken question. "It's your choice."

"Is it allowed?"

"We're both grown-ups. We can make our own rules."

Marea notices Eric move his legs slightly, giving his penis room to rise. His hair and his beard are still damp, and there are small beads of sweat on his forehead from the muggy afternoon.

"I don't know," she says.

"How could you know? It's something we'd have to discover by doing it."

"Like the clay."

"Yes, like opening the clay."

Marea looks away toward the windows and the overcast sky.

"Tell me how you feel."

She looks back at him. "The truth?"

"I would hope so."

"Curious—but also afraid."

"Are you afraid of falling in love? Because with or without sexual intimacy, this kind of relationship must at some point become an act of love."

"I'm afraid I won't come back."

Eric nods. "Yes—your troublesome habit of running away when people have expectations of you. But I don't have expectations. Whatever happens, it only happens now." He brings her hand down to enclose the bulge his penis has made in his pants.

"Come closer," he instructs.

Marea pulls herself across the rug toward him, moving from her pillows to his. She curls against him, resting her head on his thigh, as he runs his hands through her flowing hair.

"Isn't this wrong?" she asks.

"Marea, nothing that you feel good about is ever wrong."

He takes her hand to pull her up. "Come with me."

He has his arm around her back as he guides her along the glass brick wall toward the other end of his loft. They don't speak, though Marea hears his plans for her, and hears her own pounding heart.

At the entrance to his bedroom, he stops, making her take in the scene before her—his large bed, low to the floor, covered in pillows and furs. He is still her therapist; he is still making her look without flinching.

Sitting her on the edge of the bed, he goes to his bureau, opens a carved box, and takes out a pipe and a chunk of hashish. He breaks off a piece, smells it, presses it into the bowl of the pipe, and then licks the residue from his fingers. Marea looks at him. His wet beard is hanging in strings. His neck is thick. Before he lights the pipe, he pulls his shirt off over his head. She sees what she couldn't make herself look at before when he met her at the elevator—his chest covered with tight brown curls, the middle-age spread of his abdomen. Marea considers leaving, but she doesn't carry the thought further. She smells the sweet hashish as he takes a long drag off the pipe. Then, holding the smoke in his lungs, he settles down next to her on the bed, tips up her chin, and fits his lips over hers to release the smoke into her mouth.

The hashish fills every cranny of her skull, exploding her senses. He takes another hit and blows it into her mouth again. "Open your eyes, Marea. Look at me. I'm going to show you how to become one."

He helps her up and pulls off her shirt, then runs his hands over her skin, stroking her breasts, biting her nipples, digging his fingers under her waistband to grip her buttocks in his hands. He unzips her jeans and pushes them down, holding her upright because she has lost the ability to stand on her own. She wants to drop onto him, but he doesn't let her.

After he pulls off her underpants, he slips his fingers inside her and spreads the wetness down her thighs. Her head is swimming, her mind in a vortex, spinning up. He pushes his hand into her until she cries out.

"Good, good. Sex is about surrender," he whispers. "Life is about surrender."

She collapses against him, and he lays her back on the bed, spreading her thighs with two hands. "Let me look at you." She arches up. She cannot remember when she has ever been so anxious for a man to come inside her.

He stands up to untie the drawstring of his pants, which drop to the floor. He is wearing no underwear, and his penis is pointing straight out toward her. When he sees her looking at him, he says, "Don't worry about coming back, Marea. You'll be back." He kneels beside the bed, pulls her hips to him, and enters her with his tongue. She arches toward him again.

"Slowly," he instructs. "Be patient."

He moves her back to the middle of the bed, sliding her into the furs, and then lies on top of her. Pinned beneath him, she thinks of pinned butterflies. He pulls her legs out and around him, and guides his penis into her so deeply that tears spring to her eyes. She is in another world, opening herself to him as if his whole body could come into her. She wants nothing less. As he pushes into her, she flushes with heat, her head bursting with blankness, and her vagina convulses with the most intense orgasm she has ever known. He pushes again and again, until her body disappears, and all separateness dissolves, and she falls away into light, all the colors of the spectrum that she has become, life without form, being without substance, ecstatic and empty.

The loud noises and bright lights of the city night are jarring. Marea trudges back through SoHo and Greenwich Village, then east along Second Street toward her apartment, already overcome with loneliness. Will she return? She doesn't know. But she already craves more of what she has just experienced, the loss of herself.

When she crosses Broadway, she spots a Woolworth's, and the idea comes to her to buy a mirror. There is no mirror in her white room. She wants to look at her body, to reclaim it. The clerk leads her down an aisle to a stack of cheap mirrors lined up in their thin cardboard shipping boxes. In the dim light of the store, in a patch of mirror revealed by a heart-shaped cutout in one of the cardboard boxes, Marea sees her tangled black hair, her flushed cheeks, her bleary eyes.

Climbing the three flights to her room, with the mirror under her arm, her legs are lead. She knows none of her neighbors, but recognizes the dogs that bark at the sound of her footsteps. And the smells—fish fry, old dope, the urine of the Bowery men who slip inside at night to sleep.

Marea turns on the light and leans back, deeply relieved to be behind her own door. It occurs to her to count the days since her last period. She has never been pregnant, has never had an abortion. She thinks about Eric's furred chest, his muslin pants with the drawstring retied, standing with his hand braced against the open elevator door, reminding her of their next appointment on the Thursday following Labor Day, same time as always, five in the afternoon. He is confident she will be back. He has seen to that.

With a kitchen knife she cuts the mirror out of its box and leans it up against the wall. Tilted that way, it returns a distorted image. She carries it into the bathroom and props it up above the sink. She can see only half of herself, and the fluorescent bulb gives off a harsh light. She hoists the mirror under her arm once more, carries it to the middle of the room, considers her options, and then crosses to the mattress to lean the mirror horizontally against the wall so she can lie down and face herself.

She takes off her clothes and examines the bony stretch of woman looking back at her, small breasts, flat stomach, slight hips, jet black pubic hair. It's a woman's body, but a child's skin, a child's habits: Marea doesn't know when to drop a burning match, too slow to see the correlation between flame and pain. She crouches on the precipice between feeling and numbness, the battle of a lifetime. When was the moment she knew her body as a separate entity, a separate experience of pain or pleasure? When did her own corporality and its pair, mortality, come inescapably to her? Too young, she thinks, before her skin had time to thicken its layers. She was required to make a plan for survival, anticipating the walk through a blackened, desolate world. She would have to walk ahead through the smoke and steam that pumped from fissures in the contorted earth. She would have to climb over the jagged cement blocks of collapsed buildings, turn away from burnt bodies. This is what she dreamt. Tears had streamed down her skin, and she had puzzled that her feet continued to move ahead when her mind had frozen.

Marea had cried out in the middle of the night, and her mother had come to sit with her, the weight of her hip against Marea's thigh making Marea's own weight real. Her mother waited for Marea's tears to subside before drawing from her the details of the latest nightmare, kittens becoming nuclear bombs, skies full of smoke and fire, and always, as in every nightmare, the unspeakable loneliness of the search for anyone else still living.

After her mother left, thinking Marea had fallen back to sleep, Marea still looked up at the ceiling with her eyes wide open. She couldn't bear the thought of falling back into the lonely world of her dreams. She climbed out of bed and crept down the hall to her parents' bedroom, passing the framed photographs on the wall that caught sharp slivers of moonlight. She went to their door, wanting to climb between them, to be touched. Before she could knock, she had heard her mother's shrill voice: "You bring this wretchedness into our house. Bombs and violence. We can't escape it."

"It's every home, not only ours," her father had defended himself. "The Cold War is a war like any other. It's discussed in every family. Of course the children are aware of it."

"Then why don't those other children have Marea's awful nightmares?" Virginia demanded.

"Perhaps Marea is more sensitive," Jonas suggested. "She's a particularly observant child."

"Oh, you'd like the comfort of that excuse, wouldn't you? You'd like to avoid the ghastly truth of what you do."

Marea had shrunk from their door, backed into the terror of separate body, separate skin. And she had never returned.

The moon is high, shining through the window into the white room, when Marea wakes and realizes she has slept past the time to report for work. Her new mirror catches the moonlight. She thinks of Andrew, of loaves rising, his babies in bassinets, then pulls the sheet up from the end of the bed, cocoons into it, and sinks back into her dreams.

The morning residue of a new nightmare drags with her to the toilet when the sun is up. She rests her forearms on her thighs and lets her head slump down between her knees to give in to it. Because she has been here so many times—floating in murky waters after waking from nightmares—she waits for the details that will bring her dream to consciousness. When she is taken back into the stark terror in her dream, she knows she has dreamt it in order to have proof to bring to Nina Wolf.

It's a quarter after two, fifteen minutes late, when Marea arrives and finds Nina's door standing open, the cue that Marea should enter.

She sees that Nina is preoccupied, studying papers on her lap, dressed casually, almost haphazardly, in a mismatched blouse and pants. The wrap-up day at work. Phone calls between sessions to double-check the flight departure time, her lover's special meal requests, the rental car. Nina is the take-charge person in the relationship. Marea recognizes it in her squinty eyes. Marea senses that Nina has had second thoughts about scheduling this extra appointment on the day she is to leave. Marea discerns all this in the seconds before Nina looks up, even has time to feel a flash of envy: Nina Wolf will be traveling, while Marea will be standing still.

"You wanted me to come for an extra session today," Marea says, even though she knows Nina doesn't need reminding.

"You're late, and I won't be able to go past three. We'll have to make the most of the time we have."

As usual the office is a refrigerator. Marea shuts the door and takes the blanket off the back of the chair.

"Getting set for your trip?"

"Does it bother you so much?"

"Does what bother me?"

"Come on, Marea. You know what I'm talking about. Does it still bother you that you don't know where I'm going?"

Marea closes her eyes, extends her hands, aping a seer's trance.

"An anthropological theme—South America, or perhaps Central America. Yes, Central America. I see ruins. I see women weaving on back-strap looms—" Marea opens her eyes and enjoys Nina's discomfort. "Guatemala's a beautiful country. I loved it there. I'm sure you'll like it, too, if you can get past the genocide."

Nina quickly peruses the papers spread on the hassock in front of her to see what has given Marea the clue.

"It was a guess," Marea says demurely, and pulls the blanket up over herself. "I had an awful dream last night."

Nina sits back, unnerved. "Yes?"

"I think I had this dream so you would believe me about my fear of nuclear war. In a way you're right about what you said last time—it's been in my head so long, it's almost like folklore, the story of my generation. After all, we were the first ones who grew up knowing twenty million years of DNA could cook to a cinder at the push of a little red button. It's like that poem you put up with your card—about the Algerian man who walked out of his village with his body on fire—how there were no words for his pain, nothing that could describe it except himself."

Marea waits for Nina's response, but Nina has resolved to listen.

"Should I tell you the dream?"

"Of course."

Marea closes her eyes. "Okay, I'm in a building. A factory building of some sort. There are people there. We're fighting some other group of people. I'm not sure who we are or who they are, but we're enemies, fighting over an ideology, a piece of land, something. There's a railroad track that comes into the building so that boxcars can drop off shipments of materials for making weapons. We're standing in the building near the tracks, trying to decide what to do about an enemy we know is bent on destroying us. A freight train rolls up right in front of us. It should be a normal event, but something alerts me—I know how the enemy is going to attack. The train has been rigged with dynamite, and I know it's going to explode at any minute. I run to the switching box, flip all the levers, and send the train back down the tracks on the same hill it's come up. It rolls back into the valley and explodes just as it returns to the enemy camp. I feel satisfied that I foiled their plot, and we go back to our business, feeling secure. Later that same day we're all up on a high floor in the same factory building when we get word that a shipment is coming up the freight elevator. Nobody thinks anything of it, and neither do I, until the elevator doors open and a metal Dumpster is revealed. Then I know—I know how the enemy has retaliated—this huge Dumpster is a bomb—and we're all paralyzed by the instant knowledge that there's no escape. Even as we try to understand how this could have happened to us, the building is blowing apart around us, and we're engulfed in a falling inferno."

Marea opens her eyes and looks at Nina to make sure she has

her attention for the most important thing. "Isn't that the way it is? You realize the folly of your denial when it's already too late to act."

Nina's face is drawn, not quite a scowl, but clearly feeling accused of something that she does not like. "How is it that we live in the same world, with the same bombs, but I don't have the fear you talk about?"

"How is it that we have huge stockpiles of nuclear bombs that could kill the world's population a hundred times over, and no one does anything about it? It's the same question."

"You're saying I live in denial."

"Or maybe it's that we were born on two sides of a divide. I'm guessing you're around forty. You were in the generation that grew up after World War II when people were feeling optimistic about things—*your* generation never doubted the future. I grew up during the Cold War when there was a constant threat of nuclear destruction—the future is something *my* generation simply never believed in."

"Are you saying that it's impossible for me to understand you?"

"I'm saying that there's a good reason you might not want to. Your side of the divide is a happier place to be."

Nina drops her hands to her thighs, more slowly than usual. Their time is up. "We'll have lots to work with when I get back."

Marea unwraps herself from the blanket. "September, then?"

"September fourth."

"Maybe this means I'm beginning to trust you."

"Because you shared your dream?"

"No. Because I'm pissed off that you're going away."

Nina nods. "We've begun working toward a more meaningful relationship, Marea."

"That old 'we' again."

"Well, it is 'we.' I'm part of this relationship. By the way, I'm curious. How did you know that I'm going to Guatemala?"

Marea points to a travel brochure tucked under Nina's phone.

"Ah," Nina says.

"I had you going."

"You did."

That night, after Marea winds her way off Greenwich Avenue into the narrow alley that leads into the courtyard behind the bakery, she hesitates. She watches Andrew through the open door, working alone, his hair loose across his shoulders, his hands kneading in a slow and steady rhythm.

"Hi, there," Marea says breezily as she comes through the door.

He spins around at the sound of her voice. "I thought I'd lost you."

"It was only one night."

Marea stiffens as Andrew hugs her, holding his whitened hands out so as not to leave flour on her back.

"I was tired. I slept through."

"It's okay. I managed. I'd hate to think I was getting dependent on you."

"Not a good idea."

They pull apart.

"So, I'll get started," she says.

"Wait a minute. I've been wanting to talk to you. I told Tim about your offer—"

"That was pretty ridiculous, wasn't it?" Marea takes her apron off the hook.

"I didn't think so."

She looks at him and sees a sweet boy from Ohio, too nice, too sincere.

"I think I should get to work," she says again.

"We can take time for a glass of tea first. I missed you."

"Why are you making such a big deal? It was only one night. And about the baby thing, it's just something that popped out. I couldn't possibly have a baby. I'm not cut out for it. To have a baby you have to have faith in the future."

Andrew frowns. "Actually a baby *gives* you faith in the future. As usual, you've got it backwards."

"Whatever. But it's not happening. It's not something—"

He holds up his hands to stop her. "You don't have to explain. Tim warned me."

"What's that supposed to mean?"

"He sees things more clearly than I do. It comes from growing up in a shack in Appalachia. He knew you'd take off as soon as anyone expected anything from you."

Andrew removes a knife from the wooden rack at the end of the work island. He squints, eyeballing the large mound of dough he's been working on. With sure, swift strokes, he cuts the ball in half, quarters, eighths, sixteenths. Slowly, methodically, as he does everything, he takes each of the small pieces and kneads them down into individual loaves. To Marea the unleavened loaves look like worms.

Later that night, after they've spent hours working without talking, they are alerted by the whistling that signals the arrival of Andrew's friend Howie, who often visits the bakery after the Lion's Head Bar on Sheridan Square shuts down for the night. That's where Howie composes poems with the help of his friend Jack Daniels. Howie is a Vietnam veteran who believes he's a channel for the poet Siegfried Sassoon—the poems he "receives" merge the horrors of World War I with the atrocities Howie witnessed in Vietnam. He makes his living by reciting his poems on the steps of the New York Public Library and then offering mimeographed copies for sale, a quarter apiece. Usually when Howie comes whistling up the back alley, it's because he's finished a new poem, and he reads it to them with one hand against the doorjamb and the other holding his spiral pad. One poem was about an Amerasian baby who slept on a mat while his mother serviced American soldiers with fifty-cent sex; another was about a soldier who dreamed he could fly like an angel after punji stakes had shredded his feet and ankles beyond repair. Marea has told Howie her own dreams about Vietnam.

"You're going to like this one," Howie announces when he appears at the back door. He's wearing his usual uniform—army fatigues embroidered with chains of flowers and a red bandana tied around his forehead. He's muscular and stocky, and the only evidence of his injuries is the slight cant of his body as he holds the position that braces his metal leg.

"This one's called 'Green-Eyed Girl Who Dreams.'" He flips his pad open to the page he wants, then raises his hand to salute Marea. "In your honor, my lovely one." He takes a deep breath and reads.

Her green eyes dream horrors
This maimed soldier's muse
She lies down with my enemies
Dreaming them alive again
And though I love this sad-eyed beauty
I haven't legs or heart enough
To hold her safely
And close her eyes to rest
Even as she dreams me whole again
And makes my ghost leg sleep.

"Hope I didn't embarrass you," Howie apologizes to Marea.

She shakes her head. "Not at all."

Andrew says, "You write beautifully."

"Gotta write what's in your heart." Howie shrugs. "Otherwise you're no poet at all."

"I love you, too," Marea tells him.

"Sure you do." Howie points at Andrew. "Anyway, I wanted to let you know I'm heading west for a few weeks—taking the morning bus out to Seattle to see my mom. Once a year, got to show up for her Rice Crispy treats with M&M's and jelly beans. I bet you'd never guess she made up the recipe herself. She'll be on the porch waiting for me. First of August. Every year since 'Nam, that's our date."

"You're a good son," Andrew says.

"How about you and Tim? You guys planning on takin' off at all this summer?"

"I'd like to. Tim gets so frantic in August when school's about to start up again. I'd love to take him to Fire Island to cool out, but I'd have to shut down the bakery."

"The neighborhood would survive," Howie assures him.

Andrew and Marea take turns hugging Howie and then follow him to the back door to wave good-bye. After he departs, they lean on opposite jambs and look at one another.

"I wouldn't be able to pay you if I closed up shop for a vacation."

"That's okay. You should go. I won't need much money for a while. Thanks to Freud, my shrinks are all leaving town."

"But you're not going to disappear on me."

Marea puzzles over Andrew. "I didn't realize you'd miss me so much."

"You don't know much, do you?"

"So now I've got five shrinks?"

"But I'm the only one of them who loves you. Me and Howie, two guys crazy over a silly green-eyed girl."

For six weeks now, every Tuesday morning at eleven o'clock Dr. Iris has welcomed Marea into her quiet room and encouraged her to recount the stories of her travels. Dr. Iris listens intently and without judgment. That is her God-given gift. She listens as if the earth has stopped still on its axis.

Marea has grown used to the upward tilt of Dr. Iris's chin as she concentrates, her hands folded in her lap, the changing silver jewelry and changing flowers, her datebook pages that grow dark as she marks off her appointments. Each Tuesday Marea brings a basket with three freshly baked loaves and takes back the empty basket Dr. Iris has ready for her. Dr. Iris is the only one of Marea's four therapists old enough to be her parent. She is also the only one who does not reserve ten minutes between patients, but gives Marea the full hour. Each week Marea waits through the brief time it takes Dr. Iris to cross a mental bridge between two lives. When Dr. Iris is ready, she nods once, her invitation for Marea to begin.

"I bought myself a full-length mirror last week."

"Oh? What prompted that?"

"This is the first time in years I've even had a place to put a full-length mirror."

"You can look at yourself now."

"Though it confuses me to do that."

"Tell me what you mean."

"When I look in the mirror, there's a grown woman there. But when I don't see myself, I often feel like a child."

"In what way a child?"

"I have no defense against pain."

"That's certainly a theme in your stories."

"I want to tell you another story, not a story really—it's when I knew I had to come home. I don't recall what month it was, though it must have been winter because everyone on the ferry between Scotland and Belfast had their collars turned up and their caps pulled down. I wanted to travel down to Dublin—to be in the city where words worked for sound as well as sense."

"James Joyce."

"Yes. My plan was to take a bus from Belfast to Dublin. With the IRA and everything I didn't think Northern Ireland was a place I should hitchhike. So I walked from the ferry dock to the bus station, past the police barracks wrapped in razor wire fifty feet high. Children ran through the streets ahead of me, never looking right or left, as if their single-mindedness could protect them."

"You have such an interesting way of putting things."

"I do?"

"What you said about the children—their single-mindedness protecting them. Someone else might only see them as children in a hurry. Anyway, please go on."

"When the bus came I chose a seat by the window, and we drove through Belfast past all the blown-up buildings and boarded-up windows. I wondered how people found the will to carry on in such a dreary place. As the afternoon grew dark and the bus droned on down the Belfast-Dublin road, sadness came over me. I felt more alone than I'd ever felt in my life. Here I was again on a bus between cities. Here I was again trying to stay warm by a cold window—once again facing the job of finding some place to spend the night. The thought became almost more than I could bear. I had no ties to anything or anyone. Nobody knew where I was or cared.

"When I got off the bus in Dublin the city was already dark, and the air was freezing cold and damp from the rain. I wandered with my backpack through the empty streets, stood watching families moving behind windows. I was so cut off. It was like that time in the Inca city when the fog surrounded me, only this time I saw that I had done it to myself. I found a youth hostel. The custodian opened the door, handed me a blanket, pointed me to an empty dormitory room with no light or heat. I curled up on a corner cot, shivering and wondering what had become of me. I don't know if I cried. I can't imagine I would have let myself cry because the loneliness would have been unbearable. I don't know if I slept either. By morning I had made up my mind that I had come to the end of my travels. It took me six months to earn the airfare home."

"Marea, you know I'm going to be away for the next four weeks."

"Yes, we went over that."

"And what are your plans for August? Do you have any?"

"I've been thinking about going to Princeton to see my mother. Remember I called her two weeks ago to say I was back. It doesn't seem right not to see her—though I'm a little nervous about it after all this time."

"Why is that?"

"I'd like to be able to be generous toward her, but I'm afraid I won't be."

Dr. Iris waits for Marea to say more.

"I suppose I had to blame someone for his death."

"That would be natural for a child."

"I'm not a child anymore."

Marea has not seen Dr. Iris standing since their very first session when she waited at the top of the stairs. Now Marea watches her get up from her chair.

"May I give you a hug? Since this is our last session for a while."

When Marea rises to meet her, she is surprised at how small Dr. Iris is, but when Dr. Iris's arms tighten around Marea, their grip is strong.

Dr. Iris selects one of the turtles from her table and gives it to Marea. "Why don't you keep this until I return?"

Marea feels the smooth enamel of the glazed clay, bright blue, sea green. "Thank you."

Dr. Iris returns to her chair. "Take good care of yourself while I'm gone, Marea, and good luck with your trip home. There will be stories there, too, stories that will need telling. I'll see you in a month."

3

He is standing with his arms held out to her, that half-smile she remembers, his red hair combed back into a pompadour, his face as always a little flushed, the thin scar crossing his cheekbone like the track of an escaping tear he hasn't brushed away. It has been so long since she's seen him. She feels a rush of love and confusion, so many questions crowding her thoughts. His presence is thrilling, but also unremarkable. That is the odd thing, the way she accepts the ordinariness of it, her father alive and well. He hasn't come from a far distance or another time; he is here, gazing upon her, accepting her recognition of him. He waits smiling, as real as her own fingers—until a slash of sunlight falls across her face, the metallic twang of an electric guitar alerts her, and even though she shifts for more sleep, the cool sheet tightening across her flesh brings news that her waking senses have overtaken her dreaming ones. The father in her dream evaporates, a fleeting resurrection.

Dawn's Early Rising has been shut down for two weeks now, its proprietor no doubt frolicking in the water off Fire Island, at the gay beach enclave known as the Pines, while his baking apprentice has slowly returned to her normal circadian rhythm, sleeping through the nights, expectations crawling by midmorning. Each morning she has planned to make the train trip to Princeton, New Jersey, and each evening she realizes she hasn't done it.

She sits up on her elbows and recollects that her father has visited in her sleep before, leaving her, as now, oddly peaceful. Somewhere he watches over her and comes to her when she needs him.

Her collection of artifacts from her travels is spread across the floor in one corner of the room. Many times over the last two weeks she has sat cross-legged, holding one item and then another. Now she rolls off her mattress and crawls nude across the room to pick up the chunk of red coral she found planted in wet sand on the beach at Mombassa on the coast of East Africa. The evening tide had left it there for her to discover in the morning. She carried it to the dry sand and sat with her prize, studying the clustered red pipes that could have been a miniature city sheltering a thousand lives, or a still heart that pumped blood to only one.

Marea lets the shower water run over her a long time, waiting for a decision. She stands by her window wrapped in a towel. The morning sun is spreading across the cement below. She pulls on a pair of blue jeans and the T-shirt she washed and left to dry on the fire escape. Her mother will notice details. She sits on the floor to fill her backpack with only the bare essentials, none of her treasures—no stones or shards of sea glass. She would like to be as opaque as sea glass for the day ahead. She has already envisioned the examination on the doorstep. Her mother will want to evaluate what has become of her daughter in seven years. She will examine Marea for signs of happiness, unhappiness—success, failure—imagining, as mothers do, the worst.

How will Marea protect herself against such scrutiny? Her father had special dark glasses to protect his eyes from the blinding light of nuclear blasts. She had her own protection when he went off to New Mexico and California—an Atomic Bomb Ring she earned with four Kix boxtops and the correct answers to six questions about American presidents. The ring came with an observation lens, a metallic atom chamber, a secret flip-up message compartment. In the early years when the airplane trip took the whole day and Marea was still asleep at the hour her father had to leave for the airport, he would fold a message inside the ring's secret compartment—a note from Captain Caterpillar to Buck-private Butterfly—promising further adventures in the Institute Woods. Even when she was older and he dropped her at school on his way to the airport, there would be a message for her to find when she came home. There was no message the morning he left forever.

Marea hikes the quiet Sunday streets with her backpack. Passing through Washington Square Park, she notices a woman on a bench, dressed in rags and cradling a red satin high-heeled shoe in her hands. The old woman has more shoes than teeth. Her lips cave in, but they smile in rich contentment. The satin shoe is hers now and will be given a place in her cumulus of possessions, the booty in the two shopping carts that flank her. Her carts are not loaded with the shells, stones, and ocean coral that Marea collects, but with the detritus of city life. In a hip gallery in SoHo the homeless woman's creation—the ribbons, rags, socks, orange wig, mop head tied to the metal spokes of her carts—would be given its place as art.

Marea has planned her trip: At Eighth Avenue the Fourteenth Street shuttle meets the northbound IRT. At Thirty-third Street the underground tunnels lead into Penn Station and the platform where the New Jersey Transit line departs New York City. Marea grabs the railing to hoist herself and her backpack onto the Trenton train to Princeton.

The car she walks into smells of hot popcorn. Marea hadn't thought to eat before her trip, and as she moves along the aisle in search of a seat, she is also hunting down the siren smell. When she finds it, she looks so hungrily at the open box that the boy holding it pulls it tight against his chest.

"Is this seat taken?"

He shrugs.

"Can I sit here? Are you alone?"

"Yeah, I'm by myself. My father put me on the train. I'm going back to my mother."

"Funny. I'm going home to my mother, too."

"Why is that funny?"

Marea slips her arms out of her backpack, lifts it up into the overhead rack, and takes the seat facing the boy. She studies him a moment, his round Lilliputian face, feathery hair, tortoiseshell glasses, a serious little man.

"How old are you?"

"Twelve. How old are you?"

"Thirty."

"That's old."

"Twelve can be old."

"When your parents are divorced."

"When your father dies."

"Your father died when you were twelve?"

"Car accident. Smashed into an eighteen-wheeler."

"Oooh—that's *bad*." He shakes his head over the image this conjures in his mind, then holds his popcorn box toward her in sympathy. "Want some?"

"You a Deadhead?"

"You mean this?" He points his thumb back at his T-shirt and the picture of Jerry Garcia puffing on a bong. "My dad bought it for me to piss off my mom. My dad's a serious doper. That's how come she left him."

"You mind him smoking dope?"

"It's his business. I don't see him much anyway. But I'm sure not frying *my* brains like his. I'm gonna be a scientist."

"My father was a scientist."

"Yeah? What kind?"

"The kind that makes nuclear bombs."

"No shit."

Marea smiles. "Yeah, no shit."

The boy's eyes grow wide behind his round glasses, and he brings his legs up and crosses them under him on the seat.

"That's pretty cool. Did he ever see one explode?"

"Sure. When they were testing them in the desert."

"How about you? Did you see it?"

"Thirty's not *that* old, thank you very much."

"Sorry."

"We had air-raid drills, though. In school you had to get under your desk and put your arms over your head. It was supposed to protect you from a nuclear blast. Pretty dumb, huh?"

"I've seen that poster—'In case of nuclear war, put your head between your legs and kiss your ass good-bye.'"

Marea laughs. "You got it."

When the train emerges from under the Hudson River and sunlight pours in, the boy looks out and taps his fingers nervously on the window.

"Your stop coming up?"

"Yeah."

"You miss your mom when you spend time with your dad?"

He shrugs. "I don't see her that much, either. They don't like kids hanging around the ashram. She teaches yoga there. My dad never sends us any money."

"I guess when you're a scientist, you'll be able to take care of her. So what kind of scientist are you planning to be?"

"An ecologist. They protect things. If there's anything left to protect by the time I grow up."

"You're pretty smart, aren't you?"

He folds his arms across his chest. "That's what they tell me."

His attention drifts out the window again and Marea's attention follows. Praying mantises suck oil along the shoreline. Black refinery smoke twists into the blue sky. The boy consults his train schedule and checks his wristwatch several times, then climbs up onto the seat to bring his small suitcase down from the rack.

"You need help?" Marea offers.

"I'm okay."

"When do you get off?"

"Eight minutes."

He sets his suitcase on the seat beside him, flips open the top, and pulls out a fresh T-shirt. He yanks the Jerry Garcia T-shirt off over his head, balls it up, and tosses it onto the seat behind the suitcase. Marea stares at his smooth skin, pink as fingernails, until it disappears inside his clean shirt.

"Aren't you taking your present?"

"My dad thinks it's funny to piss off my mom, but I don't."

"I bet you're going to be a good ecologist."

"Probably."

"You seem to know what's worth protecting. I think my father couldn't protect things. Maybe that's why he killed himself."

"You said it was an accident."

"I've always wondered. You know how when you're a kid, people lie to you."

The boy takes a handful of popcorn and fills his mouth. "How're you gonna find out?"

"What?"

"If your father killed himself or not. If it was me, I'd want to know."

"Any ideas?"

"Didn't you say you're going to see your mother? You could ask her. You're not a kid anymore. Maybe she'll tell you the truth." He folds down the flaps on the box of popcorn and holds it out to her. "You can have the rest."

"You didn't tell me your name."

"I'll only tell you 'cause I'm never seeing you again. They named me Moon. Can you believe that shit? If you have kids, definitely stick to names like Brian and Jennifer."

"Want to hear something weird? I've got the same name as you. My name is Marea—it's Latin for moons. You think maybe we're related?"

"My mom says we're all related."

The train slows and Moon stands up for his stop. With his suitcase hanging at his side, he looks like a miniature traveling salesman.

"I think you should ask your mother about your father," he advises soberly, and then heads down the aisle, his suitcase banging against each seat he passes.

Marea watches until the metal door slides closed behind him. Something is slipping away, something she would like to keep. The train picks up speed, and she looks out the window in time to see a pale woman dressed all in white fold her son into her arms.

The walk from the Princeton station to Blossom Street isn't long, and Marea knows it well. But it's been years, and she walks slowly to let the place sink in. She recognizes the smell of summer honeysuckle, the cooling shade beneath huge maples, the emptiness of streets where children have played, left, and not returned.

The house she grew up in is in a row of identical brick houses spaced just far enough apart to allow each family a front lawn, a single-car garage, and waist-high hedges tall enough for privacy, but not so high as to seem rude. The brass numbers 117 are still tacked at a diagonal on the front door. There is still a metal awning covering the walkway from the kitchen to the garage. But the two rows of peonies that once welcomed guests like a retinue of bowing courtiers are gone.

Marea recalls a jerky eight-millimeter home movie. She was a little girl wearing a pinafore and ruffled cotton socks. Her mother wore gardening gloves, an apron over her summer dress, her shoulders bare except for the wide straps—a beauty queen with shiny black hair and full, red lips. Marea eagerly took each newly cut stem from her mother's gloved hand and carried it carefully, as if it were a lit candle, to the newspapers spread open on the cross-hatched brick path. She lined up each new flower alongside the last, so they formed two straight lines, Madeline and the orphans in their beds. Her father loved his new possession, a Brownie eight-millimeter movie camera. When her mother couldn't bear the strain of acting for the camera another moment, he apologized and gathered his beautiful wife and his toddler daughter into his arms; Marea was pressed between their warm bodies, the furthest reach of her world.

Standing on the path, Marea scans the façade of the house as if trying to place a face that should mean more to her than it does. Slowly details fill in—the eyelet curtains in the second-story window, a small room inside with a patchwork quilt on a narrow maple bed, the headboard stenciled with sprigs of holly, matching maple chair and desk.

She rings the bell, and as she hears the approaching footsteps, her mouth goes dry. The door opens slowly. There is recognition, but no leap of feeling or rush of words. The woman examining her is tired, cautious, old.

"I'm sorry I didn't call ahead to tell you I was coming. I got some time off work."

"You're working?"

"I told you on the phone."

"Oh, yes. In a bakery."

"It's a good job," Marea defends.

Virginia looks past Marea to the street. "Why are we here in the doorway?"

As Marea steps inside, they both realize that they ought to reach out to one another. It's a stilted embrace, made more awkward by Marea's backpack. Marea waits to be released, then pulls her arms out of the straps and sets her backpack on the floor.

"That looks heavy."

"I'm used to it."

"Is that all you have?"

"All I have?"

"Are those your things?"

Marea understands the question: Are you staying?

"I have an apartment in New York."

"Of course."

Virginia Hoffman is dressed in a summer suit, tailored blue linen. Her hair is pulled back into a bun. She is wearing wire-rim glasses, something Marea does not recall. There is a string of pearls at her neck.

"Were you on your way out?" Marea touches her fingers to her own clavicle to indicate her mother's necklace.

"Actually, I've just come in. I've taken to going to Meeting again. I find it—" She pauses to think how to describe her feelings to a woman so different from herself, a daughter who has never understood her. "I find it soothing."

Marea thinks back on the soothing silence of their Quaker Meeting, the smooth pine benches, the morning coolness coming through screened windows. The square room had no adornments, "nothing to distract the eye." Her mother taught that she must learn to use her "inner eye," find her "inner light." Each Sunday, dressed in clean clothes, Marea had sat flanked by her parents in the front seat of the Oldsmobile as they drove to the edge of town and parked behind the white clapboard Meeting House. The three of them filed down the aisle to their customary bench as her mother nodded in silent recognition to this friend or that, people her parents socialized with at potluck suppers in one another's homes. At those suppers, sitting in her father's lap, Marea had been perplexed by what adults called "conversation." How did they know what topic to discuss and whose turn it was to speak? When they had conversations about the "Cold War," Marea wondered how war could have a temperature. When they said that testing nuclear bombs was mad, Marea did believe a bomb could be angry. The adults' favorite subject was their famous neighbor, her Grandpa Albert, and whatever he had last written to the president or announced to the newspaper reporters who tagged after him whenever he walked out of his house on Mercer Street. A few times Marea had heard them talk about her real grandfather, an important man who had worked with President Wilson to make a League of Nations that would put an end to war, hot or cold, forever.

Though from time to time her mother had spoken in Sunday Meeting, Marea had never seen her father rise to speak until the morning she felt his body trembling. Even after all his years in America, he was still insecure about his English. He began haltingly, through a red rage.

"I do what I do—I do what you all despise me for—because God made both good and evil. You ridiculous people who do not believe that the Russians are our enemies will go to your slaughter like sheep, like my own father and mother, both murdered for the crime of being Jews." He unfolded a piece of paper from his pocket, more confident to read someone else's words than to speak his own. "'Only among people who think no evil exists will evil monstrously flourish.'" He stood waiting for someone to reply to him, and when no one did, he shouted. *"Do you not hear me? Do you not hear that your pacifism is the path of surrender?"* He had grabbed Marea's hand and pulled her up the aisle after him. By the time they reached the parking lot, Virginia was in pursuit, her face streaked with tears. *"You have brought shame on me! You have brought shame on your family!"*

He had held the car door and waited mutely for Virginia to slide into the front seat. They had driven home in silence, Virginia huddled against the passenger door, tears falling onto her lap, and Jonas gripping the steering wheel, his body rigid. For a few weeks after that Sunday Marea and her mother went to the Meeting House alone, but then they had stopped going altogether.

"Why don't I make us lunch?"

"I don't want you to go to any trouble."

"I hardly think of making lunch for my daughter as trouble. I was about to make a sandwich for myself. I brought home fresh cold cuts." She regards Marea with a worried look and presses her hand to the side of her neck as if relieving stress. "Perhaps you don't eat meat. Some of my students will only eat Hydrox. They say that Oreos are made with animal fat."

"Cold cuts are fine. I'll take my backpack upstairs. I'd like to see my room."

"Of course. Go right ahead. I'll get busy in the kitchen." She steps aside for Marea to pass. "Do you know it's been seven years, four months, and twelve days?" She forces a laugh. "Can you imagine, I've counted the days."

Marea promises, "I'll wash up and come right back down."

"Make yourself at home." Virginia shakes her head. "What a silly thing to say. Of course, this is your home."

Marea stops at the gallery of family photographs that hang in the upstairs hall, a museum her mother left unaltered even after the death of her husband. Marea examines herself with her front teeth missing, grinning energetically for the school photographer. She studies the photograph in which her mother embraces her wedding bouquet, looking as glamorous as the woman in the eight-millimeter movie. Virginia's head rests on her new husband's shoulder, a tall young man who looks more stunned than happy. There is a photograph of her grandfather with Woodrow Wilson, and next to it another historical photograph—her father's favorite—the famous scientists of the Manhattan Project, who are gathered to observe the final stages of packing the plutonium core for the Trinity test. Her father, a junior scientist in the background, was proud to recite for Marea the names of the illustrious men in front of him. He also liked to tell her the story of his assignment to climb the platform and watch over the bomb until the morning test. That night an electrical storm had traveled toward the platform from across the desert, and they had prayed that the bomb they had made by manipulating forces of nature would not accidentally be detonated by nature's own messenger, a bolt of lightning.

As this historic photograph was being taken in New Mexico, history was also being made in the maternity ward at Presbyterian Hospital in Philadelphia. In the next photograph a chubby-cheeked baby is held up to the camera. The war is over. The three of them are in front of their new home on Blossom Street. But her father doesn't look like a man relieved of worries. In the time between these two photographs, the atomic bomb he worked on killed over a hundred thousand innocent citizens of Hiroshima.

Virginia has set two places at the dining room table, mats with matching cloth napkins, two glasses of ice water, a small vase of blue campanulas. She is untying her apron as Marea comes through the dining room door.

"Come. Please take your seat." She points to the chair that was always Marea's at the table.

"You still grow flowers?"

"I have my little greenhouse out back, my escape from the world."

Marea waits for her mother to say grace.

"Thank you, Lord, for this bounty of which we are about to partake, and for the good fortune of a daughter's safe return. Thank you, generous Father, for these and all your abundant gifts."

After amen, Virginia reaches her hand across to Marea, who obliges with an open palm. Marea feels her mother's dry skin and fights the strong desire to withdraw. She hears her mother's words, "I'm so happy to have you home."

Marea replies, "I'm glad to be here."

Virginia picks up her sandwich. "Now tell me all about the bakery." She has spent her time in the kitchen choosing safe topics. She lost her daughter for seven long years and she has no intention of losing her again.

"It's called Dawn's Early Rising. I work for the owner, Andrew Martin. He's teaching me everything about baking bread." Marea pushes up her sleeve to reveal her biceps. "He insists we do all the kneading by hand, no machines. It's hard work."

"I can imagine. Well, it's always good to learn new skills. It stimulates the mind."

"How about you? You mentioned before about the Oreos. I thought you had decided to retire from tutoring."

"I wish I could. Unfortunately there's always something that needs doing on the house, and workmen are so expensive nowadays."

"But how about Dad's pension? You still have that, don't you?"

"I'm afraid with today's rate of inflation the pension checks don't go as far as they once did."

"It doesn't seem fair that they don't increase it to cover inflation."

"They do, a little. But they have to conserve, too, I suppose. They've got lots of young families coming along and they have to put money away for them. I'm grateful they've kept up the payments all these years. They don't anticipate a husband dying so young." Virginia's expression clouds. She's waded into waters she had been determined to avoid. She points to Marea's sandwich. "I didn't think to ask. Would you like mustard?"

"But that's the point of a pension, a guarantee for life. It isn't only for widows whose husbands die at eighty."

Virginia pushes back from the table. "I'd like some mustard myself."

Marea sits alone in the dining room and her morning dream returns. She looks out the window to the white birches, the hickory and oak beyond, the path that was their gateway to the woods. Virginia comes back with mustard and a bowl of fruit, and stops a moment to look out the window with Marea. "Isn't summer a pretty time of year in Princeton? Everything so lush and green." After the fruit, Virginia brings in tea and a plate of sliced pound cake. She doesn't allow Marea to help with any of it. "I want the pleasure of looking after you, if you don't mind."

Virginia asks only the safest questions and Marea answers with an appearance of openness. When Virginia says, "Tell me how you liked England—you didn't write much about it," Marea entertains her with a description of the cast of characters at the squat in Stoke Newington. She gives an upbeat rendition, skipping over the drug overdoses, the sexual promiscuity, the terrifying night when one of the squatters, high as a kite on speed, set the whole building on fire at three o'clock in the morning.

After lunch, Marea asks if it would be all right if she took a nap. Virginia is eager to accommodate. She says she could use the time to pay a sick call. A dear friend has emphysema, her lungs exhausted with every breath. Marea is lying on top of the patchwork quilt when she hears the car starting up, backing out of the garage, the motor fading away down Blossom Street. She looks up at her bedroom ceiling to the fluorescent stars she glued there many years ago, a birthday gift from Albert Einstein. Silence settles in the house. She hasn't been alone here in years.

Marea sits up, swings her legs off the bed, and hurries down the steep back stairs to the kitchen, one hand sliding down the smooth banister, the other along the familiar wallpaper, faded bouquets of bluebells tied with yellow ribbons. In the kitchen Marea is struck immediately by something that had never been there when she lived in the house—a padlock on the door to the basement where her father worked. Why would her mother lock the basement?

Marea circles the kitchen. Hunting in one drawer after another for the key, finding only utensils and string and dish towels, she grows agitated. Has her mother cleaned out the basement? Has she put the room to some other use? Have the specimen boxes been set out with the trash or sold? Of course her mother couldn't be trusted to know what was important and why. Finally Marea's gaze lands on a ring of keys hanging in the pantry. She tries one key after another with no luck. She starts over, keeping the keys carefully separated between her fingers. At last the lock pulls apart. She slips it out of its hasp, opens the door, breathes deeply. As she hurries down the stairs into the darkness, the cool air calms her.

She yanks on the chain hanging from the exposed lightbulb, and it all floods back, the room that would have been buried with him had he been an Egyptian noble, all his precious belongings that would have provided comfort on the journey to the next world. Reference books, wood and metal tools. Microscopes, binoculars, magnifying lenses. All the equipment he cherished.

With the heel of her hand she wipes dust away from one of the specimen boxes. Like life preserved below the surface of a frozen lake, the butterflies remain exactly as she remembers them. She takes an old shirt off a hook—her father's shirt—and goes to work cleaning one glass after another. There are the identifying labels written in her father's careful handwriting—the common names, the Latin names, and the names Marea chose for them. The wings still have their iridescence—blue, purple, silvery white—as brilliant as the day they were caught.

Her father's incantation: observe, describe, record. He quizzed her on the varieties of fungi and their parts—gleba, sporophore, volva. Tutored her to find the precise word to describe the stem of the Old Man in the Woods: scaly. The branches of *Ramaria for-*

mosa: toothed. He made her chart the life cycle of ferns—spore production, vascular bundle, phloem, xylem, and epidermis—and required her to diagram the rules of photosynthesis. Looking through the microscope he guided her to see: beyond every skin, within every pore, life was working.

Marea runs her fingertips across the glass to touch memory and time. She puts her cheek to his dust-covered shirt, picks up reference guides, nets. She feels an absence, something missing even before she fully registers the empty space on the shelf. That was where they kept the spiral notebooks they filled with the records of their walks together, their private thoughts, their observations of nature.

Marea knows that the attic is where her mother stores what she no longer wants to keep in sight. Virginia had emptied Jonas's drawers, put their contents in boxes, and carried the boxes up to the attic within days of his death. Marea can imagine her mother putting their spiral notebooks into a box as well and banishing them and whatever they represented to the attic. Marea fastens the lock back on the basement door, hangs the ring of keys in the pantry, and heads upstairs.

In the hall, in sight of her father's eyes, Marea positions a chair beneath a brass ring in the ceiling. This is something she has never done before. Forays through this trap door were always her mother's work; the attic was out-of-bounds.

With a firm tug, the ladder drops down. Pent-up heat rushes toward her as she climbs the unsteady ladder and pulls herself out onto the rough-hewn floor. She breathes in the musty smell, notices the sunlight filtering through small windows, revealing stacks of boxes, clothing bags, suitcases, a metal filing cabinet. From where Marea crouches she can see that the file drawers are labeled in her father's handwriting. She crouches under the eaves and pulls at the drawer labeled "1955–1957." It's locked. She pulls on the other drawers, all locked. She stills her breath to listen. Does she have time to get the ring of keys from the pantry and try them on the file drawers before her mother returns?

Carefully, backing down the ladder, she finds the rungs with the balls of her feet. At last, standing securely on the chair, she turns to step down to the floor.

"What's going on here?" Her mother's mouth is tight, fists punched into hips.

"You're back."

"Of course I'm back. This is my home, isn't it? What have you been doing in my attic?"

"Looking."

"Looking for what?"

"Looking for whatever you've got locked in those files."

"Do you make a habit of going through other people's things without permission?"

"Those files don't belong to you—they were his."

"Precisely—*his*, not yours."

"I don't have a right to see my father's files?"

"When I'm dead, you can look at anything you want."

"I'm not waiting until you're dead."

"Is this why you came back here? To snoop around and stir up trouble?"

"You know why I came. I told you on the phone. I need to know the truth about his death."

Virginia exhales deeply. "Respectable people do not go prying into other people's lives." Without meeting Marea's eyes, she retreats down the hall and into her bedroom, and pulls the door shut behind her.

Marea wakes into early evening darkness. The house is still, and she lies still. She would like not to have to choose a course of action for a very long time.

There is a soft knock on the door, the rattling of porcelain cups and saucers. A second knock. "May I come in?" The door opens, letting in hall light. "You've slept a long time. You must have been exhausted."

Marea pulls herself up to sit against the headboard and allow the bed tray to be placed across her lap.

"I made your favorite snacks from when you were a little girl."

Marea looks down at a plate of cucumber sandwiches, celery stalks filled with peanut butter and dotted with raisins, vanilla cookies, a pot of tea, a pitcher of milk, cups and saucers. She feels heat rushing toward her, as she did when she opened the attic door.

"Do you recall how you used to insist I make you cucumber sandwiches? And salt them just so. And your ants on a log? How you found that recipe in your Brownie Scout magazine and made me prepare it after school a hundred times or more? We called it your ants-on-a-log period."

She is hovering, laden with expectations and nowhere to put them.

"Shall I pour your tea?"

"I can pour it."

"The milk is hot."

"Would you like to pour it, then?"

"If you like."

Marea settles back into the pillows, settles into being a daughter being cared for by a mother working to adjust reality. Marea tastes the cucumber sandwich held out to her, and the particular mix of salt and mayonnaise and slippery coolness does the work it was meant to do.

"I'm sorry I went up to the attic without asking."

"You had a right."

"I should have asked first."

Virginia pours tea for herself and takes her cup to the window seat. She moves the curtain aside to look out onto the street, a habit.

"From time to time I've come in here to sit. I'd bring your letters and reread them. Being here helped me feel your presence—helped me imagine you—since I had begun to lose track of you—your voice, your face, what you must look like after all these years."

"I appreciated your letters in return," Marea says, only half-lying. "They were something I could count on."

"I felt it was something I could do to help."

"To help?"

"I imagined whatever was driving you on couldn't have been that easy to bear." Virginia drops the curtain and turns back to Marea. "What *was* driving you, if I may ask?"

None of Marea's four therapists have put the question to her quite like that, so directly, but Marea thinks, She's my mother, she has a right.

"Probably a lot of things."

"Was I too overbearing? Was that it? Were you trying to get away from me, my neediness—since we had lost your father?"

"I guess that could have been part of it."

"That's what I always suspected. I'm afraid I didn't know what to do about it—since it was the habit I had gotten into, depending on you, even though, of course, I claimed it was you who needed me."

Marea is pinned beneath a tea tray in her childhood bed.

"I hope you'll accept my apology."

"You don't have to apologize."

"It's my need again, not yours, I suppose. But, yes. I do need to apologize. It's weighed on me all these years. I always knew I drove you away. I keep wishing I could do it all over again, not lose you. I have no one else."

"It wasn't all because of you," Marea protests.

Virginia puts her cup aside, then takes it into her lap again, agitated. "You don't have to spare me, not at this point, not anymore."

Marea's skin is crawling. She grabs the handles of the tray, looking for a place to put it. She can't get out of the bed, can't escape this woman.

"I want to work this out with you, Marea."

She made a fist at each side of the tray, and the words burst out, *"Would you please stop? Please stop!"*

Virginia's shoulders square and her face goes cold. Marea knows she would like to scold her for speaking in such a tone—criticize her slovenly clothes, demand an explanation for why she has wasted her perfectly fine education, instruct her to find a man to marry so she can finally settle down to a reasonable life. Marea awaits her mother's harsh words, but Virginia is still as stone.

"Please," Marea begs. "I'm asking you. I need to know the truth. After all these years, I must know. Was it actually an accident—or was it—"

"Of course it was an accident," Virginia blurts. "Of course it was an accident. What else could it have been?"

Marea wants to cry—tears of frustration, impotence—but she won't. What had she expected?

"I'll leave you to yourself now."

Marea doesn't respond. It doesn't matter whether her mother goes or stays. As the door pulls shut, Marea lifts the tea tray off her bed and sets it on the floor. She lies back, wraps herself into the heavy patchwork quilt of her childhood, and accepts its sad embrace.

The three of them sat on the couch in front of the small television in its beechwood cabinet. April 18, 1955. The telephone call had come that morning at breakfast. Grandpa Albert had died in the night at Princeton Hospital. Something had ruptured inside of him, a vessel that pumped blood from his heart. He would never again come marching up the path to Sunday dinner holding a peony bud to slip behind Marea's ear. He would never again help her with her homework or watch television with her and howl at Sid Caesar doing the professor. He would never again dance her around the room whistling "The Merry Widow Waltz" through his mustache. Though it was such a very long time since they did any of these things together. Marea could not think of when he last came to visit her at all.

Walter Cronkite ticked off the achievements of "this century's greatest genius: a brilliant scientist who altered the course of history, a cultural icon whose name was synonymous with the search for world peace, a devout supporter of Israel, a generous humanitarian, a man of many memorable words, including his firm belief that 'God does not play dice with the universe.'"

From the moment her mother put down the phone and blurted out the news, tears sprang from Marea's eyes. She sobbed, sucking for air, inconsolable. Her father was puzzled by her grief. Didn't he know that children were capable of such feeling? Or was it that her grief, any grief, brought to mind the thing he refused to speak of, his own parents dead in unmarked graves? Marea was nearly ten, and she understood more than she used to. She had heard the anger in her mother's accusation: "*They* are dead. For pity's sake, why can't *you* live?"

Or maybe her father didn't understand her feelings because he didn't know that Grandpa Albert had told her secrets. Even though everyone called him a genius, the professor didn't know his times tables. He wished he had invented a refrigerator that didn't hum. He hated when people called him the father of the atomic bomb. What he hated most was that a chemical element had been named after him—einsteinium—the residue left after a nuclear explosion. Grandpa Albert had confided in his friend Marea: if he had known such terrible things would happen to the world, he would have been a locksmith instead of a scientist.

Between her father's worn corduroy pants and her mother's starched apron, between her parents who no longer touched, Marea peered at the television pictures in black and white and in her mind saw colors, his face beet red, his eyes blazing. She was clearing dishes, her job. Her mother was in the kitchen cutting slices of lemon pie. The words between her father and her Grandpa Albert were coming too fast, too loud, hurting her ears, hurting her skin. If only her mother would hurry back into the dining room to stop the yelling. Marea was scared. Grandpa Albert was grabbing his stomach with two hands. Maybe stomach pains were making him mad. She rushed back and forth, clearing a plate from one, a plate from the other, a fork from one, a fork from the other, drawing out her demonstration of loyalty to both her father and her grandpa as long as possible and trying to keep the earth from splitting.

"Finish your chores, Marea!" Her father pounded the dining table and the silverware jumped.

She ran to get her mother, who came through the kitchen door with the dessert tray clutched between white knuckles.

"Enough, enough! I've had enough of this!"

Grandpa Albert stood abruptly, bent forward from the waist, his chair crashing behind him. Virginia ran to help him, dessert tray upended onto the floor, pie plates flying, lemon curd in rug vines, shouting, accusations, and then silence.

Marea picked up Grandpa Albert's dinner napkin and held it out to him. Were there tears in his dark eyes? She went to his side, pressed herself against him, felt his body shaking. She looked back at her father, all alone, his eyes fluttering like butterflies afraid to settle. Why did they have to fight? And why was her mother hissing like a snake? "Do you see who she goes to? Do you see who she chooses?"

Grandpa Albert put his hand on Marea's head. "Good night, my dancing girl."

Then gone, doors closed, gone. Parents in separate rooms. Darkness wrapped the brick house, and Marea was alone.

She descends the stairs to tell her mother she will be leaving in the morning. At the entrance to the living room she is stopped by the strange sight of Virginia sitting alone in a pool of lamplight, looking like a lonely character onstage for the opening act or the closing one, a character who has reached the point of expecting nothing. Marea thinks of Dr. Iris sitting in her pool of light and longs for her, and for the cocoon of her velvet room.

Virginia barely seems to notice when her daughter slips into the chair opposite her. The living room curtains are drawn, and Marea cannot imagine a time they were ever open. She looks at the disheartened woman across from her, an older version of herself. If there is to be anything between them in the future, it will have to be constructed out of the words they find now.

"What's that?" Marea points to a neatly tied packet of yellowed papers in her mother's lap.

Virginia looks up at her estranged daughter. "What you were

looking for—what you came home to find." She speaks in a resigned voice Marea has never heard before. "Do you know, they advise parents that a child will refrain from asking questions until she's ready for the answers."

"Is that why parents lie?"

"I never lied to you."

"Not lied, but obscured things—so I couldn't see. And all I ever had was bits of memory."

"Could you accept that it was my way of protecting you? You had to grow up without a father. I couldn't alter that. But I could try to protect you from the despair that overcame him."

"It's true, then."

"What's true?"

"That he killed himself."

Virginia holds the packet of papers out toward Marea on the altar of her opened hands. "Nothing so clear as that. More difficult, more complex." Virginia rises. "I'll be in my room, if you wish to talk."

Marea recognizes his handwriting and feels a start. It returns her to her morning dream—his presence vital and real—and now she sits with him in her hands. She unties the string, untying a child's bonnet. As she rotates the pages to face her, she sees that each is headed with date and place, in the same way he headed the entries in their forest notebooks. Habits of a careful man. Does a careful man kill himself? She bows her head, asking his permission and forgiveness. She does not want to degrade him or turn him to dust. She moves to her mother's chair so the lamp will cast light on the pages. The first entry is July 16, 1945, Compañia Hill. Marea knows this place. She knows where her father was the morning she came into the world, and thirty years later she settles in to unearth his memories.

Jonas Hoffman, a tall, red-headed Austrian Jew of twenty-six with barely an ounce of extra flesh on his bones, a man still adjusting to a new language and a new life, aimlessly wandered through the remainder of the day that had changed everything. The war would be over soon, the second great war of the century. But for Jonas the triumph did nothing to ease the anguish he woke into every morning, fell asleep with every night. Though many shared his fate, there was no solace in comradeship. The loss of one's parents was particular, appalling, and it left a gaping void even if they were among thousands, hundreds of thousands, some now speculated millions of Jews exterminated from this earth.

Sometimes, like on the morning he had just experienced, when science was put to the service of furthering man's ability to kill, Jonas thought of how his parents, Viennese intellectuals, had brought him up to believe in the enlightenment of humankind through science. They were not secular Jews—they attended synagogue, said Shabbas prayers over bread and candles, insisted Jonas become a bar mitzvah—but they worshipped more at the altar of liberal idealism than at the Torah. Perhaps that's why they sent him to America, but didn't believe it necessary that they emigrate themselves. They still believed that reason would somehow prevail over the violent anti-Semitism unleashed that awful morning, March 13, 1938, the Anschluss, when red-and-white bunting dropped down from every apartment window along the Ringstrasse and Nazi flags were suddenly on sale at every street corner. March 13, the day squadrons of German bombers flew continuous relays over Vienna in a terrifying drone, and swastika lapel pins appeared on every Christian's topcoat—the day photographs of Hitler were hung in Christian shops, while the word *Jude* was slapped in black paint on every Jewish store. March 13, 1938—the day Austrian citizens lowered their own flag and welcomed Hitler's stormtroopers with open arms.

Jonas, a young university student, stood by helplessly on that freezing morning and witnessed his parents dragged from their home, forced to their knees along with all the elderly Jews in the neighborhood, and made to scrub the city's sidewalks with toothbrushes and burning acid. Otto Hoffman, a fifth-generation Austrian who had gone to the front in defense of his country in

World War I, was kicked in the ribs by a teenage boy wearing the uniform of the Austrian Nazi Youth, who screamed at Herr Hoffman that he wasn't working fast enough. Jonas's mother, scrubbing on her knees beside him, held her mortified husband in her arms while he shook and cried.

Jonas was in the habit of restricting how much he allowed himself to think of them. If he thought of them too much, the pain might kill him. He also limited his thoughts of his new wife, the beautiful, dark-haired Virginia Pell. Jonas's life was a delicately balanced scale—despair in one cup, hope in the other.

Virginia—he is trying to learn to call her by her nickname, Ginny—had insisted that a baby would ease his pain. Now he permitted himself a few moments of imagining his baby daughter in her bassinet. The telegram was folded neatly in his pocket. It had arrived two hours ago. *Girl born 9:23 A.M. STOP Ten fingers ten toes STOP What shall we name her STOP* He was making a family to replace the one torn from him. If there was a God, would he forgive Jonas for this act of forgetting?

Jonas thought of his own birth, his own childhood. He grew up breathing science the way other children breathed air. His mother taught chemistry at the gymnasium until her teaching credentials were revoked because she was Jewish. His father was the leading theorist in tensor calculus at Vienna University until his professorship was stripped from him under the Aryan Paragraph, well before the annexation by Germany. Jonas, the Hoffmans' only child, demonstrated an affinity for numbers even before he could speak. He and his father would sit for hours with pencil and paper playing the game they both loved, trying to stump each other on the properties of a chosen number. But when it came time to enter university, Otto Hoffman would not permit his son to matriculate in mathematics. With the Pan-German Party beginning to dominate every institution in Austria, Otto Hoffman insisted that a Jewish boy must study something that would be considered useful to any party that came to power. He made a joke for his son: "Even the Führer needs a physicist to explain which way the world is spinning." Peering over his gold-rimmed spectacles, Otto comforted his son. "You will find the order you love so much in physics as well as mathematics." Years later, when Jonas sought order in the natural world, he recalled his father's promise that in order there was meaning.

Jonas tried to impose order on the events of the historic morning he had just witnessed: the cold hour before dawn, men keyed up and waiting, mouths blowing hot breath, Dr. Teller spreading white cream on his face and neck to keep his skin from burning, his ledge of eyebrows turned to snow. "Use, use," said Dr. Teller, pushing his bottle of lotion at the men nearby, an immigrant army of brilliant scientists, but none smart enough to wear a jacket, so they beat their arms against the bitter cold. These scientists, with the biggest invention of their lives, were the boys who had once played with silver balls to calculate their speed against the inclination of the slope, dropped coins into oil and then water to compare the resistance of molecular structures, begged for chemicals and Bunsen burners and permission to use fire.

When Jonas watched Dr. Teller that morning, he couldn't help remarking on the contrast with his own father, a soft-spoken, almost timid man. Jonas wondered what his father would have said about the monster they had created. But there was no way to ask his father's opinion about anything, not since the gray day the small steamer floated into the strong current of the Danube, taking Jonas from his homeland forever. After months of taunting, Jonas had been beaten bloody by the young men wearing stormtrooper uniforms, who made a daily practice of lining the entry hall of the university's main building waiting for Jewish students whom they could attack. With shouts of *Tod den Juden*—Death to Jews—and armed with leather whips and brass knuckles, they set upon their prey, and no police or university officials stopped them. After the bloody beating, which left Jonas the thin scar that ran from near his left eye over his cheekbone and down his cheek, Otto Hoffman hastily arranged for his son to continue his studies in America. Alone at the rail of the steamer, Jonas watched his parents grow small, until suddenly his father broke away and ran down the dock, flailing his arms as if frantic to tell his son one more thing before he was gone into the fog. Until this very morning Jonas had received only one other telegram in his life. *Father taken to Gestapo headquarters at Hotel Metropol STOP Shot dead STOP Do not come home STOP.*

So many of them working there in the desert had lost their fathers in the Nazi pogrom. So Dr. Teller became their father. Dr. Oppenheimer became their father. Fermi and Bethe were their fathers. Staub, Weisskopf, Segrè. They were the men who trusted science to save the world from evil. They were the fathers who marshaled all these young men working together in secret toward the single purpose of insuring that America would be the first to have the atomic bomb.

Even though they had been instructed to lie facedown in the sand with their arms folded over their heads, Jonas had no intention of missing a nuclear explosion. Like everyone else his attention was focused on the tower twenty miles from where they waited—the wooden platform where he had camped out the previous night, baby-sitting Trinity, a sleepless child.

Jonas kicked his boot heel into the desert dirt again and again, standing close to Dr. Teller, who was mumbling to himself, his worries knocking around in the echo chamber of his mind, success or failure, two poles with nothing in between. Jonas had his own worries. His group had been responsible for setting the detonators to explode according to the microsecond timing required to squeeze the plutonium core and initiate the nuclear reaction. There was another worry on his and everyone else's mind—a thought beyond conception: Would the bomb ignite the earth's atmosphere and feast on oxygen and nitrogen until it incinerated the planet? The betting pool was their black joke. Where would the debts be paid, in heaven or in hell?

After the Trinity test was a resounding success, a holiday was declared in Los Alamos, champagne bottles were uncorked, and the merrymaking began. For hours Jonas wandered by himself past the empty labs and Quonset huts where acetylene torches were cold. The morning's observations ran over and over in his mind—the blinding light against a black sky, the massive fireball growing and growing, and then the roiling desert sea below rising up and slowly taking the fireball into its mouth. The sight of such unbridled power was terrifying. Dr. Oppenheimer's words were solace to some of those around him. "Lord, these affairs are hard on the heart." But Jonas was not conversant with his heart. It had become a stranger to him the day he received a letter smuggled through a German guard, no doubt at considerable expense. The letter arrived months after his last postcard from his mother, from "Lake Forest," the fake address Jonas had learned that Jews were required to put on mail sent from Auschwitz. The smuggled letter informed Jonas that on January 16, 1941, his mother, Hilde Hoffman, had been hung by the neck until dead for the crime of stealing a potato.

Jonas returned to the telegram in his pocket, to humble thoughts of his young wife, the woman to whom he was indebted for her faith that his heart might someday be a Lazarus. He had gone to a college social on the advice of his professor, who told him that a physicist without a wife would be a very lonely man. "You are tall and good-looking with your head of thick red hair. American ladies like boys who are tall and handsome." Jonas was a stranger to what ladies liked. He never had a woman before Ginny. He never wanted one. The only woman he wanted was his mother.

When he reread the morning telegram, he saw that Ginny had asked him to name their daughter. Jonas looked at the night sky and saw the moon hanging. The nuclear blast of the Trinity test had been reflected as a bright spot on the moon, but the dark seas on the other side—the marea—were safely distant from man's lethal power. Jonas whispered his baby daughter's name: Marea, Marea, the dark seas of the moon.

August 9, 1945

When the atomic bomb had been dropped on the Japs three days earlier, the news had spread through the barracks like wildfire.

Jonas was wedged among the crowd in the mess hall examining the photographs that came by courier. The photographs were laid out on the mess hall tables in chronological order, each labeled in the upper right-hand corner with the military time to the hundredth of a second. The pictures of the mushroom cloud were breathtaking. It was the view they hadn't gotten from Compañia Hill. The Hiroshima photographs were taken by the tail gunner of the *Enola Gay*: the mushroom cloud looked close enough to touch. Jonas's only regret was that the Nazis surrendered before the Allied forces had had a chance to drop the bomb on Germany.

The courier had also brought aerial photographs taken in the first fly-by after the mushroom cloud cleared. Using key landmarks to measure distances, the legend showed that four square miles of the port city of Hiroshima had been flattened along its seven branches of the Ota River. To Jonas the river and its tributaries looked like black ribbons lying across a dredged sea—the radio-linked parachutes dropped to measure the explosive yield looked like drifting jellyfish. He shook off these poetic images, remembering his father's instruction: observe, describe, record. As he compared the photographs taken moments before the bomb was dropped with photographs taken moments after, another set of photographs came to mind. To bolster enthusiasm for their work, General Groves had ordered distributed around Los Alamos a dozen copies of an issue of *Life* magazine with aerial photographs taken in the hours after the Japanese had torpedoed the USS *Indianapolis*. Hundreds of sharks circled the men desperately trying to swim to the safety of floating debris. Out of more than two thousand sailors on board, all but two hundred and eighty-four had been eaten alive or drowned. The same issue of *Life* had time-lapse photographs showing a Japanese soldier burning to death. The caption read "When Japs refuse to leave their pillboxes and surrender on the Pacific islands, the Allied forces use flame throwers to flush them out."

That evening in the barracks they had argued over whether the atomic bomb was simply more efficient than bombing with massive amounts of TNT or if it represented a quantum leap in the technology of war. To settle the argument, one of the men was dispatched to the research library to bring back aerial photographs of Tokyo taken earlier that year when a hundred B-24s killed 124,000 Japs in a single foray. The room stilled while the young scientists compared them with the photographs from Hiroshima. In the Tokyo photographs there was still a visible grid of streets and buildings left standing: there was still a city. In the photographs of Hiroshima, at least near the epicenter, there was nothing left, as if there had never been a city there at all.

That night Jonas had trouble sleeping. On the table beside his bed there was a photograph Ginny had sent of herself holding their new daughter. Nearby was the leaflet handed out that afternoon, a sample of what was to be distributed across America to head off criticism about dropping the atomic bomb on innocent civilians. The pamphlet was entitled "We Had No Choice." Under a picture of a handsome American soldier was the pronouncement "We didn't want *your* son to be killed while we waited for the Japs to surrender."

Jonas had no son, but he had a daughter now. Would he tell her that he had helped make a bomb that killed children who were riding their bicycles or still dreaming in their beds in order that no American family would have to imagine that its son had died in vain? Would he be so ashamed of what he helped create that he would tell a monstrous lie?

August 12, 1945

Jonas stood alone outside the mess hall after dinner watching the hills fade from orange to gray. In a few weeks he would be on his way home. They were all packing up for the return to civilian life. They had not been soldiers, but for months every waking moment of their lives had been devoted to the imperatives of war.

He was startled when out of nowhere Dr. Oppenheimer appeared in front of him. Though Oppenheimer was often surrounded by those who admired him, and had a beautiful wife and child, Jonas detected in him the habits of pain he himself was familiar with—a deep preference for his own solitary mind, and what some might call an unmanly aversion to a fight of any kind. Oppenheimer had a feminine slenderness not unlike Jonas's own, and delicate facial features almost too beautiful for a man.

Never having exchanged even two words with him, Jonas retreated a step when the director of the Manhattan Project stood before him, tipped slightly off center, , smoking a cigarette, a martini glass in one hand, cocktail shaker in the other. He handed the cocktail shaker to Jonas. "Would you mind accompanying a tired philosopher on a desert hike?"

Oppenheimer set out into the desert with long strides, confident that the young man whose name he did not know would follow him. When the sky grew dark and the stars began to dance, Oppenheimer paused a moment, poured himself another drink from the shaker, and sighed, "How we have desecrated this holy place with our presence."

As he marched on, stopping from time to time to refill his martini glass and light a new cigarette, Oppenheimer discoursed to the young scientist, clearly expecting no reply. Jonas recognized some of the literary references—the Sanskrit quotation Oppenheimer made famous after Trinity, "Now I am become Death, the destroyer of worlds," and the story of Prometheus and his guilt. Oppenheimer shook his head wistfully. "God gave us a magnificent gift in our capacity for remorse, and look at how we squander it."

Oppenheimer tipped the shaker to see if he'd gotten the last drop, then let his empty glass fall from his fingers to the ground. "Do you want to know the truth? The Japs who got incinerated were the lucky ones. Wait till they see what the radiation does to the survivors." Tears slid down his high cheekbones. "I had a teacher named Herb Smith—at the Ethical Culture School in New York City—he taught me that it was my job to make the world a better place. I wrote him a letter yesterday and asked him to forgive me." Oppenheimer stumbled and fell against Jonas, who had no idea what to do or say to the man sobbing against his shoulder. He didn't even know how to open his arms to hold him.

"I want to go home. Can you please take me home to Kitty?"

At the door of the ranch house in the Pecos Valley, high in the Sangre de Cristo Mountains, Jonas returned Robert Oppenheimer to his grateful wife. Jonas saw a woman like his own mother, a woman who did not judge a man for being overwhelmed by the world. Before shutting the door she asked Jonas to keep this encounter to himself. Now that her husband was preparing to take a position against further development of nuclear weapons, it would be difficult if people thought he was taking that position because he had lost his nerve.

September 17, 1945

Jonas was studying the waves of grain through the tinted window, traveling home by train instead of by air force transport because he needed time. He wrote Ginny that he wished to get a look at his adopted country, but the truth was that he needed to prepare himself for his new responsibilities. Everything seemed to have happened so quickly—a wife, a child, a job—and Jonas had never been at ease with the rush of life. As a boy in Vienna, when Gentiles still made friends with Jewish students, Jonas's closest companion had been a muscular Christian boy who protected him when they were required to play sports at school. Their son was "sensitive," the headmaster of the Realgymnasium reported to Oscar and Hilde Hoffman with pity. But they understood when Jonas explained to them that his mind was full of numbers and the balls the boys threw came at him too quickly. His mother never hurried him when he needed to stop a moment and listen to the hum of the natural world.

Now the world of people—the one he understood less well—had caught up with him. He was a married man, not because he had imagined it or sought it, but because a woman had approached him aggressively and made it possible for him to do it. Ginny had crossed Broadway from her dorm room at Barnard College to his room at Columbia without an invitation, and without giving him time to prepare his room or himself. When they were side by side in his narrow bed, he had no time to ask forgiveness from his dead parents for giving himself to a woman who was not a Jew. As he swam into her, accepting what she offered him, he decided that her being Gentile might save him. She would never fully comprehend his experience, never fully believe the savage hatred that had obliterated everything he loved. Her disbelief might help him; it might blot out his memories and bring him back to life.

Jonas was pleased that he had already accepted a civilian job a day before Norris Bradbury, who would soon replace Oppenheimer at Los Alamos, started through the barracks attempting to persuade the men to stay. Suddenly everyone was worried that the Russians, no longer trusted allies, were close to having an atomic bomb of their own. Dr. Teller, infused with hatred of Russians from his childhood in Hungary, was trying to drum up support for building a hydrogen bomb; he insisted the United States must never lose its lead to the Communists in the development of thermonuclear weapons. Jonas could have been drawn into this. He agreed with Teller's position that the Russians were every bit as anti-Semitic as the Germans. But Jonas had already accepted an offer from Dr. John von Neumann in Princeton, New Jersey. Von Neumann had heard of Jonas's work at Los Alamos and of his remarkable ability to see through—in his mind—to the solution of complex mathematical problems, and then work backward to structure the steps of the calculations. That sort of mathematical intuition was exactly what von Neumann needed for the development of his digital electronic computer. When Jonas agreed to join von Neumann at the Institute for Advanced Studies in Princeton, Ginny went immediately to Princeton to find them a place to live. A week later she sent a photograph of a small brick house at 117 Blossom Street, "a lovely new home," she wrote, "where our life together will flower."

As the train raced eastward, Jonas ran his fingers over a keepsake he had tucked into the pocket of his corduroy jacket, the memento given to all the men during the closing ceremony at Los Alamos. Along with certificates of appreciation from the secretary of war, General Groves gave each man a pin with the word "BOMB" spelled out inside a silver letter "A."

Jonas twisted the pin in his fingers. He was amused to think of it as the badge they were given to warn people of their presence among them, the scientists who gave the human race its tools for self-destruction. In Oppenheimer's parting speech he warned that if America proceeded to stockpile an arsenal of atomic bombs for future wars, the time would come when people would curse the words "Los Alamos." Jonas picked up a slim volume of poetry from the seat beside him, his other souvenir, a gift from Kitty Oppenheimer, delivered to him several days after his adventure in the desert with her husband. "I wonder if you know the work of Wilfred Owen," she had written in delicate handwriting on rose-colored stationery. "Please accept this gift of gratitude from Robbie, little Peter, and myself." How she discovered his name, or where to find him, Jonas never knew.

The sound of the speeding train restored him. He leaned back and closed his eyes. Perhaps someday he would consider himself an American. Maybe someday he would learn to live without his dear mother and father. Maybe, in time, with Ginny's belief in him, he could learn the words and actions of a happy man.

October 5, 1947

It was an Indian summer evening, and everyone was spruced up to welcome the new director of the Institute for Advanced Studies. Though other names had been put forward, Dr. Oppenheimer was the man they all wanted. Von Neumann, Einstein, Oswald Veblen, Kurt Gödel had all put him at the top of their lists. So, after only two years at Cal Tech, Robbie and Kitty Oppenheimer had returned to the east coast to make their home.

Fuld Hall was decorated with flowers, the French doors opened to the temperate October air. Ginny and Marea were in the garden where Marea was chasing butterflies, while Jonas joined his colleagues to discuss Truman's plan to create a Central Intelligence Agency to stop the spread of Communism across Western Europe. Jonas listened with half an ear. His attention was on his little girl, now squatting on the lawn with her skirt hiked around her waist, tossing the petals of a daisy into the air. Jonas noticed his wife fight her impulse to scold their daughter. They had discussed this many times. He had begged Ginny to allow Marea to pursue her curiosities, even when she made a mess of things. He couldn't forget that in his own childhood he'd been obsessed with examining everything. Perhaps he was putting thoughts into her head, but already he saw in little Marea the makings of an acute observer of nature. She examined every leaf and caterpillar with singular intensity, insisting Jonas crouch down beside her to share her wonder.

Someone tapped Jonas on the shoulder. He turned to find Kitty Oppenheimer smiling at him, even more striking than he remembered her. She had Ginny's dark hair and lovely features, but there was a softness in Kitty Oppenheimer that his own wife did not have.

"I wanted to say hello. We were delighted when we heard that you're here working with Johnny von Neumann. Robbie was so pleased."

Jonas was certain she had mistaken him for someone else, but she put her arm through his and led him directly across the room to her husband.

"You remember Jonas Hoffman," Kitty prompted.

"Ah, yes, the unfortunate witness to my wrestling with the angel."

Oppenheimer examined him, and Jonas imagined he was surprised at his transformation from the skinny and awkward young scientist who worked at Los Alamos to the tweed-jacketed, cigarette-smoking protégé of the renowned von Neumann.

"I see they've done a good job of fattening you up here at the 'intellectual hotel.'" Oppenheimer patted his own flat stomach. "Maybe they can make something more of me as well."

Jonas shook Oppenheimer's hand and felt its delicateness.

"Welcome to the institute, sir. We're all so pleased that you accepted the appointment."

"And tell me how you and Johnny are progressing on his contraption that will do our thinking for us."

"It will never think, Dr. Oppenheimer. All it can do is calculate."

"Yes, and isn't it marvelous that there's still a difference?"

At that moment a flurry of activity at the entrance to the parlor claimed everyone's attention. Albert Einstein had arrived, accompanied as always by an entourage of relatives, friends, and reporters. He was making straight for Robert Oppenheimer, his thick white mustache, long nose, and twinkling eyes leading the way like the bow of a ship breaking through ocean waters. He was sporting his signature T-shirt and suspenders, baggy pants, and sandals without socks, and he grinned with pleasure as he pumped Oppenheimer's hand. "Now we are all rounded up in one place—in the case they are wanting to give the lions a good feeding."

Oppenheimer laughed. "At Cal Tech they warned me I'd be thrown to the wolves back here."

"Wolves, lions, FBI."

"Tell me about your health," Oppenheimer said.

Einstein pressed his hand over his abdomen. "Veyizmir. Miss D. makes me eat broccoli and spinach."

Jonas, standing nervously at Oppenheimer's side, ran his fingers through his hair, wondering how he could gracefully back away. Though he had worked down the hall from the man for the last two years, he had never dared speak to Professor Einstein, and he doubted Einstein had even noticed him.

"Have you met Jonas Hoffman?" Oppenheimer asked, picking up on his wife's nonverbal cue to introduce the young man. "I've heard he's going to get Johnny's computer to talk to us one of these days."

A look of annoyance passed across Einstein's gentle face. "I am told Dr. Teller wants you to make a better computer so he can test the new thermonuclear calculations for his fusion bomb."

Jonas was taken aback. He had been told that the plan to run the new set of calculations was still secret. But Einstein was correct. In the last six months Teller had been pressuring them constantly to complete their work on ENIAC's successor, a new computer with an internal operating system that should be able to do calculations at a thousand times the speed of their ENIAC computer. Only then would it be possible to accomplish the theoretical studies Teller needed in order to evaluate his new design. This was critical because if a fusion bomb was built and the test failed without the computer work, there would be no way to know if its design was flawed, if the required ignition conditions were not met, or if a fusion bomb was simply not feasible.

When Jonas had confided misgivings about aiding in the development of even more powerful nuclear weapons, von Neumann told him that the new computer would most likely demonstrate that Teller's design was flawed. Jonas accepted that reassurance, since it freed him to tackle the problem of predicting fusion as a purely theoretical question. Fusion brought to bear a dozen interrelated problems about the behavior of matter under conditions of tremendous chemical change. New elements not present in the original configuration would be created. They would affect the behavior of an increasing density of neutrons and alter the rate of the reaction, but exactly how?

Jonas often slipped out of bed after midnight to go to his basement office to work. He found he needed to use his mind the way a long-distance runner must run. Working also allowed him to forget the demands that always lay in wait for him on the floors above. In the morning, when his mind was dull with exhaustion, he had to look away from Ginny. How could he deny that as the months passed, his body had grown cold beside her—that the more she drew toward him, the more he wanted to pull away? He had accepted that he was incapable of giving her what she was asking from him, that her campaign to transform him into a living soul could only fail. Why couldn't she accept it, too?

Jonas replied to Einstein, "When the new computer is ready, sir, we will only be testing Dr. Teller's hypothesis."

"Epimetheus—I believe he was also only testing a hypothesis."

Jonas looked to Oppenheimer for help.

"Epimetheus allowed Pandora to open her box," Oppenheimer explained. "And thus escaped into the world all the evils that have since afflicted man."

Einstein shrugged wearily. "But the young scientists are so busy with their new inventions that they do not worry about such a thing as evil. They believe in technical solutions to all of the problems of mankind."

"I do believe in evil, Professor Einstein. Both my parents were murdered by the Nazis."

Quiet fell over the small circle. Kitty touched Jonas's elbow and then covered his hand with hers. The horrors of Nazi atrocities filled the newsreels in every movie house in America. The piles of suitcases, shoes, gold teeth, the lampshades made of skin.

Einstein reconsidered Jonas. "Please tell me your name again."

"I am Jonas Hoffman. I work in Fuld Hall, at the other end of the corridor from you, sir."

"How can it be that only now we are making our introduction?" Einstein offered his hand to the timorous young man before him. An idea occurred to Professor Einstein. "Tell me, do you think you could give an ancient professor an hour of your time? I am not such a good reader, and they have sent me a very big report from the School of Medicine of Yale University. Can you come to help me read what men do one to another when they think that weapons will solve the problems of civilization?"

"I will come to your office first thing tomorrow morning, Professor."

"No, no. That is not good. What is good is that you come to Mercer Street. You come tomorrow at five o'clock. Miss D. will make us a strong cup of tea."

"You won't feed this young fellow to the wolves," Oppenheimer chided Einstein. "Better to fatten him up a bit more for the lions."

Einstein emitted the lighthearted, high-pitched laugh he was famous for. "Yes, yes. Better the lions. All good men of science to the lions."

Ginny was at the French doors, holding Marea's hand too tightly, and Jonas saw the irritation in her face. Jonas promised Einstein he would be prompt the following afternoon and made his way toward his wife.

"You were speaking with Albert Einstein," Virginia said.

Jonas whispered, "I'll tell you on the way home."

As soon as they were on the steps of Fuld Hall, Virginia asked, "Did you say how pleased I am that he's accepted the chairmanship of the Emergency Committee of Atomic Scientists?"

Jonas laughed.

"Why are you laughing?"

"I suppose Albert Einstein wants to know every Princeton housewife's opinion of his position on nuclear disarmament."

Ginny scowled and walked ahead.

Jonas caught up. "Now what's the matter?"

"I am not just any Princeton housewife. I am Harold Pell's daughter. I am quite sure Albert Einstein knows the work my father did with Woodrow Wilson to form the League of Nations."

"Well, perhaps he does."

"Of *course* he does. My father was revered by all who seek peace. He believed in a world government and never shied away from standing up to warmongers and misguided government men."

"I think you ought to go for tea instead of me."

"What are you saying?"

"Professor Einstein invited me for tea tomorrow afternoon. It seems you'd have much more to discuss with him than me."

Virginia stopped in her tracks. "You're going to Mercer Street?"

"Indeed I am."

"Then you must reciprocate and invite him to our home for supper."

Jonas laughed again. The brief encounter with Albert Einstein had cheered him.

"Very well, I'll ask him to come for supper. I'm sure Albert Einstein has an evening free to spend with the daughter of the great Harold Pell."

When Jonas swung Marea up and over his head and onto his shoulders, the daisy petals she'd been holding in her tiny fists floated softly before his eyes.

October 6, 1947

Miss Dukas examined Jonas through the screen door of the old clapboard house on Mercer Street. Fumbling and uncertain, he repeated that Professor Einstein had invited him to come for tea. She left him outside on the porch, and after a lengthy interval returned and opened the door. "You are the mathematician who is making a computer?"

"Yes, ma'am."

"Professor will see you in his study."

Jonas followed Miss Dukas up the narrow stairway and down a dimly lit hall. She tapped at a closed door, then went back down the stairs, leaving Jonas to wait alone in the dark. He twisted a pencil stub in his pocket and listened to the sound of violin music behind the door, a plaintive melody he recognized, a European folksong or perhaps the tune of one of the prayers from synagogue. Jonas understood that Professor Einstein would play his music to the end before opening the door for him, as his own father had completed whatever proof he was engaged in before answering Jonas's knock. Jonas was flooded with the memory of making himself utterly still outside his father's study so that the magic of his father's mathematical proofs would enter his own mind as well.

The door opened, and Einstein stood holding his violin with two fingers at the scroll. His stomach protruded like a volleyball between the suspenders that held up his baggy pants. He was barefoot, and Jonas towered above him.

"I forgot that you are such a giant. You will have to bend like time to fit into my study."

"You had a report from the Yale Medical School you wanted to go over with me, sir."

"Sir, sir. What is always this 'sir'? As far as I know I have not been knighted by Her Majesty the Queen."

Large windows along one wall of the room looked out on an overgrown garden below. Bookshelves were stuffed with scientific journals, piled in neat stacks as if someone had imposed order, though not the professor himself. If anything, Einstein appeared at odds with the neatness of the room. He stood a moment with his chin in his hand, as if perplexed by what to do with this young man who crouched awkwardly to keep his head from grazing the low ceiling.

"Sit, sit. You are making me feel like a dwarf." He pointed Jonas to the chair in front of his desk.

Removing his cardigan from the music stand where it was hanging, Einstein settled into his own chair. "How about the rest of your family? Brothers, sisters? Did you lose them, too?"

"I'm an only child. My parents married late in life."

"I am told you are from Austria."

"Vienna."

"I am sure you know that the Austrians were the very worst."

"Yes." Jonas nodded.

"And how is it you managed to escape the Nazis?"

This was not a conversation Jonas wanted to have, and yet he felt compelled to speak by the sad and piercing eyes that bore down on him.

"My father decided I had to leave Austria after I was beaten up by Nazi students at the University of Vienna. He knew someone in the physics department at Harvard University, so he arranged for me to study there. When I arrived at Harvard, they already had too many Jewish immigrants, so they sent me on to the physics department at Columbia."

"What year was that?" Einstein encouraged Jonas to continue.

"I left Vienna on April 30, 1938, six weeks after the Anschluss. The Nazis were still allowing Jews to leave, but my father didn't believe it was necessary for him or my mother to go yet. He had

Gentile friends from his days of teaching at the university, and he thought they would protect him. A month after I left, he was arrested in the first roundup of Jewish intellectuals. Most of them were transported to Dachau, but for some reason my father was shot even before they left Gestapo headquarters in Vienna. My mother wrote that she found his body piled with other corpses on a donkey cart. When they cleared the rest of the Jews out of our neighborhood, my mother was sent on a train to Poland. She ended up at Auschwitz—where they killed her."

Jonas dropped his chin to his chest. There were times when his pain blinded him with a cold, white light. Silently the two men looked out at the garden below, where the summer green had given way to yellow, orange, and brown. Jonas was surprised to have told Einstein details of his life that he rarely spoke about to anyone. Whenever Virginia pressed him to talk, he recoiled. He saw no point in discussing it, even though he knew his memories were an infection that weakened him with every passing day.

"Tell me," Einstein instructed, "what was your contribution to Robbie's 'unholy endeavor in the desert'?"

Jonas was grateful for the change of subject. "My group worked on the high-voltage capacitors that fired the detonators."

"I heard that it was very difficult to get the timing right."

"Until Dr. Alvarez figured it out."

"He is a good man, Luis Alvarez. And then he had to witness the awful business with his own eyes. You knew he flew in the observation plane over Hiroshima?"

"We saw the photographs they took."

Einstein leaned forward and rummaged through a stack of papers on his desk until he found the manila envelope he was looking for, and handed it across to Jonas.

"When one examines photographs taken from the sky, there is no way of understanding the suffering of the people below."

There was a tap on the door. Miss Dukas backed into the room carrying a tea tray, and used her elbow to push aside the day's newspapers to make a place for the tray on the desk.

"My dear young man," she addressed Jonas. "You have sugar

in your tea, if that's what pleases you. The professor means well, but he has an unfortunate habit of telling people what is good for them."

"I am not the only one in this house with such a talent," Einstein replied. As soon as the door closed behind Miss Dukas, he leaned forward and held out his open palm to Jonas. "I noticed that you were smoking a cigarette at Robbie's party."

Jonas put his pack in Einstein's hand and watched him remove two cigarettes, slit them open with a pen knife, and methodically pack the loose tobacco into a pipe he pulled from beneath the cushion of his chair.

"Now, you smoke a cigarette," Einstein said. "If she comes sniffing, it will be you who gets the scolding."

Einstein waited for Jonas to light up, and then put a match to the bowl of his pipe. He breathed in deeply, closing his eyes to savor his rebellion. He pointed the stem toward Jonas. "Please, my friend, read. I wish to learn what you think about how your detonators were put to use."

With a cigarette in one hand and a cup of tea in the other Jonas settled in to read a report prepared by Yale pathologist Dr. Averill A. Liebow, a member of the Japanese-American commission that had spent months studying the impact of the atomic bomb on Hiroshima. The first pages of the report summarized the findings: At 2.3 miles from the hypocenter the surface temperature of human skin rose to 120 degrees Fahrenheit. People living within half a mile of the fireball burned to ash after their internal organs boiled. Black packets of incinerated flesh that had once been individual bodies were discovered stuck to metal poles and fences everywhere. Several days after the blast, radiation was found to cause spontaneous bleeding, hair that came out in handfuls, flesh that crumbled like drying clay, failure of kidneys, thyroids, livers. As Jonas read about a girl who found her dead parents curled around each other, he thought of his own little Marea.

Einstein's eyes drifted closed for a catnap. Jonas listened to his raspy breathing. He knew what Einstein was up to. Just as Einstein had once warned President Roosevelt of the danger to humanity if the Nazis were the first to build an atomic bomb, he now warned anyone who would listen about the horrifying consequences of a nuclear arms race. Jonas examined Einstein's sunken eyes, his drooping eyelids, the deep furrows in his brow—and he wondered if Einstein had examined him as well, observed the uncertainty of a man with no father to guide him.

Jonas fit the report back into its envelope and cleared his throat to wake Einstein.

"I had no idea."

Einstein roused himself. "And do you happen to know what is the predicted explosive yield of fusion as compared to fission?"

"It could be a thousand times greater."

"The most rudimentary version, before Dr. Teller improves upon his design."

"But there's no proof at this point that any design will work at all."

"I am wondering if you have heard the term 'backyard deployment'?"

Jonas shook his head.

"That is what Dr. Teller explained to the military men at Los Alamos, that a hydrogen bomb could be made so big that they might as well explode it in the backyard because it would destroy all life on earth. He was proud to tell them such a thing. Do you see what madness this is, making bigger and bigger thermonuclear weapons? Do you understand what I am saying? This is a disastrous situation for everyone, this belief that the problems of countries can be solved in a technical way. This preposterous idea of creating security for America by having the strongest weapons will lead only to war. Roosevelt had a big insight into this. He understood that you cannot prepare for war and for peace at the same time. Unfortunately now that he is dead, we have the military men making these decisions."

Einstein leaned back to wait for Jonas's response.

"My wife is an ardent supporter of your efforts to stop nuclear proliferation, Professor Einstein. She feels your work with the

Emergency Committee of Atomic Scientists is our best hope. She inherited a deep commitment to pacifism from her father—you may have heard of him—the late Harold Pell. Dr. Pell worked closely with President Wilson on the creation of the League of Nations. My father-in-law was a believer in world government, like yourself."

Einstein nodded vigorously. "Yes, yes. I know the important work of Harold Pell. You are telling me you have married the daughter?"

"She asked me to invite you to our home for dinner. I told her that you're much too busy to accept every invitation you receive, but she insisted I invite you anyway."

"Tell me, is she a pretty girl, this daughter of Harold Pell? And more important, do you deserve her?"

"My wife is beautiful, Professor Einstein, but I'm afraid I do not deserve her."

"Please tell your beautiful wife that I would be a very happy man to accept her invitation. On Sunday I will come. And I don't mind, please, if you will tell the daughter of Harold Pell that I have had enough broccoli and spinach for three lifetimes."

"We're at 117 Blossom Street. Shall I write it down?"

Einstein put two fingers to his temple. "This brain may not yet know how to unify electromagnetism and gravity, but it retains three-number sequences."

Einstein stood to signal that their visit was over. At the door to his study, he touched Jonas's arm. "My new young friend, may I please explain? The story of Pandora's box is a tragedy because of one thing. You see, once Pandora opened this box, it was quite impossible for Epimetheus to get it shut ever again."

October 12, 1947

When they spotted Albert Einstein coming up the front walk, Jonas and Virginia were taken aback to see that he had come alone, no escort or entourage, as if he were nothing more than a family friend arriving for Sunday supper. Not knowing what to expect,

Virginia had laid the table with several extra settings. She had ironed her only linen tablecloth, polished her mother's silver, taken her good china from the glass breakfront. Tension had filled the house all afternoon, and Virginia wouldn't allow Jonas and Marea to go out on their Sunday afternoon hike in the Institute Woods. Albert Einstein was coming for dinner, and their home was too small, too dark, too dreary. Virginia harvested all the flowers in her greenhouse and filled every vase she owned.

While Jonas escorted their honored guest into the living room, Virginia quickly removed the extra place settings from the table. When she reappeared to tell the men that dinner was served, her apron had been removed, she had applied fresh lipstick, and her dark hair was unpinned to fall across her shoulders. When Jonas saw Einstein's frank appreciation of his wife, he was more uncomfortable than proud.

Marea, holding Virginia's hand, was dressed in her favorite yellow pinafore with a matching yellow bow in her own long, dark hair. Marea looked up at her mother. "Is he my grandpa?" Einstein's eyes sparkled as he leaned forward in his chair. "My pretty madela, given what we now understand about time and space, why couldn't I be your grandpapa? It is possible. Why not?"

Jonas and Virginia were formal as they began the meal with their distinguished guest, and Virginia bowed her head to say grace. But Marea continued to eye her "grandpapa," his paintbrush mustache and lion's hair. What sort of funny man was he? Virginia had decanted a bottle of sherry for the table. By the time she had finished her second glass, her cheeks were flushed, and she had relaxed enough to expound on the role the United Nations must play in putting a stop to nuclear testing.

"I see that you are your father's daughter," Einstein commented, enjoying her.

"And that awful General LeMay!" Ginny exclaimed. "Can you imagine? Advising our president that America must have a first-strike capability—telling him that the way to win a nuclear war is to be the first to drop the bomb!"

Though Jonas was relieved not to have to speak, he was embarrassed by his wife's boldness.

"But there is no such thing as the winning of a nuclear war," Einstein pointed out quietly. "With the means of destruction incomparably greater than at any time before in history, we have a new situation."

"These generals are leading us straight into disaster!" Virginia exclaimed.

"Yes, Mrs. Hoffman. This is what I have tried to say to your husband. As long as they are saying that we must make our armaments as strong as possible to protect us from another war, they are doing everything that will make such a war inevitable."

Virginia sat up with excitement as she asserted that the most critical issue in the regulation of nuclear energy was the necessity for civilian, not military, control.

"Mrs. Hoffman, I can assure you that I am in complete agreement on this matter. I have recently sent a letter to President Truman insisting that we must have civilian control of the Atomic Energy Commission."

The discussion continued as Einstein accepted second and third helpings of Virginia's homemade lemon meringue pie. Marea, who was up well past her bedtime, crawled onto her new grandpapa's lap, tucked herself into his arms, and was soon fast asleep. The warmth around the dining table was not something Virginia and Jonas had ever managed on their own, and as Virginia cleared the plates and Jonas gathered Marea from Einstein's lap to carry her upstairs, he felt an uncommon lightness. He pulled the quilt over Marea's small body and rested his hand on her warm forehead. He no longer believed in God, but still each night he sang the Hebrew prayer his father had sung over him at bedtime to prepare him for safe sleep.

When Jonas returned downstairs, he was surprised to find Einstein in the kitchen beside Virginia, with a dish towel in his hand.

"I am not so useless," Einstein insisted to Jonas proudly. "Even though at Mercer Street they think I am to be treated as if I am an exhibit in a museum. And I am still capable of using my own two legs to carry me to work each day. Why don't you come by Mercer Street at eight o'clock tomorrow morning? We'll make the walk to the institute together."

When Miss Dukas opened the door the following morning, she pointed her finger at Jonas. "Young man, I will have no more smoking in this house."

Refreshed from a night's sleep, Einstein used the walk to grill Jonas on the new calculations von Neumann would do for Teller. Proud and humbled to be walking the neighborhood streets alongside Albert Einstein, Jonas found it difficult to refrain from answering whatever Professor Einstein asked him. On the steps to Fuld Hall, Einstein smiled. "It is sounding to me as if Dr. Teller's neutrons are not so very happy to cooperate in giving mankind the tools of its self-destruction."

October 28, 1949

Jonas sat alone in his basement office, bent forward in his chair, his back to his desk, his head in his hands. On the floor beside him, where he had accidentally brushed it from his desk, lay the card Marea had made for his thirtieth birthday. She had spelled out "Daddy" and "Marea," drawn a red heart by each word, and added a bold red line connecting them.

It was the wretched night of a wretched day in an ever more wretched world. No one at the institute had been surprised by Truman's announcement that the Russians had tested an atomic bomb in Kazakhstan, but even so the news had polarized the institute into two camps, those with Albert Einstein who saw a solution in sharing nuclear secrets with the Russians, and others who considered Joseph Stalin to be another Hitler. Churchill's ringing alarm that an "Iron Curtain had descended across the continent" raised the specter of a new era of European fascism, but Einstein insisted it was in America, with its red-scare tactics, where fascism was to be feared. Lately Jonas found himself more in sympathy with Edward Teller, who believed Stalin was determined to rule both East and West. However, Jonas kept his doubts about Einstein's position to himself and always spoke up in Einstein's defense when people whispered about his sympathy with the Communists. In two years, over more than a dozen intimate Sunday suppers, Professor Einstein became a beloved visitor to the Hoffman household—a playful grandfather for little Marea, a needed father figure for Jonas, and most of all, a treasured confidant for Virginia. They were two peas in a pod with their animated discussions about the dangers to be feared from what Einstein liked to call "the worst outcrop of herd life"—the military. "Heroism on command, senseless violence, and all the loathsome nonsense that goes by the name of patriotism. There can be no true freedom under the militarization of a nation."

Jonas often wondered what Marea made of all this talk when Einstein came to dinner. Jonas liked best when dinner was over, and he, Einstein, and Marea were allowed to retire to the living room while Virginia retreated to the kitchen to wash up. Jonas smiled when Marea hung on to Einstein's suspenders as if they were the halyards on a sailing jib and insisted her Grandpa Albert waltz around the room. He felt a sharp tug of loneliness after Einstein left, Marea was put to bed, and he and Virginia were by themselves again.

The year Einstein turned seventy he was in constant demand for celebrations. Newspaper reporters hounded him day and night for interviews, and one university after another wanted him to accept an honorary degree. After a long stretch during which he hadn't had a single free Sunday evening to come for supper, Virginia pressed Jonas to stop by Einstein's office at Fuld Hall to say that Marea missed her grandpa.

Jonas knocked at the office, but got no answer. There was light coming from under the door, so he knocked again. When there was still no answer, Jonas tentatively pushed opened the door. Einstein sat at his desk staring at the floor.

"Are you all right, Professor?"

When Einstein looked up, Jonas saw a tired and discouraged old man.

"Can you please explain to me, Jonas? Why is it that everyone is saying they like me, but no one is understanding me? The newspaper men never stop asking, when is my unified theory coming? What do they believe? That my work is like making a recipe for a cake?"

"Ginny wanted me to tell you that Marea won't stop pestering her about when 'Grandpa' is coming to visit. Ginny says you missed her rhubarb pie in August and her grape preserves in September. She's worried you're losing your appetite for her cooking. She says you can come by for a few minutes without Miss D. sending the police to look for you."

"For your beautiful wife's cooking I never lose my appetite. For my fellow man, that is a different matter. Very well. I come. I have Marea's present here in my office since her birthday." He dug through a pile on the shelf behind him and retrieved an envelope tied around with a red ribbon.

"A young scientist must have stars to paste onto her ceiling to help her go to sleep at night dreaming of the universe."

Einstein turned off the lights in his office, and he and Jonas walked out along the quiet corridors of Fuld Hall. As they passed empty offices, Einstein shook his head. "What use so many brilliant minds when not one studies how to abolish war?"

When they turned onto Blossom Street, Einstein said, "Robbie telephoned me before he left for Washington this afternoon. He says he's going to try to talk the government men out of their plan to build the H-bomb. The trouble is Robbie worries so much about everyone liking him that sometimes he forgets what he himself believes."

"I don't imagine he'll get much of a hearing in any case. Everything's changed now that we know the Russians have tested their own bomb. We have to assume that they're working on fusion as well."

"This business of the Russians testing an atomic bomb is of little importance, my friend. Much more important is how we are to arrange for countries to be reasonable with one another. Unless all countries see the benefit of a world government, I can't imagine how any of us will survive. In any case, I am not so sure how this news of the Russians having an atomic bomb has come to light. Our military men might have their own reasons for saying such a thing. There is nothing so reliable as fear when the military men want the government to do their bidding."

"Even so, you can't discount the aggressive policies of the Communists. And you won't dispute that whoever masters fusion first is going to be in a position to rule the world."

"My dear Jonas, the Russians never were aggressive, never in history. They were always the ones to be invaded. The Russians are more convinced of their weakness than of their strength, and they are right on that matter. They do not have a strong economy. They lost twenty million in the war. Communism is not like Nazism, it has no policy of aggression. Do you think the Russians imagine they can subdue the whole world? Why do you listen to those Hungarians, Teller and von Neumann? Listen to our friend Robbie instead. He says we are two scorpions in a bottle. Both scorpions will be dead. Do you know that Dr. Teller has been lecturing the congressmen and senators in Washington? He tells them that if the Russians get the hydrogen bomb before us, we will all be locked away in prison camps. Mr. Teller lost his foot to a streetcar in Budapest, so he thinks every man wants to mangle his other foot. If only Sigmund Freud had taken him for a patient and saved the rest of us from his derangement."

"I don't see how you can deny the importance of who has fusion first. It's 1945 all over again. America must be the first to build a hydrogen bomb."

Einstein threw up his hands. "This stupid thinking makes me want to lie down in my grave. And if a smart fellow like you is thinking such foolishness, what then a president with a corncob for a brain? There was a time when you impressed me with your good mind, and now you are making me think of the story of the fool who finds another fool to follow and calls that man a king."

In the darkening evening, Einstein didn't notice how deeply he had insulted Jonas.

"Do you know what people are saying about you? Do you know that they call you a traitor to your adopted country?"

When Virginia opened the door, Einstein was laughing. "Your husband informs me I am a traitor to America."

"Jonas!"

Einstein handed the ribboned envelope to Virginia. "For Marea's birthday. Tell her I am sorry it comes so late." He turned to go, but Virginia held his arm and returned the envelope to him.

"Marea would be so much happier if you gave it to her yourself."

Virginia steered Einstein across the doorstep and into the house, leaving Jonas to stew in the dark. Jonas turned down the cement path that led to the back of the house, let himself in through the kitchen door, and went directly to his basement. Tears of hurt filled his eyes, but he denied them. Instead he told himself that the great Albert Einstein would give America to the Russians on a platter, and he'd still be laughing when they locked him in his cell.

June 26, 1950

Virginia sat at her dressing table with her back to Jonas while he methodically packed the suitcase lying open on his bed, boxer shorts, socks, T-shirts, khaki pants, his clothes for Los Alamos. An argument that had gone on for weeks had now been put to rest, not because Jonas and Virginia had reached an accord, but because they were weary with the debate and with each other. Jonas would do what he believed he must do, and Virginia would remain unyielding in her disapproval and disappointment.

At Los Alamos they had been working on a duplicate of Princeton's new digital computer, and Teller was desperate to have it operating so that, under his own direction, he could perform his thermonuclear calculations. After Truman's January announcement of the crash program to develop a hydrogen bomb, Teller had had the audacity to accuse von Neumann of prejudicing the computer calculations done at Princeton. Teller was in a rage after von Neumann announced that igniting the liquid deuterium with heat from a fission explosion, as Teller proposed, would require an unworkable amount of tritium. If this was true, neither Teller's old "super" design for a hydrogen bomb nor his new "alarm clock" configuration would work.

On an afternoon in May when Teller was visiting Princeton, he had tracked down Jonas, who was working alone in the computer lab. Teller backed Jonas against a wall and wagged his finger in his face. "You are a young man, not like Johnny. Old men believe you go out and slay the dragon once and he is dead. Young men know that evil changes faces. You will come to Los Alamos. You will work on my computer. I will tell you the secrets the government keeps from your Mr. Einstein and your Mr. Oppenheimer. I will tell you what Stalin does to Jews. I will tell you what Stalin does to any man who disagrees with him. You are young, Jonas Hoffman. A young man is not afraid to see the truth. President Truman is calling me on the telephone, asking what day we can announce that we will never lie down at the feet of Communists who want to terrify the Western World."

Jonas did not report this encounter to John von Neumann, but he did suggest to him that if he went out to Los Alamos for a few months to help get their MANIAC computer operational, there could be no more accusations of biased calculations. The truth was that after working so long in von Neumann's shadow, Jonas was anxious to be his own man. Edward Teller seemed to be the only one who understood that von Neumann had assigned Jonas the critical work of sequencing the operations.

Virginia flatly refused to consider accompanying Jonas for the three months he would be working at Los Alamos, but it pained him more to think of being away from his daughter at a time when her curiosity was expanding like a supernova. In preparation for her fifth birthday he had sent away for the best-quality specimen boxes, cherry wood with hinged glass covers, to house her burgeoning collection of butterflies. Marea absorbed the world directly through her pores with a natural intelligence. It was her idea to keep four separate notebooks—for plants, butterflies, birds, and insects—and Jonas gave them a special spot on a shelf among his books and papers. Sometimes, when he was busy with his own work, Marea sat on a stool, her dark hair tied back in a ribbon, industriously drawing pictures to accompany their observations. These were Jonas's truly happy hours. What would Virginia have said if he admitted to her that Marea was the only person in the world he knew how to love?

They had been lying awake in their separate single beds when Jonas told Virginia he planned to spend the summer in Los Alamos working with Edward Teller.

"Does Albert know about this?"

"I haven't had a chance to talk to him."

"Of course you haven't."

"He'll understand that I have no choice."

"You certainly have a choice whether or not to assist in a project that escalates the Cold War beyond all reason."

"I appreciate your commitment to pacifism, but unfortunately it is no response to the realities of the modern world."

"Because the world has gone mad, you feel you must go mad right along with it?"

"I'm weary of your lectures, Virginia. When I'm away, you and your professor will have plenty to discuss."

Virginia's sparrow body and Jonas's long frame made rigid contours under the covers of their separate beds.

Almost inaudibly, Virginia said, "I suppose they would be proud of you."

"What was that?"

"I said they would be proud of you. Your parents. Your beloved ghosts. The two corpses you've yoked yourself to. Yoked me to. Yoked our marriage to. I suppose they'd be proud that you want to save the world from Stalin—since you failed to save them from Hitler." Virginia twisted violently, sat up, yanked on the light. "I am a very lonely woman. Do you know that? Do you have *any* idea? And you wonder why I look for attention from another man."

She was crying now. Jonas couldn't bear to look at her, at the need he could not fill. When she continued to glare at him, he raised himself off the bed, found his bathrobe, and slid into his slippers. Before leaving, he stopped at the door. "I am sorry, Virginia. I'm sorry I will never be the man that you deserve."

February 4, 1951

Jonas stepped into the morning sunlight and stretched his arms to the sky. He was in a heightened state. Everything around him was crisp, clear. The desert mountains were ocher and rust, the sky above streaked with crimson. After months—no, years—of frustration and failure, they had accomplished the impossible—they had unlocked the secret of fusion.

The work had gone on so long. Traveling back and forth from Princeton to New Mexico had become routine. In the last months Jonas ran more calculations and more permutations of calculations than in all the previous years of his career. The pressure was unrelenting. Teller's tyrannical rages brought everyone near the breaking point. And Teller was ungenerous, to say the least, when it was Ulam and not he who had made the critical breakthrough with his proposal of a two-stage explosion—using the neutrons heated by a primary fission bomb to compress the deuterium with such force that it would create a secondary thermonuclear implosion. But in the end it was Teller himself, in a startling moment when he appeared to be struck by a supernatural force of pure inspiration, who fit the last piece into the puzzle. From the depths of his despair Teller rose phoenixlike. "Forget neutrons! Neutrons will never work. We will use the *radiation* coming off the fission primary to compress the thermonuclear!" With a few swift strokes of chalk, he drew out his vision on the blackboard—simple, elegant, and perfect. Contentment transformed his shadowed face and he announced that he would go home to play piano and have dinner with his wife, while the rest of them stayed behind to test his theory.

Testing was a gargantuan task. With MANIAC still not fully functional, they had nothing but their clumsy Frieden and Marchand desk calculators to do the work by hand. Through the night they ran thousands upon thousands of computations. At dawn, their eyes burning, they fell into one another's arms like marathon dancers, delirious, spent, but with the certain knowledge that in one night the hydrogen bomb had been transformed from an idea into an inevitability.

Teller crowed like a rooster, ignoring Ulam's critical contribution, but Jonas was not offended by Teller's egotism. On the contrary, he was in awe. If Teller had not kept the candle burning all those years when so many condemned him as a madman, who knows how far behind the Russians they would have fallen?

December 12, 1953

In the middle of the night Virginia removed her bathrobe and slipped back into bed.

Jonas whispered, "Has she gone back to sleep?"

"You heard her?"

"Of course I heard her."

"I thought you were asleep."

"Did she tell you what it was this time?"

Virginia's voice was strained. "It's always the same."

"Where does she get such fears?"

Virginia sighed deeply. "I'd like to try to get some sleep now, if you don't mind. These nightly bouts are exhausting me."

"I can go to her. It doesn't always have to be you."

"I prefer to deal with this myself."

"To protect her from me, isn't that it?"

Virginia did not answer. The only sound was a fierce December wind that shook the branches of the sycamores.

"You think I don't know that you consider me a carrier of despair—'a disease like any other'—didn't you once put it to me that way?"

"Say what you will. Your daughter dreams of nuclear annihilation night upon night—while you spend your days dreaming up new nuclear weapons. I suppose there's no connection."

Virginia put on the lamp again and crossed to her bureau, removing an envelope from her top drawer. "Tell me, please," she asked, holding the envelope out to Jonas, "when did you plan on letting me know that you're following Teller to California?"

Jonas put on his own light to examine the return address, Teller's new laboratory in Livermore, California.

"I didn't know you made a practice of opening my mail."

"This letter came addressed to me. Apparently you listed me as your next of kin on the life insurance form. It does make me wonder why one needs life insurance for work on nuclear weapons. In any case, I'd like to know when you decided to go to California. I'm well aware that we have little to say to one another, but I would think you'd have the courtesy to inform me of such decisions."

"I haven't decided yet."

She pointed to the envelope. "Apparently you have."

"I've only agreed to go out once or twice to help set up a computer operation."

Virginia scowled. "And you have the gall to ask why Marea has nightmares."

"That's nonsense. Marea is not the only eight-year-old in America who's aware of the Cold War. She's not the only child who's required to practice for air raids in school—or sees television announcements warning us what to do in the event of a nuclear attack. I know it would suit you, but I don't think you can blame Marea's nightmares on me."

"For God's sake, Jonas. Haven't you already done enough for that wretched man?"

Jonas had once thought of his wife as beautiful. Now he saw a bony woman with a sharp tongue, curled lip, tightly narrowed eyes. What if he tried to explain to her why he must go to Livermore? What if he took her into his confidence and explained the need for a new facility that would take up the work of increased megaton delivery? What if he tried to make her understand why this was critical to the Cold War strategy of deterrence? The trouble was that anything Jonas told Virginia would go straight to Einstein's ears, and Einstein was now under suspicion of being a traitor to America and watched constantly by the FBI.

"I'm quite sure you're happier when I'm away in any case."

She did not respond.

"I've been wondering if there's something I should know about your friendship with Albert that you haven't had the courage to tell me."

Virginia looked away. "There's simply no way I can hold this marriage together if you're determined to destroy it."

"Is it me or is it you who's given up?"

"Oh, please," Virginia replied wearily. "Has it never occurred to you that you repeatedly pursue the path most certain to drive us apart? Your guilt about abandoning your poor parents has made this marriage impossible."

April 15, 1954

Jonas knew he had lost everyone, even his own daughter. When the wretched fight had broken out at dinner, her green eyes had darted back and forth until she finally made her choice and went to stand beside her Grandpa Albert. Despair now caught up with Jonas, dark water closing up around his chest, his neck. He sensed the cold, but otherwise he was numb.

Jonas was the one who had provoked the argument. He should have left well enough alone when Albert lectured him once again about the "rising tide of American fascism." Einstein was fired up after speaking to reporters, to condemn the government's decision to revoke Robert Oppenheimer's security clearance. Virginia had, of course, hung on Einstein's every word, and after she'd left the table to prepare dessert, Einstein had turned to Jonas to castigate him, once again, for his work with Edward Teller. It was Teller, after all, who had offered the Atomic Energy Commission the testimony it needed in order to justify revoking Oppenheimer's clearance without having to prove any specific transgression. Slyly Teller had testified that he didn't believe Oppenheimer would knowingly endanger America, but that his behavior in the years after the Manhattan Project indicated that his personal beliefs might lead him to *unwittingly* betray his country. Teller still held a grudge—Oppenheimer had adamantly opposed the development of the hydrogen bomb.

"Before he walked into the hearing room, he took Robbie aside and promised he would support him. Your friend Teller, he stabs a man in his back."

Jonas examined Princeton's white-haired saint, the man who had come into his home seven years ago, worked his wiles, and driven a wedge between Jonas and his wife and daughter. Jonas had seen a side of Albert Einstein that most people never knew—the modesty that masked his rigid obstinacy, the passion for social justice that substituted for too much direct contact with humanity, the trick of dispensing advice to acolytes in order to distract himself and everyone else from the failure of his unified theory. With Virginia in the kitchen preparing dessert and Marea clearing the dinner dishes, Jonas looked across the table at Einstein and saw only a sour old man who for too long had treated Jonas like a hapless pupil.

"Frankly, I think Teller did Oppenheimer a favor," Jonas interjected. "He gave the AEC a way of dealing with Oppenheimer without dragging his name through mud. I imagine I respect Oppenheimer as much as you, but his sympathy with Communists is widely known. He's no Klaus Fuchs, I'll grant you that. But he shouldn't be trusted with classified information about nuclear weapons development."

"Sympathy with Communists? That's preposterous!"

"The record is clear."

"Robbie is a humanist, not a Communist."

"Communist operatives prey on humanitarian impulses."

"Why do I think that Dr. Teller is here in this room?"

"Say what you will about Teller. He lived through the Red Terror in Hungary. He knows what Communists are capable of."

"The old song he sings to justify his fascism."

"You can't accuse every anti-Communist of being a fascist. *I* am not a fascist."

"No, Jonas. Not a fascist, but sometimes a dreadful fool."

Marea froze, clutching the stack of dishes she was clearing from the table.

"Call me a fool, but I respect a man who has the courage to endure the ridicule of men like you and Oppenheimer in order to do what he knows *must* be done to save this country."

"You call building more weapons to blow up the world *courage?* What has become of you that you let that madman tell you what to think?"

"No one tells me what to think! In fact, let me tell you exactly what I think! I think you've spent thirty years pursuing a theory that every scientist in the world considers ridiculous, and still you have the nerve to judge a man who pursues a dream to protect this great country that has taken us in!"

When Jonas barked at Marea to get along with her chore of clearing the table, tears sprang to her eyes, and she ran through the kitchen door.

"They all whisper behind your back. They say you can't bear the uncertainty of quantum behavior because you're mired in the naïve notion that the physical world is rational. They say your work of the last thirty years has failed, not because you're old and tired and no longer have the genius of your youth, but because you cannot tolerate the most obvious principle of the universe, something that every second-year graduate student knows—that a scientist who clings to a belief in an ideal world is no scientist at all. Your precious fantasy of a unified field theory is blind denial. *Yes, there is no God, there is no inherent meaning, and we are surrounded everywhere by the banality of evil.*"

Einstein nearly lost his balance as he bolted upright and his chair clattered to the floor behind him. The kitchen door swung open, and Virginia, gripping the dessert tray, shouted at the two men to stop. When Einstein doubled over and braced himself at the edge of the table, Virginia rushed to help him. Marea stared at this terrible scene, wringing her hands, until she spotted her Grandpa Albert's cloth napkin on the floor. She hurried to get it, as if it were something important he must have. She held the napkin out to him. When he took it, she stepped forward and tucked herself against his side.

"Do you see who she goes to?" Virginia spat at her mute husband. "Do you see who she chooses?" Virginia drew up her small body in contempt. "Go! Go now and leave us here in peace."

April 18, 1955

They got the call at breakfast. Einstein had died in the night. Jonas felt as if a cold wind were blowing between his bones. Virginia and Marea cried all day, but he did not.

He and Einstein had not spoken once in the year since their terrible argument. Jonas had written a note of apology, blaming his inexcusable behavior on extreme fatigue. There had been no reply, but for her ninth birthday Marea received from her Grandpa Albert a small microscope and a note urging her never to forget that a scientist sees more when she looks at the world with love. This gift to Marea had emboldened Jonas to walk to Mercer Street, but Miss Dukas would not let him past the front porch. Jonas was certain that Virginia had found her own way to stay in touch with Einstein, that she visited him from time to time. She would have kept that secret—not to spare Jonas's feelings, but to protect the solace she got from that relationship, a solace she desperately needed.

Jonas had no idea who had made the telephone call to their house that morning, but it must have been someone who understood that his wife would want to hear the news personally, not on the radio or television. When Virginia came into the kitchen to tell Jonas and Marea the news of Einstein's death, Jonas and Virginia had stared at one another with the blankness of strangers momentarily stopped at the same stoplight.

July 16, 1956

Marea's eleventh birthday. The three of them ate birthday cake and tried to muster a cheerful front, but no one had anything cheerful to say. Marea had come home from school that afternoon with tear-stained cheeks. At school two girls had taunted her about her father's outburst at Sunday meeting. One girl reported that her parents said Marea's father should see a psychiatrist; the other girl's mother was sure Marea's parents would be getting a divorce. Marea would have kept this to herself, except that a boy she went to summer camp with, the boy who wanted to marry her, had explained sadly that he wouldn't be able to come to her birthday party on Saturday after all. His parents didn't want him to go to the home of a man who continued to make nuclear bombs.

When Jonas returned from work, Virginia confronted him with the facts of Marea's terrible day. It was one thing for his work to pollute their home, but why had he been compelled to make a public display at Sunday Meeting?

That night, after Marea opened her birthday presents and went to bed, Virginia knocked on the door of Jonas's basement office, a place she would not enter. Standing in the half-light, she delivered her ultimatum: "If you don't put an end to this unconscionable work you do, I *will* divorce you."

September 4, 1957

Jonas canceled his planned trip to Livermore, and Teller phoned daily to pressure him to come back. Then John von Neumann informed Jonas that he had gotten a call from the Atomic Energy Commission to say they were considering an investigation of Jonas's security clearance. Of course Jonas knew Teller was behind this, that it was blackmail, but the prospect of being put through the public humiliation that others had suffered sickened Jonas, and he could not face it.

Jonas begged Virginia's indulgence to allow him to go to California for the week it would take to finish work on the Livermore computer. He hoped she would understand the predicament he laid out before her, Teller's threat, but Virginia only left their bedroom. When Jonas came back from Livermore, his clothing had been moved into the spare room across the hall.

"Why have you done this?" he asked.

Virginia replied, "Do you remember I once told you that nearly every choice you made seemed calculated to destroy our marriage? If I have to live here alone, as I've done all these years, I prefer to be alone by myself."

October 29, 1957

Near midnight Jonas knocked at Virginia's door. He had finished reading and signing Marea's report card, the last chore on Virginia's written list of things she wanted him to complete before leaving for California in the morning.

His eyes were unfocused. He could barely look at her. He hadn't shaved. He hadn't slept at all since a nightmare had woken him the previous night. He dreamt of his parents' bodies atop a pile of corpses being carried away in a donkey cart. His mother sat up, and the pile of dead bodies jostled her so that she had to steady herself by grabbing the thick cloth of her husband's coat where a brown stain of blood spread from his heart. Hilde Hoffman called to her young son, who tripped and fell in the rutted road as he frantically tried to catch up to her. The cart was always just beyond reach even though it traveled slowly with its heavy load of corpses. What was she trying to say to him? Her mouth moved, her eyes implored, but there was no sound. Then he saw that his mother was Virginia, her long dark hair twisted around her neck like a black silk scarf. Jonas now knew he would never reach the cart. He gave up running and watched it grow small. He looked down at his stalled feet where blood filled the ruts of the road, the dark crimson blood that had drained from the cart as it passed.

"What is it?" Virginia demanded impatiently.

He stood outside the door, head bent, hands hanging at his sides. He hadn't been able to finish packing. Every time he tried to choose a pair of socks or a shirt, he was overwhelmed with an exhaustion greater than he had ever known in his life; a tremendous weight had been given him to carry, and his muscles had turned to lead.

Virginia was in her robe. He examined the outline of her slender body, her dark hair spread across her shoulders. It had been more than two months since he had seen it fall to her shoulders as she prepared for bed. He remembered the time so very, very long ago, another lifetime, when he had been the one to remove the pins and let her hair drop into his hands.

"I'm going to bed now," she said.

Jonas reached out to grab her narrow wrist.

"Is it really necessary?" he pleaded. "Must we divorce?"

She yanked free. "I'm not going to discuss this anymore. It will be better for all of us. Perhaps in time you'll find someone you are able to love."

"You are the one I love," he protested.

"No, Jonas."

He stared at her, imploring.

"What is it? I'd like to get some sleep."

"I don't suppose you'd let me stay with you this last night?"

She looked at him for a long moment, then shook her head. "No, Jonas, not tonight. And never again."

The ink is smeared on the last page of Jonas's diary. Marea understands that her father was crying as he wrote it. She is crying now, and the ink runs fresh. She knows there will be no more pages to read. October 30, 1957, was the day her father's Buick smashed into a semitrailer truck as he drove to Idlewild Airport. She ties the pages back into the neat packet her mother presented to her, and sits quietly for a very long time holding the packet in her lap. She does not have the answer she was looking for, but she has answers to other questions.

Upstairs, in the hall outside her mother's bedroom, Marea waits a moment before knocking. She thinks about waiting outside this door, the night air on her calves and arms, fear on her neck, her mouth dry. The only deliverance from the panic of her nightmares was her parents' touch. And then she had stopped calling them, stopped going to them in the night, and their touch was gone.

"Is that you?"

"Can I come in?"

"Please, yes. Of course."

Virginia is sitting up in bed, wearing a silk bed jacket. The pillows are propped up behind her. Her eyebrow pencil and lipstick have been removed, and she has applied night cream that makes her face pale. Her bedside table is crowded with books, pill bottles, an eye mask, a pitcher, and a glass of water. Marea sees a woman who has taken a caliper to the width of her narrowed life and confined herself to its measurement.

"Did you finish reading it all?"

Marea looks around the room, a place she hasn't seen in years. She doesn't know whether to sit or stand. And where to sit? On her mother's bed? At the dressing table where she used to sit while her mother combed her hair and tied it back with ribbons? The upholstered love seat cluttered with clothes to mend or give away? It's the same choice of chairs she has been confronted with at each therapist's office, though here there are years of history.

"Where did you find this?" Marea asks.

"After the accident the institute cleaned out his office and sent me his file cabinet. I had a cursory look, but I couldn't make heads or tails of his work. I didn't have any use for his papers, but I couldn't imagine throwing them out, either, so I had a young man come over to help me put the cabinet up in the attic. I never gave it much thought after that, not for years."

"You found his diary in those files?"

"Yes, but let me explain. It was something you wrote in one of your letters that got me thinking. Do you recall that you wrote that sometimes you scanned the faces of strangers looking for him? All those years I focused on helping you cope with the loss of your father—it never occurred to me that someday you might want to find him—metaphorically, I mean—to find out who he was. He was always running away from us, from home—from himself, I suppose. I could understand how you might have imagined that he had run away for good. But it wasn't until you called on your birthday last month and asked your question about the accident that I went looking in that file cabinet again."

Marea watches her mother move one hand between the pillows and her back, pressing to relieve tension, an image Marea recalls, her father away, her mother alone in bed, the strain of maintaining the appearance of happiness.

"I know you adored your father. As he wrote in his diary, you were the one person alive he allowed himself to love. I also worshipped my father, you know. Perhaps I passed this on to you, the way I made my father the standard for everyone. In that way I was unfair to Jonas. How could he measure up to my mythic father—or to your 'Grandpa Albert' for that matter, since Albert was the man I put in my father's place? When you and your father went off on your Sunday afternoons, I was jealous that he was closer to you than me, but I suppose I also preferred it that way. Perhaps I married a man who could never allow any woman to replace the mother he lost, because I also didn't want a husband to replace the father I worshipped. I hope you don't mind my talking to you this way. I thought it was time. Is it all right?"

"Of course."

"I'm not sure it's fair to burden you with my doubts. My guilt."

"Guilt?"

"That I asked for the divorce. That I didn't appreciate the complex situation in which he'd found himself, that I didn't realize how growing up with such terrible anti-Semitism led to his deep fear of Stalin and the Soviet Union—to his sincere belief that he was protecting us from another evil regime. Reading his diary helped me understand more."

"And it turned out he was right."

"I don't want to debate right and wrong, Marea—not at this point. It was all so secretive. There was so much he had to keep to himself—so much he chose to keep to himself. Maybe he did that to protect me from the full force of his despair, but it contributed to our alienation from one another."

Marea's head is swimming with all her mother is spilling out to her, but the fragments are settling into a logic she cannot escape.

"Do you suppose I inherited this from him? Do you suppose I became obsessed with nuclear bombs destroying my world because he was obsessed with how the Nazis destroyed his?"

"Honestly, I don't know the answer to that, Marea. It's been a century of such violence. It's hard to imagine how anyone could be immune."

Marea touches her father's diary. "At least there's no evidence here that he committed suicide."

Virginia's silk jacket has fallen open, and through her thin nightgown Marea sees the ivory skin of her mother's breasts. Marea takes note of the moment of untended exposure—her mother as a woman—and then the return of modesty, the jacket pulled closed again.

"No, at least not in any deliberate way."

"What do you mean?"

"From what I've read, and what I've been told, it takes enormous determination to commit suicide."

"But—"

Virginia raises a hand to stop Marea. "Please give me a moment here. This part is not easy for me."

Marea moves aside the clothes on the love seat, and sits with the diary in her lap.

"You see, I don't believe he deliberately set out to kill himself that terrible morning. But there's another kind of suicide. Life is so fragile, so much can go wrong. If some part of you is distracted, you can easily become vulnerable to the dangers the world presents every single day. Perhaps some internal instinct for self-preservation shuts down, and things can happen—tragic things. I don't believe your father willed his death, but perhaps he no longer willed his life either. Do you understand what I mean?" Virginia leans forward, intent on making herself clear to Marea. "I've thought about this ever since you telephoned on your birthday. I've thought about it night and day. Perhaps now that you've read his diary and know more of what went on between us in those last months, you can understand why I needed to hang on to the belief that it was an accident. But you asked the question, and you deserve an answer. This is the best I can come up with for you. No, I don't believe your father committed suicide. But yes, I do think that in a certain way he contributed to his own death. He had become indifferent to his own survival, and he was driving on a highway, going at high speed. At the last moment, when he was sandwiched between those trucks, did he realize what was happening to him? Did he have a moment when he was either relieved or regretful? I suspect both. He was a brilliant man, Marea, too brilliant not to realize what he had done. This is not a tidy answer, but I've not found life to provide tidy answers."

Marea lifts the papers from her lap. "Can I keep this? Would you mind?"

Virginia sighs. She is reluctant.

"Why do you want it? What for?"

"To have something of him."

"It's probably what he would have wanted. You were the one light in his life."

"I'd like to go to bed now."

"Are you all right in your old room?"

Marea is puzzled by the question.

"So many memories," Virginia says, explaining herself. "And your dreams."

Marea gets up and goes over to her mother. She bends to kiss her. Virginia holds her daughter a moment, and then lets her go.

It is morning, and the branches of the birch trees are lit by a low-angled sun. A squirrel quivers, front feet in nut-prayer. A blue heron stands perfectly balanced on one leg, studying the stillness of the gray-green pond. The morning is cool, full of promise. The forest and its inhabitants have come through another night.

Marea knows she will find him here. That is why she has come out walking. He once told her that morning was the time when all the creatures of the earth faced each other new. When he appears, parting tree branches and stepping carefully, he is weighted down with equipment—binoculars hanging around his neck, a magnifying monocle attached to a string looped around a shirt button, tattered reference guides stuffed into his front pockets, his canvas specimen satchel slung over one shoulder, a butterfly net over the other. Marea's heart leaps at the sight of him, a tall young man with a shock of red hair, deep in concentration, absorbing the woods and the new morning.

He stops and cocks an ear, then lowers his eyes so he won't be distracted by any sense except hearing. Turning back toward the pond, he examines a thicket of vegetation, then crouches down onto his hands and knees in front of a feathering fern. He slips the satchel and the net off his shoulders, spreads the fronds apart, leans forward into the fern. Delicately he inserts his hand among the fronds, then withdraws it palm side up, cradling a baby bird. Has it fallen from a nest above? He must have heard it chirping. Still kneeling, Jonas cups the bird in both hands and brings it close to sing to it. Marea recognizes the melody, the Hebrew prayer, her own surrender into sleep.

But soon Jonas's singing is drowned out by the rising sounds of a gathering storm, and the bird begins to bleed. Blood flows from its tiny beak and fills the cup of Jonas's hands, spilling through his fingers, running down his arms onto the ground around his knees. Marea sees the baby bird floating in blood in her father's hands, and she startles like a deer, fleeing as the sky blackens overhead and there is nothing left of the morning. A battalion of crows slap wings, and screeching caws break from their open beaks. Marea runs hard, her feet pounding, as the forest transforms into a dark river. There is no escaping because the river takes in everything, and everything becomes it.

The window lets in the first light of morning. Marea wakes out of her dream that leaves its residue clinging like magnetized shavings of steel. In a few moments she recalls where she is, her childhood bed, her childhood home, the brick house where two women lie distant from each other, a house of memory. Marea does not feel love for her mother, but she does feel compassion, and compassion is a better feeling than anger because it has a future.

She pictures her mother sleeping—eye mask keeping out the dawn, bed jacket folded over her dressing table stool, thin body barely disturbing the mattress.

Marea looks through the drawers of her childhood desk for a pencil and paper. She is wearing only the T-shirt she slept in, and she sits, bare-bottomed, feeling the cool smoothness of her childhood chair. She wants her note to be kind, and she thanks her mother for the gift of her father's diary, and for her honesty. She promises to call and apologizes for not having a telephone number where she can be reached. She acknowledges that it must be difficult to dredge up the past, thanks her again.

Marea slips into her blue jeans, her sneakers, and then, using what she knows about protecting the artifacts of life, fits her father's diary carefully into the front pouch of her backpack. She pulls on the backpack and shifts the weight to get it balanced. She is anxious to get outside, to feel the coolness of an August morning. She is anticipating walking the streets, riding the train, movement. The kitchen clock on the old GE stove says six-fifteen. Marea sets her note against the sugar bowl. She glances toward the lock and hasp on the basement door. It is clear to her now—the lock wasn't put there to keep intruders out, but to keep memory locked in.

4

Marea sits on the step of Dawn's Early Rising beneath a hand-lettered sign taped inside the window, "Sorry, We're Closed." Her chin is cupped in two hands and her elbows are on her knees. She is used to leaving people, but she is not used to people leaving her. It's more than a week since Andrew was scheduled to return. She sits on the step as the evening becomes night. Hours ago she felt the cloak of disappointment wrap around her once again. Andrew has not returned, and neither have her four therapists. Marea is waiting for them all.

She watched the last sunlight of the afternoon reflected in the window of Flower Fantasies across the street, followed as it shrank from trapezoid to triangle to a golden slash, and disappeared. The shop girl has come outside to gather up the buckets of day lilies and the potted trees, walking them inside one by one, each pot and bucket hugged to her chest like a sleepy child. Marea observes the shop girl sweep the floor, wipe down the glass doors of the refrigerated cases, turn off all but the grow-lights, back her way out the front door carrying trash to the curb for the morning pickup. To Marea, this flower shop girl is a whole world of responsibilities, intention, purpose. To the girl, who has already walked away up Greenwich Avenue, Marea is an odd woman sitting alone on a cement stoop, staring at her.

Marea drifts down to Sheridan Square, which is always alive through the night. The neon signs give off a droning hum, and there is the din of the crowd of cruising men and stoned hippies—the seedy West Village movable feast. The sidewalks are lined with things for sale, some on makeshift tables, other merchandise spread out on blankets on the cement—sticks of incense, leather belts and sandals, hash pipes, silk-screened T-shirts, carved beads. One stack of T-shirts shows Dick Nixon as Pinocchio; another has Bob Marley as an angel. The street merchants share jug wine. The selling is more important than the sales.

The street commerce reminds Marea of her travels. There are the same woven coca pouches and alpaca ponchos she's seen spread on mats in *zócalo* markets. High in the Andes the markets smelled of burning charcoal and roasted meats; here the smells are hashish and marijuana. In the Andes the women had children tied to their backs; here there are no children.

A young woman sits on a tall stool behind a table with a dozen notebooks arranged like the petals of a large daisy. Each notebook is covered in a different color of batik cloth. The woman is also a flower, a narrow stem through her waist and shoulders, frizzy rosette of hair, a bud face, small glass earrings like drops of dew. Her back is straight, and her hands are held prayerlike between her knees. Even on this warm August evening she wears a long blue silk scarf wrapped around and around her neck and, hanging from a beaded necklace, a golden Buddha sits between her breasts.

"The notebooks are pretty," Marea says.

"Thank you. I make them."

"You make them?"

"Yes, the only thing I buy is the rice paper. I sew the bindings, dye the fabric, glue the covers. I learned to do it in Nepal."

"May I?" Marea points to a yellow notebook.

"Go ahead."

Marea turns the notebook in her hands. She opens it. The paper is rough, a brownish color. She moves her fingers across a page to get the feel of it.

"Can you write on it?"

"You have to use the right pen. Ballpoints usually work."

"When were you in Nepal?"

"Last year, after I left India."

"How long were you in India?"

"About a year, until my guru went to California."

"How much are your notebooks?"

"How much do you want to pay?"

"How much do you charge?"

"I don't do it that way."

Marea cocks her head. "What's that mean?"

"You need to decide why you want it. That way it will have more value to you—and then whatever you decide to give me for it will have more value to me as well."

"You support yourself this way?"

"It works out."

The woman's serenity puts everything else on the street—even sound—at a distance. Marea examines the yellow-covered notebook again, and pictures her father's diary on the floor beside her mattress. She has read his diary a dozen times, knows his memories as intimately as her own.

"It isn't only money I'm supposed to offer," Marea guesses. "I have to make you a promise or something."

"Whatever you like."

"But I'll probably never see you again, so whatever bargain I make with you has to be the honor system."

"That's right."

"Do you sell a lot of notebooks this way?"

"Just the right amount."

The notebook is already Marea's. It belonged to her before she saw it, before she turned down Seventh Avenue. It is hers in the way that the shells she painted on the Algarve in Portugal were hers before she found them, the way the red coral from the Indian Ocean waited for her, the way the red satin shoe was waiting for the homeless woman with her carts. And yet Marea could put the notebook down and move on without it, a tributary passed by.

"Do you have a use for it?" the woman prompts.

"I think I do," Marea answers, surprising herself. "Would three dollars be enough?"

"It's up to you."

Marea puts the yellow notebook back on the table, closer to the edge, closer to herself. She digs into her jeans and pulls out crumpled bills. She has never had much use for money. Now she wants this notebook, feels she must have it, is disturbed that she could easily have passed it by. A five-dollar bill is wadded up with the rest. She flattens it out and puts it on the table.

"Thank you," the woman says, taking the money. "And you said you wanted to make a promise."

"I guess I'll write in it."

"Yes, but what sorts of things would you like to write?"

"What I see, what I observe."

"Okay."

"But I can't promise. I haven't been very good at keeping promises."

"Is it an intention?"

"Yes, I could say it's an intention."

The woman studies her customer. "Okay. I'll accept an intention."

"This is a little weird, you know."

"But interesting, right?"

She offers her hand to Marea to seal the bargain and holds it there, as if allowing something to pass between them. When she lets go, Marea prepares herself for the coming good-bye. This has been the nature of her travels, everything said and shed in passing, people let go of almost as soon as they are found.

Marea takes the notebook from the table. "I like it."

"I'm glad you do."

At the newsstand beside the Sheridan Square subway entrance Marea buys a ballpoint pen and then hurries down the subway stairs to look for something to describe in her new notebook.

Four boys burst onto the train at Thirty-fourth Street, electric guitars strapped across their backs. They are rail-thin, with bell-bottom jeans that mold to their genitals like Saran Wrap. Their arms are filigreed with tattoos. Safety pins pierce their ears. When they spot Marea, a pretty woman sitting alone, they surround her.

"Such a luvly bird to be by her lonesome." English accent, north country.

"Come along for a pint?"

"We're openin' at CBGB's. They're payin' us in greenbacks."

"We're all alone in a foreign land."

"We're good boys. Bring flowers to our mums."

They have her up in their arms at Forty-second Street, falling on each other up the steps. They laugh, light a joint, press it to her lips. She sucks in deeply. She is happy about her new notebook, in a mood to play. "Your mums know you're stoned out of your gourds?"

Times Square is lit like day. Triple and quadruple X's are plastered across blacked-out windows. Neon thighs and breasts flicker on marquees. Marea goes along as they duck into "Live Girls, All Requests." The five of them jam into one booth where a chicken-limbed girl, nowhere near a woman, waits behind scratched Plexiglas. Her T-shirt, printed with the stars and stripes of an American flag, doesn't cover the red tracks up and down her arms. Through a talking tube, she asks in a flat voice, "What do you want me to do?"

"Can you put yer finger up yerself, show the pink inside?"

She is barely old enough for pubic hair. Marea aches for her.

"'Ey, little pussy, the sign says 'All Requests.'"

The girl nods. No need to remind her. She opens her legs and obliges. The boys unzip and wag their erect penises at the Plexiglas, laughing and elbowing one another.

Marea lets the booth door slam shut behind her, feels her way back down the hall, unpeeling the fingers of the one boy who's come after her.

"What's the problem? We were only 'aving a bit o' fun."

Marea remembers her problem, her porous skin. Back at the subway station she waits until the attendant is busy in his booth, then ducks under the turnstile and slips along the wall to wait for a northbound train to take her in.

At dawn Marea comes out of the subway to the thud of a stack of newspapers landing on the sidewalk outside the locked metal grating of a newsstand. It has rained in the night, and the wheels of the departing delivery truck make the sound of splitting fabric as they cut through the puddles in the street. Marea breathes in the flowery smell of August. In her hand, against her chest, she holds her yellow notebook. She has kept her promise, her intention, and is looking forward to sleep.

In the late afternoon, she wakes into someone else's skin, jittery, distracted. She goes to the bathroom and then returns to her mattress. She is nude. She always sleeps nude. Fully awake, she feels edgy, waiting for something, what? It's Saturday. Monday is Labor Day. Marea looks across the floor to where Dr. Iris's ceramic turtle has a place among her shells and stones. On Tuesday morning she will climb the stairs to Dr. Iris's room. On Wednesday she will return to Colin Ross, and later that day to Nina Wolf. On Thursday she will ride the elevator up to Eric Silas's loft. Will these encounters satisfy this edgy desire she cannot name?

Marea rolls over to pick up her father's diary, unties the string, and turns to a line she has read again and again. *I have lost everyone, even my own daughter.* Marea will never forget going to Einstein's side the evening of their fight, joining the jury that pronounced her father guilty. *"Do you see who she goes to? Do you see who she chooses?"* If she hadn't slipped away from the father who had begun to frighten her, would he have found the desire to keep on living?

Marea ties up the pages, gets dressed, and sticks her new notebook into her shoulder bag. She knows how to soothe her loneliness. Within a half an hour she is riding the subway, north to Harlem, and then back south all the way out to Brooklyn. When the speed and the traveling calm her, her loneliness subsides, and she opens her notebook.

Something calls to me and comforts me here in the subway. Perhaps it is the fact that struggle is the common ground. Survival, transit, pulling through the eye of another day. There is every sort of person here except the rich, since the subway scares them and they don't need it. I like it when people press in, when shoulders touch. I like the human weight, someone's life leaning against my own. Forgiveness is the nature of the place. I watch, but I do not judge, and am not judged. I am at last doing the work my father prepared me for. I am becoming a scientist. I am observing and making field notes. I feel a new and tentative sense of purpose. What matters to me most is detail. Chipped front tooth, sagging socks, the puffy flesh closing up around a gold wedding ring. People are my species to behold. As I watch them hours pass with the intense focus of held breath. From time to time lately, since my money is running out, I walk the aisle with my palm held out, grateful to receive quarters or nickels or whatever people give me. With their money they earn the right to examine me, to worry over me. It is a way of being the best kind of scientist, using my own body and skin to gather data. My notebook will fill up with what I see in their eyes.

Dr. Iris waits at the top of the stairs the way she did the first time Marea came to her in June. As Marea peers up from the darkness below, Dr. Iris looks like a cautious landlady tracking the movements of her tenants. When Marea reaches the landing, and the light from inside falls on her face, Dr. Iris is a queen in a castle.

"How nice to see you, my dear. Come ahead."

"I'm sorry I don't have any bread for you. Andrew is still on vacation."

"I admit I've been looking forward to that luscious smell."

"Next time," Marea promises, and moves toward her accustomed seat.

Marea takes in the room, glad to be back, her eyes grazing over the things she has held on to in her mind over the month away. She stops at sunflowers in an urn on the floor, something new.

"Those flowers are pretty."

"Sunflowers have a special place in my heart. They're always so proud and tall in summer. But then their heads bend with the changing season." She rests her cheek against her hand, thoughts of changing seasons, the unstoppable passage of time, herself in the autumn of her life. Marea sees all this and feels a love for Dr. Iris.

"I forgot to bring your turtle back," she apologizes.

"Keep it as long as you like."

"Did you have a good vacation?"

"I did, thank you. I'm curious to hear how things went with your mother. Did you go for a visit as you had planned?"

"Yes, I went. When I first got there, I regretted going. I didn't know what to say to her, and she didn't know what to say to me, either. We've never been at ease with each other, but after all my years away we were almost strangers. She was desperate to ask me the question that's apparently bothered her all this time—whether I left to run away from her. She seemed determined to get me to agree so she could apologize and get it off her chest."

"She felt guilty."

"Yes, but I think it was to cover up a guilt that made her feel even worse."

"What was that?"

"The way she treated my father."

"You've said they didn't get along very well."

"I knew something was wrong between them, but it was tied up with my own fears. She blamed him for my fear of nuclear war, but in retrospect I think my fear of nuclear war got mixed up with my fears about their marriage. When they argued, I felt alone. And loneliness was what I dreaded most when I thought about nuclear war, the loneliness of seeing everyone around me gone. Children mix these things together, don't they?"

Dr. Iris nods. "Children are both blessed and cursed by the

limits of their perception. Without the fuller picture they take the essence of what confronts them straight into their hearts. In some ways they understand less than the adults around them, but in other ways they feel more of the essential truth of things."

"My mother gave me my father's diary to read."

"Your father kept a diary?"

"I never knew about it. She says she didn't either. She went looking in his old files after I called her on my birthday and asked about his accident—remember when I asked her?"

"Of course."

"That's when she went looking in his old files and found his diary."

"She let you read it?"

"I think she wanted me to understand what caused the problems between them. I don't know if I ever told you that my father lost both parents in the Holocaust. I don't talk about it much—I guess because he almost never talked about it either. Reading his diary was the first I even found how they were killed—his father was shot by the Gestapo in Vienna in the first roundup of Jewish intellectuals. His mother was killed later in Auschwitz. She was hanged for stealing a potato. Reading his diary I finally understood how something died in him, too. I guess I should have figured it out for myself, but my mother didn't talk to me about it, either. Maybe he wouldn't let her tell me. In his diary he wrote about wanting to protect me from his despair. He knew his despair had destroyed his marriage. How could he love and let himself be loved when he'd left his parents to die?"

"Do you think this could explain the car accident?"

"I don't know," Marea says softly. "I really don't know." She looks down at her hands folded in her lap, hands like her own mother's. "And my mother doesn't know, either—so I guess it will always be a mystery."

The two of them sit quietly, digesting the finality of this, a loss that can never be fully understood or put to rest.

"I bought myself a notebook."

"Oh?"

"My father and I kept notebooks to write down what we saw when we went exploring in the woods. In his diary he wrote that he wanted to teach me the lesson his father taught him—that there is exquisite beauty in the natural world, and you could always look there to find meaning in life, even when the actions of people led you to despair of meaning. After he died, I never went back into those woods. Sometimes I think that's why I traveled—because I had lost faith in what he taught me."

"Did you really lose faith in it?"

"Why do you ask that?"

"I'm thinking about the collection that you carry in your backpack, all the shells and bits of nature you told me about. And your stories about your travels. The way you have observed things so carefully and in such detail, you seem very much to have used the lessons your father taught you."

"I've been writing about the people I see on the subway. People, not nature."

"There can be beauty in people, too, don't you think? Your father's lesson was a good one, you know."

"But it's a risk, isn't it? To see beauty, to be willing to see it, to risk trusting to the meaning in it and then losing it all over again."

On Wednesday morning, a few minutes before ten, Marea sits like a college girl waiting for office hours with the English teacher on whom she has a crush. The night before, to prepare for her return to Colin Ross, she took a long shower, tried on a pair of earrings she had bought from a sidewalk merchant on Eighth Street, washed her clothes so she'd have a clean shirt and jeans. The loneliness she felt in the days after coming back from Princeton has been supplanted by anticipation, though she doesn't know what she anticipates or why. The days are longer, her breath shorter.

She flips through magazines in the waiting room of the New York Psychoanalytic Institute with an eye on the person beside her, a young girl in her early twenties, dressed in an organdy blouse and white painter's overalls, crouched over the application on a clipboard as Marea herself was crouched almost three months back. The girl's blond hair is woven into a ropy braid. Marea wonders if she will be assigned to Colin Ross, and examines her again with a more critical eye. When the girl gets up to hand in her application, Marea shares a conspiratorial look with the receptionist she dislikes.

The door opens, and Colin Ross waits for Marea. His brown curls have been clipped to a cap. His tie is too tight. His smile looks as if it were purchased in a dime store.

"Hello, Marea."

"Hi." She goes through the door without looking back, embarrassed to have competed over such a loser.

"How have you been?" Colin asks as they head down the hall.

"I'm okay."

Marea does not go immediately to the couch.

Colin waits and then asks, "Hard to get started again?"

"I suppose."

He gestures toward the couch to encourage her.

"Might as well," she says, to make light of her discomfort.

She touches her feet to the end of the couch, reaches her hands back to the headrest, looks up at the ceiling.

From behind her she hears his voice. "I was concerned after our last session that you might not come back."

Marea recalls their last session when she abruptly canceled their final appointment before the break.

"I guess I was a little mean."

"You were irritated with me, and perhaps you had a right to be."

"I did?"

"Have you forgotten? You said you wished you could hear something from me that didn't sound like what I'd been taught to say. I was quite angry with you at first. I told myself you didn't understand the psychoanalytic relationship. I decided that you couldn't accept my being in training, that it was impossible for you to put your faith in my professional ability. I tried quite a number of ways to avoid what you were saying, but in the end I faced up to the fact that if what you said upset me so much, there must be something to it. It took awhile, but I realized how important your criticism was, and I have to thank you for it. It's what they teach us, after all—that if you're not really there in the room, nothing of value will happen."

"I like your haircut."

"It's shorter than what I wanted."

"It's not so bad. Hair grows back."

"I suppose that should be some comfort when your barber turns your head into a bowling ball. Anyway, now that I've gotten that off my chest, I'd like to hear what's been going on with you. What have you been doing, thinking? Any important dreams?"

"You're going to be proud of me."

"Oh?"

"In our last session you said that because my father died when I was young, I never had the chance to see him as an ordinary man with faults. I guess I also had to face the fact that if something you said made me so angry, there had to be some truth to it. I decided to try to find out what I could learn about him. I couldn't think of a better place to go looking for his faults than from my mother."

Colin laughs. Marea likes to make him laugh.

"I went back to my house on Blossom Street, slept in my old room. It was strange."

"Strange in what way?"

Marea looks through the snapshots in her mind: the encounter at the front door, brushing the dust from the specimen boxes, her mother's stricken face at the bottom of the attic ladder.

"I found out that my father kept a diary. He began it when he was working on the Manhattan Project."

"Was it about his work on the bomb?"

"That and other things."

"How did you come across the diary?"

"I had gone up into the attic to try to find some scientific notebooks my father and I kept. I thought I might find some other things as well, some clues about his life. My mother freaked out when she saw me coming down the ladder, so I knew there had to be something she was hiding. Later that night she gave it to me. I think she realized that if we're going to have a relationship, it has to be based on truth. It makes me wonder why I let all those years go by without demanding the truth from her." Marea looks at the pattern of spines in the bookshelves, and then up to the milk-glass ceiling fixture and the shadows where dead flies have collected inside. "Maybe I didn't want to know the truth."

"Yes."

"Or maybe I didn't want to dissect him."

"Dissect him?"

"Even though he taught me to put everything under a microscope, I didn't want to do that to him."

"Did you find the truth you were looking for in his diary?"

"You mean whether he killed himself or not?"

Colin waits.

"Maybe I should let you read it for yourself."

She hears him shift in his chair. She knows he's waiting for her to decide.

"But I don't want you to dissect him either. Is it weird to be so protective of someone who's been dead for eighteen years?"

"Marea, in a certain way for you he's not dead at all."

Marea tries to manage the strong feelings that come over her when Colin's verbalizes this essential fact of her existence.

He interprets her silence in a different way. "You don't have to share his diary if it's not something you feel comfortable doing. But if you ever feel ready, I'd be interested to take a look."

"Were you close to your father?"

"Why do you ask?"

"Just curious."

"Are you trying to decide whether you can trust me with the diary?"

"I wanted to know more about you."

"I see."

"And you're not going to tell me."

"No."

She sits up. "It's about time for me to go, right?"

"Not quite."

"I feel like getting going."

She stops halfway between the couch and the door.

"What is it?" Colin asks.

Without turning back to face him, she says, "It's too bad we can't be friends."

She hurries along Third Avenue to catch the bus to Central Park West. When another pedestrian accidentally bumps up against her to avoid a messenger on a bike, Marea feels a flash of anger and wheels around to bark at him—but he has already disappeared into the oncoming crowd.

On the crosstown bus the seats are full of children returning from their first half-days back at school. The green trees arching over the Central Park transverse have a few errant boughs of yellow and red, autumn scouts. When Nina opens her door into the waiting room, she is full of the energy of the changing season and greets Marea energetically, ready for work. Nina's office has been cleaned and straightened in her absence, knickknacks arranged in little groupings, window-seat pillows squared up like attentive guests.

"What's the report?" Nina asks. "What's happened in your life over the last month?"

Marea shifts in her chair. "Not much."

"Not much?"

"No, not too much."

"I see. Well, is there something you'd like to get started with?"

"Not really."

Nina folds her arms. "All right."

"How did you like Guatemala?"

"We had a wonderful time. It's a beautiful country with such an interesting history."

"I know. Isn't it interesting the way they're killing off the indigenous population?" Marea says this with such a straight face that it takes a moment for Nina to catch her sarcasm.

While Nina was traveling in Guatemala, Marea remembered her own time there when she fell in love with the Mayan people and became heartsick at their predicament. She stayed at a boardinghouse on the banks of Lake Panajachel, and in the hot afternoons she joined the women who wove blankets on their back-strap looms as their babies napped on mats around them. The women spoke of whoever had last been taken in the night, husbands found in ditches, sliced open with machetes. The military men said these were guerilla fighters, but the Mayan people knew that the government of Guatemala was on a campaign to destroy them. Marea spent her first Christmas away from home in Panajachel and was witness to the one day each year that the local police allowed the Mayan peasants to protest the genocide. They paraded through the streets hidden inside gigantic puppets that caricatured President Osorio, his henchmen, and the local politicians who turned a blind eye to the killing. And then after sundown, when the women finished steaming the fruit tamales for after midnight mass, everyone went back into the streets to join the procession behind the wooden statue of their patron saint, a march of sorrow for the souls that had passed over during the year.

"Truthfully, I didn't get the sense of any killing. Of course we kept to the tourist spots."

"They kill Mayans in the tourist spots."

"If that's true, I didn't see any evidence of it."

"Trust me. It's happening."

Nina gathers her hair and pushes it back off her shoulders. "So what would you like to talk about, Marea?"

"Actually, I'd like to talk about Guatemala. I'd like to talk about how a political person like you could visit Guatemala and be indifferent to the genocide taking place there every day."

"That sounds like an accusation."

"Call it an observation. You say you're political. It surprises me, that's all."

"If something is bothering you, Marea, why not just come out with it?"

"I thought I did."

"I'm talking about something between you and me."

"Here we go again. What bothers me doesn't count because you've got something else that's supposed to be bothering me more."

"Do you realize you've taken a hostile tone with me from the moment you sat down?"

"Or perhaps you're a bit defensive."

Nina works to rise above her irritation. "Not everyone is as preoccupied with violence as you are, Marea. I was in Guatemala on vacation. Perhaps I wasn't attuned to these other things."

"Too bad genocide doesn't take vacations."

Nina squares her shoulders. "I assume your hostility is some sort of punishment for my going away. Wouldn't it be better to deal with your feelings directly?"

"The therapeutic relationship as a microcosm of power and authority."

"Sarcasm avoids the real issues."

"The *real issue* is that it bothers me that you could visit Guatemala and not have a clue about the horrors being done to the Mayan people. You advertise your brand of therapy as a way of seeing the world more clearly, but when I describe what *I* see, you twist it into some cockeyed notion that I was sexually abused as a child. Frankly, I think your 'politics' is a bunch of intellectual garbage. It has nothing at all to do with what people suffer in the world—*not a goddamn thing.*"

"Yes, Marea!" Nina punches the air as if cheering a goal. "At last we've uncovered your anger."

"Fuck you."

"Why are you so afraid of your anger?"

"You think my anger is some big accomplishment?"

"It's a wonderful accomplishment."

"Right. Anger at *you,* the oppressor," Marea snaps back.

"Anger at me because I can't fix the world for you."

"Such bullshit."

Nina takes a long centering breath, a tool of her trade.

"Do you suppose you could learn to express your anger and still show regard for me as a person?"

"I thought you 'welcomed' my anger."

"I do welcome your anger, but I don't wish to be your whipping boy. All that does is allow you to postpone facing the underlying reasons for your feelings."

"Who the hell are you to judge the reasons for my feelings?"

"Marea, I don't wish to be a transference object for your abuse. I don't believe that's helpful for either one of us."

"You are so full of shit."

Nina rises up, as if a burst of helium has inflated every limb. "We've reached the point where this session is no longer productive. We'll put a punctuation point here and make up the time another day." She checks her clock. "Twenty minutes. We'll keep it in the bank."

Marea spreads her fingers against her chest. "You're kicking me out?"

"I think we could both use some time to cool down."

"So *that's* your prescription for anger—you ice it?"

"Call it what you wish. I'm not prepared to go on with this session right now. We'll continue next Wednesday."

"Maybe. I'll call you."

"All right."

As Marea hurries down the steps of the old synagogue, she shakes off the unpleasant encounter as if it were a buzzing fly.

It is late afternoon, and as the elevator clanks up to the fourth-floor loft, Marea wonders whether Eric Silas will even remember he made love to her. It's been five weeks. He's been to the Himalayas and back. Marea suspects she doesn't weigh down even one minute corner of his life. If he were asked to recall her physical features, would he get any part of her right?

When the elevator door opens, she sees him standing at the far end of the entry hall with the telephone receiver pressed to his ear. With his free hand he makes a circle in the air to suggest that the person on the other end is going on and on. He points to the front of the loft and gestures that he will join her momentarily. She's relieved he wasn't waiting by the elevator to embrace her. In fact he seems indifferent. Either he has forgotten, or sex with a patient is not particularly remarkable.

Marea slips off her sneakers and goes inside to wait. Looking out at the other reincarnated buildings of SoHo, she listens with half an ear while Eric's voice hardens and softens, impatience, conciliation. Marea guesses he is speaking with his mother. Above the buildings the sky has an orange glow. Marea likes the late-afternoon hour when expectations subside, her favorite time to ride the subway. Commuting home, people are more patient with themselves and with each other. If they stare at one another with glazed eyes, no one is offended.

She turns away from the window back to the room she has visited now half a dozen times. Without Eric there to observe her, she examines it as a habitat, pillows and rugs, tall grass tamped down after deer have spent the night. Though they have moved on, their dreams remain.

Marea notices one stack of pillows set apart in a darker corner. She is always on the edge of sleep these days now that her nights are spent riding the subway and writing in her notebook. She yawns deeply. Eric is still engrossed in what has evidently become a difficult conversation. She goes to the corner, pushes over the pillows, and folds herself into them. She pulls one pillow to her chest and wraps her arms around it. The light from the window is turning purple as she succumbs to sleep. When she senses a presence approach and then drift away, she imagines a gull floating by on a swelling sea.

Her sleep is full of dreams. She sees an oxbow in a river far below. In every direction the sky is iridescent blue. She spreads her arms and arches her back to catch the rising wind. Is this a secret, that flight is possible? But flying is what she does, what she desires, what she knows. Rising and dipping along the contours of the land below, she recognizes the yellow fields and green valleys where she has flown before.

There is rustling, stocking feet padding on wooden floors, people gathering, greetings. The sounds slowly bring Marea through to the other side of sleep, and she opens her eyes to the legs and backs of people settling into a circle among the pillows at the center of the room. Eric is already seated, back straight, eyes closed, yogi-style, preparing himself for the coming session. The others close their eyes, too, to come together from their disparate lives. Marea watches from her dark corner, but does not budge. So far no one seems to have noticed her.

"Who'd like to get us started?" Eric asks.

There are seven people in the group—three men and four women—and they look around to see who will be the first to speak. A woman who appears to be the youngest in the group holds her head in her hands, tears dropping down onto the front of her oversized man's dress shirt. Her hair is cropped and tinted to a bluish bristle, and her toenails are painted black.

"Josie?" Eric asks gently. "Do you have something you need to say?"

"I went home. My parents wouldn't let me in the house."

The others wince at this report, at the coldness it implies. A woman with bulky shoulders and thighs that strain the seams of her pants hunches forward. "Why did you even go?"

Eric nods. It's the right question.

Josie tucks her hands into her armpits and rocks, comforting herself.

Eric adds, "They told you that's what they'd do."

"I miss them," Josie whimpers. "They're still my parents, and I miss them."

One of the other women asks, "Do you miss them enough to become the person they want you to be?"

She shrugs, bows her head again. Maybe.

"Or were you hoping that they could change enough to accept you as you are?" This man is the only one who appears to have come from a job in the business world. His black socks are held up with garters, and his jacket and tie are laid out neatly on the floor behind him.

"It's not like you didn't know this would happen," the fat woman continues.

The businessman comes to Josie's defense. "That doesn't mean she's not allowed to hope things could be different."

"Or maybe you get off on having them hurt you," the fat woman harps.

Josie's tears are coming steadily now with little hiccups.

"Or maybe *you* get off on hurting her," Marea says from her pillows in the corner.

All eyes turn toward the intruder.

"Who is *she*?" the fat woman demands of Eric.

"Ask her," Eric suggests.

"Is she new?" asks a black man in leather pants, who worries his earring. "I thought seven was the maximum."

Eric looks over to Marea. "Would you like to come into the circle and introduce yourself?"

Marea gets up and joins the circle. "My session is before your group. I didn't plan on being here. I fell asleep."

"Are you going to join our group?"

"Didn't you say it was full?"

"But if we invited you, would you want to join?"

It's a trick question. She will not be invited unless she says she's not interested. Is she interested?

"Tell us about yourself," Josie says between sniffles. "That will help us trust you."

Marea recalls that Andrew said she would describe herself differently to each of her four therapists according to how each of them saw the world. Here there are seven different perspectives on the world.

"My name is Marea Hoffman. I guess the main thing about me

is that my father may have killed himself when I was twelve—it was a car accident, but there's no way to know for sure. He worked on nuclear bombs, and when I was a child I had nightmares about nuclear war. What else do you want to know?"

"Are there any questions for Marea?"

"Why do you see Eric?"

"A friend told me he thought a Jungian could help me."

"But what's your problem?"

"I wander. I used to wander around the world. Now I wander around the city."

"Would you like to be part of our group?" the man with the earring asks. "We could take a vote or something, see if people are willing to expand to eight."

The sky has grown dark, and Marea misses the subway.

"What would I do here?"

"The only rule is to listen with respect," Eric explains. "Other than that, it's an experiment."

"And why would I join?"

"To be part of something."

"If I wanted to be."

The "Closed" sign is still taped inside the window, but Marea spots a light. She hurries down the side alley and her heart leaps when she sees the back door held open with a potted geranium. The pot has been watered, but the geranium has not revived.

Inside, shirtless and with his back to the door, Andrew is hunched over his kneading, his shoulders tightening and releasing in a steady rhythm. A slower rhythm of piano jazz is playing softly on the radio.

"Andrew!" Marea exclaims. "You're back!"

He opens his floured arms as she rushes to him and rests her head against his bare chest. His smooth skin comforts her as she admits, "I was worried you wouldn't *ever* return."

"Isn't that your trick?" Andrew teases.

Marea puts a fist to her hip. "You were supposed to be back

here two weeks ago. I was worried sick about you. Totally out of character, but it's the truth."

"I'm sorry, Marea. I didn't know how to get in touch with you. So much has happened." He points his floured index finger toward the pantry.

It takes a few moments for Marea to make sense of what she sees, a bassinet set across the tops of two large drums of flour. "What's that?"

Andrew puts his arm around Marea's shoulders and guides her into the pantry. Side by side they look down on a baby sleeping on its back. The baby's eyes are closed, its long lashes lie against its cheeks, and its pink arms are spread out as if awaiting an embrace. Perhaps sensing the proximity of human warmth, it puckers its mouth before quieting again.

"Whose baby is this?"

"She's Tim's and mine now." Andrew touches the baby's head with his finger, leaving a track of flour on her dark hair. "Tim had to go to a teacher's conference, so I decided to try bringing her here to see if I could get back to work. You wouldn't believe the expenses with a baby."

Marea slips out from under Andrew's arm and retreats from the bassinet, distancing herself from it and from Andrew. "Would you mind telling me how this happened?"

The baby stirs again. Andrew puts his finger to his lips, points toward the back door, and then plucks his T-shirt off the hook and pulls it over his head. Outside in the alley he gazes up at the sky. A tipped moon is pouring stars into the night. Andrew settles his long body into a lotus position and leans against the painted wall. The rings of Saturn jutting out at each side of him give him wings. Marea slides down the opposite wall among the geraniums that were left to die.

"It's been a very bad time," Andrew begins. "A really horrible thing happened. We never got to Fire Island. The morning we were packing we got a phone call from the police in Kentucky. Tim's sister and her husband had been in a car accident." He takes a deep breath. "We lost them both. The awful thing is that it was their very first night out since their baby was born in April. They had worked so hard to get her—dozens of fertility doctors, I don't know how much money—they never wanted to leave her for a minute. On their way home a pickup truck swerved across the road and hit them head-on. The driver was drunk—of course, he only broke his leg. We couldn't believe it when we saw their car, totally destroyed. Tim's been in very bad shape, as you can imagine. His sister and brother-in-law, and his new niece, were his only family in the world."

Andrew massages his neck, and Marea notices the tiredness in his eyes.

"We spent two weeks in Kentucky seeing to everything, arranging for the funeral, emptying their house. We had to sell their things to pay off their debts. And then we brought Rebecca home with us. We've been back a little over a week. Tim's beginning to be able to sleep again."

"You're keeping the baby?"

"Of course."

"How do you plan on taking care of her?"

Andrew looks puzzled. "The same way anybody takes care of a baby."

"You both work."

"We'll figure it out. Rebecca is Tim's niece *and* his goddaughter. She's our responsibility."

"There was no one else to take her, some couple?"

"Tim and I are a couple."

"But wouldn't it be better to find a family to adopt her? Wouldn't that be best for *her*?"

Andrew turns away to the dark end of the alley.

"I'm not saying this because you're gay, Andrew. I wouldn't care if you and Tim were Martians. A baby isn't for a week or a month. It's for your whole life—for *her* whole life. You're a hippie—like me. We know nothing about providing a future."

Andrew looks back at Marea. "I don't understand you."

The sound of Rebecca's whimpering comes through the open door, and Andrew gets up to go back inside, informing Marea, "It's time for her evening bottle."

Marea pulls her knees to her chest and listens as Rebecca's whimpering grows into an angry cry, and then slows and stops. Marea imagines that Andrew has her in his arms now, quieting her, feeding her. The yellow light from the kitchen spikes into the dark. Marea belongs nowhere and to no one. The baby is crying again and Andrew is soothing her. Marea pushes off the cold cement and goes inside. Andrew has Rebecca's bottle sticking out of his pants pocket as he holds her against his shoulder, burping her. How has he learned these things?

"What do you want me to do?" Marea asks quietly.

"You sure you're in a mood to work?"

"Of course I'm in a mood to work," she snaps back.

"The dough absorbs everything."

"I don't need to hear that. I came to do my job."

He circles the kneading table, dancing lightly from foot to foot as Rebecca's eyes drift closed.

"How about you finish the kneading I was doing? Then you can tackle the eggs. We need three dozen eggs cracked for Portuguese sweet bread."

Marea contemplates the mound of dough, a cow's swollen udder.

"It's had ten minutes so far," Andrew says as he continues to walk and rock Rebecca.

On the radio Otis Redding is singing "Dock of the Bay." The slow rhythm of the song is maddening against the rhythm required for kneading. Marea shuts the music out of her mind, shuts Andrew and the baby out of her view, throws herself into the work of pushing and turning and doubling with much more force than necessary.

Andrew's hand clamps down over hers. "You're driving the dough crazy. Leave it to rise. We'll work together on the eggs." He settles Rebecca into her bassinet to sleep. "I'll get the mixing bowl. You get the egg cartons from the fridge."

Marea's hands are trembling as she lifts three cardboard trays of eggs off the stack. She knows she is losing control. She knows she will not make it from the refrigerator to the bench where Andrew is waiting. Two steps from the refrigerator the trays tumble out of her hands. Eggs fly everywhere, little missiles that hit and crack. Within seconds the cement floor is a swamp of slimy albumen, yolks, shattered shells. Mortified, Marea lurches forward to try to save the only tray that still has eggs intact. Her feet fly out from under her and her body slides straight across the slippery floor into the shelves against the wall. The shelves rock, and a tall stack of bread pans crashes to the floor. The blood-curdling cry that rises from the bassinet is so pained and helpless that for a moment Marea and Andrew stare at one another. And then Andrew rushes to gather Rebecca into his arms. She is safe, her world is safe—what scared her was nothing but a noise.

Marea is on her knees with her shins in slick albumen, frantically trying to scrape the eggs back together, seeking a miracle, that the eggs will go back into their shells, that the cracks will knit together, that the mended eggs will fit back into their cardboard sockets. But the yolks break into yellow rivers between her fingers, and she rocks back on her legs, rocks and cries, crying for what is broken, for all that is broken and cannot be fit back into an unbroken shell. With Rebecca in his arms Andrew watches dumbfounded as Marea stands up with eggs dripping down her calves, yanks off her apron, and runs out into the alley and the night.

The white room is as silent as a swim underwater when Marea closes the door and leans against it, out of breath. She goes straight to the mattress and curls herself into a fetal position. She could lie there forever, no engine, no rudder, no map.

Cool air blows through the open window. Fall is coming and with it shorter days. Winter is a hard time to be on the road. Drivers are not friendly. They speed by, spraying cold mud, and with the dark descending so early, the need to figure out where to spend the night presses down in the afternoon.

Before she realizes that she has made a plan, Marea finds herself filling her backpack. Once she understands what she is doing—packing up, moving out—she considers it resolved. She empties the small fridge and the overhead shelves of her few provisions and packs the food into the side pouches. She will have to live out of her backpack again. She folds her clothes, collects her things from above the bathroom sink, puts a rubber band around the remaining money she has saved. With care she wraps each shell, stone, and piece of coral, Dr. Iris's ceramic turtle, and fits them between the folds of her clothes where they'll be safe. Finally she ties the string around the pages of her father's diary and zips it into the front pouch, together with her own notebook.

It's nearly midnight when she tightens the straps across her shoulders and trudges down the three flights. She's got her sights set on the entrance at Spring Street, a shorter walk than Union Square. Tonight she will ride the subway; in the morning she will consider a destination.

Once in London I put my hand up to the window of the squat and felt the sound of a passing truck. I could not hear it or see it, but I could feel it. The train I'm riding picks up speed, and I feel sound in my feet. I sit with my backpack on the seat beside me, my notebook open in my lap. When I join the moving train, I go beyond feeling *sound, and I* become *it.*

In the morning Marea gets off the Broadway local at West Twenty-third and walks down the street to the YMCA, where she rents a locker so she'll have a place to store her backpack for the day. She takes a shower, talks with other women in the locker room, and then settles into a deep chair in the library to sleep until it's time to go uptown to the Psychoanalytic Institute.

"Did you decide to bring your father's diary?" Colin asks as Marea pulls her notebook from her shoulder bag before lying down on the couch.

"This is mine."

"Your diary?"

"Not really a diary. I've been writing about things I see, and also about some stories from my travels. There's something I want to read to you. Would that be okay?"

"You could read it, or you could tell it to me."

"I'd like to read it, if you don't mind."

Marea looks for the page she wants, feeling Colin's eyes on her in a new way. Is he thinking about her parting words at the last session? Or is he noticing a change in her now that she is unmoored and traveling again? She sits up on the couch to cradle her notebook in her lap. "It's about a man I met in Scotland. Since you've talked about the reasons I haven't been able to sustain relationships with men, I wanted to read you about one relationship I did have."

"Go ahead."

Marea opens to the page she's marked and reads.

I decided to go to Loch Ness in Scotland. It was silly, but I thought I might as well try to get a glimpse of the famous Loch Ness monster. Almost anything served as an excuse to go somewhere. It was less about having a destination than a way of moving on.

It was the most beautiful time of year. The trees were blazing with fall colors, and Loch Ness was smooth as glass. I was walking along with my sweater tied around my waist, my backpack riding high, feeling good the way you can on an autumn day that's perfect. I was even singing, entertaining myself with old camp songs—"Kookaburra Sits on the Old Gum Tree," "They Came on the Sloop John B"—singing so loud I didn't notice at first when a van rolled up alongside me.

The driver tapped his horn to get my attention, and when he pulled to a stop what I noticed first was the disfigurement of his chin, clay that someone has partly shaped and partly left as an unformed lump. He had the hooded eyes of a troublemaker out of Charles Dickens, but for some reason I wasn't scared. He asked me if I wanted a ride, and I told him I wanted to walk for a while. He said I'd want a ride eventually, so why not take one now? When I asked what direction he was going, he pointed to the door to indicate I should open it and come in. I looked into his van, a hitchhiker's habit, to sense whether it was a safe ride to take. I spotted two metal canes in the back, strapped down to keep them from rattling around, and then I noticed the stick he used to work the gas.

When I insisted on knowing his destination, he told me he was headed to the Isle of Skye off the northwest coast of Scotland. Then he reached over to slide back the side door so I could stow my backpack. I saw a mattress on the floor, crumpled blanket, piles of clothes. I put my stuff in the back and climbed into the front seat, and he drove on.

A few miles up the road, he stopped to go to the bathroom. He pulled his canes out from the back in a spasm of clattering and twisting, and I watched him head off, flinging forward his atrophied legs as his body dipped and lurched, and his head swung like a floating pendulum.

The moon was up by the time we drove onto the ferry to Skye. At the first town we found a restaurant and ate fish chowder and bread, and as we left the restaurant he lifted his nose to the air. A glimmer of pleasure came across his face. He explained that the burning peat of Skye was why he had to come, for that sweet smell. Ever since his bones began to pulverize inside his useless hips, he'd been on the dole and traveling. When he told me that a scent could be a destination as much as anything else, I knew I'd found a kindred soul.

That night he parked the van off the road on a high bluff that looked out across the dark channel called the Minch. The wind sang through the holes in his van, an eerie song, flutes, oboes, a call of wolves. I knew we would share his blanket and sleep side by side on his mattress, but I didn't know that in the howling wind I would unbutton his pants, slip them down his deformed legs, and pull him toward me. Even in sex and sleep, his body was a twisted tree.

Over the next weeks I made love with this crippled man many times. Not out of pity. Out of true affection. When I stepped down from the van one morning and turned back to tell him it was time for me to go, he didn't ask for a reason, or ask me to stay. He had long since lost interest in the fight of life. As I walked away down the winding road I did not understand why I was overcome with grief.

Marea closes her notebook and sinks back down into the couch. She wants Colin to say that he liked what she read, to say he likes her.

"It's about my father, isn't it?"

"Tell me what you mean."

Marea doesn't answer. She wants to hear Colin's voice, not her own. She looks toward him, then quickly away because now her strong feelings are for the earnest man who is leaning forward to give her his full attention. Longing moves up her thighs and burns where she wants his body pressed to hers.

"What's wrong?"

"Nothing."

"Why did you look at me that way?"

"I have to go. I'll see you next time." Marea is up, out the door, and gone.

Her next scheduled appointment with Eric Silas isn't for a few days, but she needs to carry her sexual desire somewhere, to carry it away from Colin Ross, away from that room, away from the Psychoanalytic Institute, where it will only do harm. She dismisses the thought that Eric might be busy with another patient. She envisions him shirtless, barefoot, the string of his pants hanging loose. He is not waiting for her, but he will not be displeased when she shows up at his door.

She checks her reflection in the window of the subway train and runs her fingers through her unkempt hair. She is a stranger to herself, a woman with desires. She pulls out her notebook and pen and looks around the car to find someone's worries or sadness to invade. But all she sees are passengers, dutifully reading their schoolbooks and newspapers. Not even a beggar or a child with whom to share a skin.

Marea doesn't want to ring and have to announce herself. She wants to catch Eric off guard and present herself as a woman, not a patient. She waits for someone to leave the building so that she can catch the door. When a thin and nervous young man emerges, sight inward, Marea wonders whether Eric takes boys to bed as well.

Rising up in the industrial elevator, Marea feels like a shipment of raw materials. The elevator door opens and Marea steps into the entry hall. It is noon, and there are none of the sounds she is accustomed to hearing, one half of a phone conversation, the kettle whistling for Eric's mug of green tea, the time-bending hum of Gregorian chants—there is only a heavy silence.

She steps in farther and checks out the therapy side of the loft. The room is dull and gray, and the pillows and vacant chairs seem oddly cold. She peers down the hall toward Eric's living quarters, then slips out of her shoes, drops her shoulder bag to the ground, and waits for more courage. Her sexual desire has evaporated, replaced by the desire for restitution. She is going to take back what was taken from her.

She starts down the hall, wondering now if he's there at all. Has he gone out on an errand? Will he come up the elevator and discover her in his home? To her left is the kitchen with a long work island, pots hanging overhead, open shelves stacked with plates and mugs. A bachelor's life. She continues toward his bedroom, sure now that he is out, wanting to spy on him while he is absent.

At the bedroom door she gasps at the unexpected sight of him lying on his back, totally nude, penis soft, arms and legs stretched out like Leonardo Da Vinci's "Vitruvian Man." She starts to withdraw, measuring her good fortune that she's found him sleeping and can quietly leave. It was enough to see that his penis is too small for his large frame, enough to examine him when he has no idea that he is being seen. But he is too still, too indifferent to the cool air, and Marea acknowledges to herself that something is terribly wrong.

"Eric?" She goes to his side and touches his arm. "Eric? Wake up." She lifts his hand, and it falls like a dead weight. She scans the room until she spots a small length of rubber tubing, spoon, matches on his bureau. "My God," she says aloud, and shoves him hard. "Eric! Wake up! *Wake up!*" She puts her ear to his chest, thinks she hears his heartbeat, but it could be her own racing pulse.

She uses the phone beside his bed to dial the operator, who coaxes her through the crucial information—the address, that someone is unconscious or perhaps dead, that the likely cause is drugs. Marea hangs up and stares at him. This is not the restitution she wanted.

In minutes a siren is bouncing off buildings. Should she have left? She's done her job—she called for help. But she needs to find out if he's alive or dead.

She buzzes open the front door and shouts into the intercom, "You have to work the elevator yourself. There are instructions on the wall inside."

She puts her shoes back on and then waits by the door, relieved not to have to stand over Eric's motionless body anymore. Should she have covered him, covered his small penis?

They jog past her, two men in uniform, necks draped with medical equipment, lugging a folded stretcher, a plastic box of supplies. Marea follows and observes from the bedroom door. One of them puts two fingers to Eric's neck. They wait for a verdict. The waiting goes on forever. The emergency worker nods. Marea doesn't understand what this signifies. He flips open the supply box, withdraws a large syringe, takes aim, and jabs the syringe straight through to Eric's heart. Eric's eyes pop open, bewildered. Who are these men? Who is the woman in his doorway? His eyes close again. He prefers his sleep.

"Come on, come on! Nap time's over, buster."

Eric opens his eyes to a piercing light flashed straight into his eyeballs.

"You're gonna make it, old man, whether you like it or not."

His partner holds up the three glassine envelopes of white powder he's found in a dresser drawer, then drops them into a plastic bag. He tells Marea, "There's bad shit on the street. Your buddy's our sixth overdose since midnight. I take it you're the girlfriend."

"He's my therapist. I found him lying here when I came for my appointment."

"Well, he's gonna make it, thanks to you. We had two others today who weren't so lucky. I guess your therapist owes you a free session or two—or maybe you should look for someone else to tell your troubles to."

"Do I have to go with you?"

"Not with us, but when the police show up, they're gonna have questions. My advice to you is to make yourself scarce before you end up devoting the rest of your day to the NYPD. They'll be here ten minutes after we notify them, which we're required to do."

"Who will you say found him?"

"We'll figure something out. Go ahead, save yourself a hard time."

His partner has opened the stretcher and fit the cross bars to hold it rigid. "Mikey, would you quit trying to get laid and come help me lift this motherfucker."

Mikey scribbles his name and number on a scrap of paper and presses it into Marea's hand. "If you need someone to listen to your troubles, I'm good for a beer and a pizza."

They wrap Eric in a sheet and lift him onto the stretcher. His eyes drift open again, and he reaches out toward the door. "Marea. You're Marea."

"You sure you're not the girlfriend?"

Marea shakes her head. "I'm definitely not the girlfriend."

Mikey uses the same phone Marea used. As he waits for the police station to answer, he cocks his thumb. "Go ahead, beautiful. And don't lose my number."

As Marea rides the elevator down to the street, the words of a nursery rhyme come into her head. *There were four little Indians, and then there were three.*

Nina Wolf doesn't do much to hide her mixed feelings about Marea's return. "You said you were going to call. I might've already rescheduled your time."

Marea feels no need to apologize to the grasshopper perched against the door jamb.

"Is my session taken, then?" Marea asks from the waiting room couch.

"The point is it could have been."

"Should I come back some other time?"

"You're here. I can give you the hour."

As she follows Nina inside, Marea thinks about how little changes in this room, and how little changes in Nina Wolf, who has fixed on her style of dress, taste in furniture, sexual preference, politics.

"I have something I want to read to you. I've been writing about my travels. Would you mind?"

"Why don't you leave it for me to read when I get a free moment? We should use our session for talking."

"Actually, I don't want to talk. I want to read."

"Therapy is about talking."

"Robert's Rules of Therapy?"

"Talking seems to be what most people find helpful."

"I find writing helpful."

"Writing is something you do alone. Therapy is something you do with a therapist."

"When I'm here it feels like I'm alone anyway."

Nina folds her hands in her lap. Last time Marea got her goat. She won't let that happen again. "Why did you come back here if our sessions are so unhelpful to you?"

"Because I wanted to read this to you. When I wrote it, I had you in mind."

"Perhaps you're not as indifferent to me as you'd like to think. Go ahead, then, if you think reading it will help you."

"I'm not saying it will help me. I'm saying it's what I want to do."

Nina raises her hands. "However you like. Go ahead. It's your show."

Marea takes her notebook from her shoulder bag. "I told you about that time in the London Underground when everyone was terrified by the sound we thought was an IRA bomb. This is from that same winter." Marea looks at Nina to be certain of her attention, then opens her yellow notebook to read.

In February the squat was so cold and damp that the best thing was to go outside to walk and warm up. One evening I went out walking along the narrow sidewalks in Stoke Newington. It was raining, as it had been non-stop for weeks. A man waiting for the light to change turned to me and asked if I thought it was ever going to stop. I thought about rain that never stopped, gutters running like rivers, wool coats smelling like socks, life behind windows, the constant yellow glare of tungsten light. Would the adjustments creep up so slowly that people wouldn't even realize that what caused their misery was the constant rain? What about the generation born into an endless rain, melancholy children who would never see a sunrise?

At the next intersection I felt a pair of eyes on my back. I turned to see an ancient woman with a plastic sheet draped over her head and shoulders who whispered to me that she couldn't cross alone. I offered my arm. Her feet were turned in so she couldn't flatten them. Trucks and buses blared their horns after the light had changed against us.

The urine smell that rose from her carried me all the way back to the nursing home where my schoolmates and I were taken to sing "Deck the Halls" and "Silent Night." But was there ever a silent night for these old women whose bedsores and loneliness ate away what remained of them? I was brought up to show respect for elders, and I walked up to one bed to touch the woman's hand and wish her Merry Christmas. The nurse's shriek went off like a fire alarm. She came screaming that we must not touch the patients. I was nine, only just learning to fend off other people's sorrows.

On the opposite side of the street I helped the old woman to the curb and offered to take her farther, but she did not want my pity. I watched until I lost sight of her, and then turned into a shop to look for something to eat. Bells hanging from the door announced my entrance, but no one came out from behind the shower curtain that separated the living quarters from the store. The shelves were empty, only a few matchboxes, candy bars, tins of beef. I heard the scratchy sound of the evening news and smelled the sourness of boiled cabbage. At last an old man pulled the curtain aside and braced himself with one hand on the counter. In the other hand he held his supper fork, a weapon to protect his last tins of beef. The fork began to tremble until his whole body was shaking. I wanted to apologize, to explain I meant no harm, but his wife ducked out from behind the curtain and hissed at me that they didn't need my kind coming round. I thought again of endless rain, of endless rain and endless fear.

Marea looks up. Is it her imagination, or does Nina Wolf seem distracted?

"You can't help me, can you?"

Nina isn't offended by the question.

"Perhaps not."

"What do you think about what I wrote?"

"Maybe I can't help you because you want us to solve the world's problems rather than your own."

"But I thought that was the point of your kind of therapy—that I am formed of the world's problems."

"We're not a good match, Marea. I'm sorry. Sometimes that happens. Things don't click."

"Click?"

Nina leans forward and extends her hand to Marea. "Good luck to you. I'm sure you'll work things out. Clearly you are a very determined young woman."

Marea packs her notebook into her shoulder bag and goes to the door.

"I think you should take down that poem by Adrienne Rich. Put up your own poem, if you have one. You don't understand that poem. Putting it up is a lie."

When she reaches the subway entrance at Ninety-sixth Street, Marea hurries down the stairs, thinking, *There were three little Indians, and then there were two.*

At the West Eighty-first Street stop near the Museum of Natural History, a group of schoolchildren fills the car. They have been to see the dinosaurs. They have romanced a dead species, answering questions on their school worksheets about herbivores and neck strength. The children bounce in front of Marea like superheated atoms, and they bring to mind her own class trip to the Museum of Natural History. They sat on cool marble floors while the teacher led them in a discussion of what could have caused the extinction of such glorious creatures. Were they done in by a cataclysmic event—unleashed forces of nature—or was it a mystery of their own arrogance, some aspect of the way they lived that caused their end? Marea watches the schoolchildren on the subway car. The girls hold hands and the boys punch, but there are a few who look puzzled. For them the movement of life is a little too fast. Marea knows her father was that kind of child, and she was that kind of child, who did not go easily with the rush of things. Marea watches a boy standing apart, his eyes glazed. Is he still pondering the question of the dinosaurs, how inexplicably things vanish forever?

Marea needs three loaves of Andrew's bread to bring to Dr. Iris. She pictures joining the long line of customers that forms outside Dawn's Early Rising each morning. Thinking of Andrew, she longs for him. She steps into a shower stall in the locker room of the YMCA and lets the water and steam enclose her, turning it up hotter and hotter, a glove of heat. She goes back over the absurdity of their last encounter, the eggs dripping down her shins, the playground fountain she found where she splashed her legs with water. Children had gathered around, fascinated to examine the odd adult intruder, until their mothers and nannies, antennae twitching with something not right, called to reel them in.

Outside the row of shower stalls, on wooden slat benches, women and girls dry the crevices of their bodies, bare shoulders bent to their knees. Smells of lotion and perfume hang in the steam. The younger women with smooth skin chatter about television shows and the men they date. The older women, whose skin has stretched, are solitary, mulling over what troubles them, or planning the day ahead. Swimming has energized them all. They have stretched their arms, tensed their legs, traveled up and back between ropes in the clear water. Marea has come from her night of swimming in the subway, in and out of sleep, in and out of words.

At this early hour the streets are full of students on their way to school. As Marea walks down Greenwich Avenue, she catches herself expecting to go around to the alley door to work. It's been two weeks. She wonders if Andrew has hired her replacement.

The line from the bakery reaches down the sidewalk, a fresco of sleepy Greenwich Village types, not at all like the fresh flesh of the shower room or the industrious students hurrying toward their schools. Andrew's people are peaceful souls for whom the pursuit of a superior loaf of bread is a worthy and sufficient endeavor for a weekday morning. They wait and drink coffee from paper cups, reading their newspapers on the quarter fold. Some make conversation or study the chalkboard hanging on the open door to find the day's offerings. Cat Stevens is singing "Moon Shadow" on the radio inside.

Marea peeks to the front of the line, where Andrew is talking with one of his customers. How will she face him after her miserable behavior?

As the line moves forward, Marea pulls her hair back and slips a rubber band around it, then changes her mind and pulls her hair free. Andrew gives his full attention to each new customer who appears before him, and so he only sees Marea when she is first in line.

"I thought you'd be halfway to Australia by now." He opens his arms to enclose her, and she lets herself be hugged.

"I need some bread to take to Dr. Iris."

"Sure. Take your pick."

"I'm a paying customer."

"If you like."

"What happened to your hair?"

Andrew feels his neck where his ponytail used to be.

"Rebecca kept pulling it. It was killing me."

"Sounds like fun."

"It is a lot of fun."

"Have you found someone to help in the bakery?"

"Do you want to come back to work?"

"I've got another job now," Marea says, and realizes that in a way she does.

"So why don't you pay Dr. Iris instead of bringing bread?"

"She likes your bread."

"That's a nice compliment."

Andrew contemplates his shelves and then chooses three loaves. "Pumpkin rye, whole wheat sourdough, and a walnut raisin. How's that?"

Marea offers money, but Andrew won't accept it.

"I told you I want to pay."

"You pay her in bread. Why not pay me in talk? Come visit some night. You don't have to do any work. I miss you."

Marea wants to admit that she misses him, too, but instead she asks, "How's it going with the baby?"

"Honestly, it's been hard. She wakes almost every night. I tried keeping her here with me in the bakery, but that didn't work out, so Tim has to get up with her. He's exhausted all day when he's got his classroom of kids screaming at him. We'll get through it, though. We're figuring it out."

"You've got other customers," Marea reminds him.

Andrew starts to wrap Marea's bread until an idea occurs to him. "Wait here a minute." He reappears with an empty basket and a checked dishcloth, then carefully lines the basket with the cloth, sets the three loaves inside, crosses the corners of the cloth over the bread, and hands the basket to Marea.

"Isn't that how you like to take it to her?"

"But it's your basket."

"So you'll have to return it."

"I'll need more bread next Tuesday. I'll bring it then."

Andrew still has one hand on the basket handle.

"Do I get to know why you ran away?"

She shrugs. "Maybe I wanted to be the only woman in your life."

Marea waits as Dr. Iris lifts the cloth to smell the loaves.

"Whole wheat sourdough, walnut raisin, and pumpkin rye," Marea tells her proudly.

"It's getting to be the season for pumpkins, isn't it?"

Marea settles into her chair, happy to be back in Dr. Iris's world.

"Well?" Dr. Iris asks.

"Well, what?"

"Well, what's the reason for that lovely smile?"

"I'm smiling?"

"You certainly are."

"I guess I've been feeling hopeful. I suppose most people would consider that an ordinary thing."

"But not you?"

"I feel a sense of anticipation—though I have no idea why."

Marea reaches down to her shoulder bag and rummages through it for her notebook.

"I'd like to read you something. I've been using my notebook to write down memories from my travels."

"Very interesting."

"This is another time in Peru. I told you that after I left Machu Picchu I went down into the jungle. This is from that time in the Amazon jungle."

"Your bravery amazes me."

"I hardly think of myself as brave, Dr. Iris."

"Go ahead, Marea. I want to hear about your experience in the jungle."

For the third time in a week Marea opens her notebook to read aloud.

Izcocazín was a tiny jungle settlement that grew up around the cattle trade, a collection of shacks, a grass airstrip, a rooming house, a small store, and a cement slaughterhouse. Single-engine Cessna planes landed once a day to carry the raw meat out to the markets in Lima. People were allowed to ride on the planes only if there was room after loading the beef, so visitors like me sometimes spent days in Izcocazín waiting for a chance to leave.

Izcocazín was so hot and humid that even breathing was an effort of will. Days passed in an unending stream, nothing to mark one from the next. In the river that ran through the settlement, boa constrictors slept in deep pools, and local people caught catfish that weighed as much as humans. German immigrants ran the settlement. They disdained the local people, who feared them, envied them, and were perplexed at how these Germans had been able to get so rich. The jungle pressed in, dark green and dense, and when families emerged from it to trade at the Germans' store, chickens for nylon string, oranges for fish hooks, Don Franz cheated them with such consistency that they barely noticed anymore.

I'd been waiting to get a seat out on the plane for three days, numbed by the humidity and the hot sun and the morning-to-evening sameness. When my body rebelled against too much sleep, I woke one morning well before dawn. I lay in the dark listening to the grunts and scraping of Don Franz's military regimen of exercises and his wife barking at her kitchen staff of Indian girls. Finally I got up and went over to the slaughterhouse, where I was in the habit of washing up each morning.

I had never been there so early before. I pushed through the door and headed toward the sinks, but then froze and turned to what I had blindly passed, what I could not now avoid. Thirty feet from me a cow was strung up from the ceiling, her head cut off, blood gushing from her neck, black-red blood, overflowing the buckets set to catch it, blood spreading across the floor, a blood lake. I pressed my back against the cement wall. Men in black rubber boots and aprons were waiting for gravity to suck the blood out of the carcass. Then something else came into focus. I saw the metal gate that opened into the holding pen, and peering through the rungs of the gate, her head dropped low, was another cow looking on as the blood ran out of its companion's shrinking neck. I saw the full, brown, despairing eyes that looked in on the slaughter. I had never before seen such anguish in any living thing.

Marea closes her notebook and rests it in her lap. She wants to look up and see Dr. Iris's reaction, but instead she studies the texture of the batik cover.

"Is something the matter?" Dr. Iris asks gently.

Marea can't look up now. Her feelings are raw as she waits for Dr. Iris's response.

"Marea, can I tell you something that your writing made me think about? Back when you first came to see me, you said your problem was that your skin was too thin, that you couldn't keep out other people's pain. Do you recall that? Of course you do. It's your life, isn't it, this managing of your skin and your perception?"

Marea feels a flush start from deep inside her, working its way outward.

"What you've written is both moving and upsetting, in the best way."

Marea raises her head. "You liked it?"

Dr. Iris has her chin in her hand, her elbow on the arm of her chair, the posture Marea has grown to know and trust. "Oh, yes, my dear. I liked it very much."

"I don't believe you have an appointment for today." The receptionist pushes the pause button on her tape recorder but does not remove her earpiece.

Marea holds out a large envelope. "I wanted to leave this for Dr. Ross. It's something for him to read."

"We're not set up here to receive packages from patients. Bring it to your next appointment."

"I need him to see it before my next appointment."

"It's so important?"

Marea knows she is being punished for her dislike of this woman.

"Please," Marea pleads.

The receptionist purses her lips, as if considering Marea's request, but clearly gratified to see her humbled.

"I suppose if it's *so* important, I could make an exception this once." She reaches for the envelope, but now Marea can't part with it. It is all she has of him.

"Do you want to give it to me or not?"

"There's no chance it will get lost?"

"If you're that worried, perhaps you ought to keep it and give it to him yourself."

"Do you think you could give it to him right away?"

"Dr. Ross is finishing up his morning appointments. He'll be done in twenty minutes. Is that soon enough?" She is making an exception, but she is certainly not forgiving Marea.

"Yes. Thank you."

"And you'll be coming in at your regular time on Monday?"

Marea nods.

"Very well, then." The receptionist puts the envelope on her desk, and softens enough to give the envelope an encouraging pat.

Marea returns to Sheridan Square on Sunday night at about the same time she purchased her notebook almost three weeks ago. With the evenings growing cool, the street merchants have thinned out, and the carnival aspect is gone, a summer thing. Only the hardcore are left, and they sit hunkered down on stools, silent.

Marea is disappointed when the notebook woman isn't at her spot. She wanted to show that she has kept her promise. In the woman's place a man is selling chunks of crystal, agates, and precious stones.

"There was a woman who used to sell notebooks. She made them herself." Marea removes hers from her shoulder bag. "Like this one. Do you have any idea where she might be?"

"You need another notebook?"

"I have something to tell her."

"Something about a promise?"

"You know her?"

"I had to make a promise before she'd give me her spot."

"Do you know how I can get in touch with her?"

"No clue. She said she was leaving."

Marea digests her disappointment as the man rearranges some of the stones. He is muscular and compact, like a Greek fisherman, broad shoulders, olive skin, forearms covered with dark hair.

"What was your promise?" Marea asks.

He lifts his eyes to take a better look at the woman who has not moved on. "I promised I wouldn't sell my stones to people who don't need them."

"Who needs stones?"

He folds his arms in a show of feigned indignation. "A lot of people need stones. They need something beautiful to keep with them, to touch."

"I'm like that. I have a collection—stones, shells, coral."

"So what was the promise you had to make?" he asks.

"To write down what I see."

"Have you kept it?"

"Yes, I have."

"I'll make *you* a promise. If you give me your telephone number, I'll take you out to dinner."

"I don't have a telephone number."

"Then give me your address. I'll come and get you and take you out."

"No, you give me your telephone number, and maybe I'll call you."

"What if I give you one of my stones, and in exchange you keep your promise to call me."

"I didn't promise."

"No, but you're going to."

"I am?"

"Sure you are."

He looks over his stones and picks up a smooth piece of jade the size of an almond. "I got this in New Zealand. It's traveled quite a distance for you. It matches your eyes." He sets the jade apart from the rest, and then fishes in his pockets for a scrap of paper. "Do you have a pen?"

Marea hands over the ballpoint she uses for her journal. "Have you got a name?"

"Paul."

"Marea."

"Marea. That's a beautiful name—to go with your beautiful eyes."

He writes his number on the paper, puts it on the table, and sets the jade on top of it. "Do you promise to call me?"

"And what do you promise?"

"I promise to love you."

Marea shakes her head. "You're a little off the wall, you know."

"Not at all. You've got the most extraordinary green eyes I've ever seen, and you came back here so you could tell someone you met once that you'd kept your promise to her."

Marea slips the jade and the piece of paper into her pocket.

"So you think I have a good track record on promises?" she asks.

"Either that or you've made a start."

Marea laughs as she starts up Seventh Avenue. Before she realizes it, she's walked all the way back to the YMCA on Twenty-third Street without going into the subway.

Standing in the shower room, one of the pearls on the necklace of female bodies wrapped in white towels, Marea clears a patch on the mirror over the sink. Is she someone a man could love?

For the first time in two weeks she has not gone into the subway to spend the night, but slept instead on a narrow cot in the YMCA dormitory. The girl in the next cot cried in the night, and when Marea asked her what was wrong, the girl apologized for waking her.

Marea smoothes the wrinkles in the skirt and blouse that had been stuffed into her backpack, the outfit she purchased back in June with her first bakery money in order to make a good impression at her interview at the Psychoanalytic Institute. This is how Colin Ross first saw her. She has decided that this is the way she wants him to see her again.

Sitting on the bench in the locker room, her hands pressed between her knees, her skin dampening in the steam heat, Marea is stalled. She feels foolish in her rumpled skirt and blouse. She feels ridiculous with her high school crush on Colin Ross. He has a life apart from her, maybe a girlfriend, maybe even a wife and child. She knows nothing of his life. To him she is nothing more or less than a patient he sees twice a week at her regularly scheduled times. Marea returns to her locker, digs out her jeans and a T-shirt, and changes back into the clothes that say who she is, a woman too skittish for love.

By the time she has made the trip uptown, sat stewing in the waiting room, and followed Colin Ross down the portrait-lined hall, she has worked herself into a cyclone ready to touch down. He is indifferent to her as a woman—sees a client, not a person, the challenge he has to overcome in order to get the "Dr." before his name. She flops down on the couch, folds her arms, digs her hands into her armpits. She is silent, loudly silent, until Colin says very gently, "I read your father's diary over the weekend."

She sinks into a blue regret. Why had she given it to him?

"It's an extraordinary story."

She is livid: Her father's life is a *story*?

"I found it especially interesting the way the child perceives things at one level and not another."

And now I am *the child*.

"So, Marea, I'm curious. What was your reaction when you read his diary?"

Marea's mouth is sealed shut. Her eyes are fixed on motes tumbling in the sunlight streaming through the airshaft window.

"Marea?"

"I'm not cut out for psychoanalysis." She says this in the most detached voice she can muster.

"What do you mean by that?"

"I don't like relationships with rules."

"All relationships have rules," Colin points out. "They're just more explicit in some than in others."

"Straight from the textbook."

"Is it that you'd like more from me than I can give you? Like your father?"

"And what's *that* supposed to mean?"

"Your father had a limited ability to love. That might help explain why you have so much trouble trusting me, because of the limits built into this relationship."

"Transference," Marea says dismissively.

"We don't have to give it a name. But perhaps we ought to talk about your disappointment in your father."

"What disappointment is that?" Marea demands, still fixed on the motes in the light.

"You told me you always thought it was his shame about making nuclear bombs that might have explained a suicide. I wonder if you hoped he felt more guilt about his work than he actually did. After all, you grew up with a terrible fear of nuclear bombs, and it's affected you so deeply."

"I had a dream the night I read his diary."

"Would you tell it to me?"

"If you really want to hear it."

"You know I want to hear it."

Marea turns from the motes in the light to the motes in her mind.

"My father is in a forest—a young man—carrying binoculars, nets, guidebooks, all the supplies he'd take when we went out together into the woods. I observe him from out of sight. He rescues a baby bird from a clump of ferns where it must have fallen from its nest. Then he holds the bird in his hands and sings the prayer he used to sing to me at night before I went to sleep. Then there are loud noises, the sound of a gathering storm. Hundreds of crows fill the sky. The sun and the morning are blacked out. The baby bird starts to bleed. Blood fills my father's hands and overflows onto the ground. Soon he's kneeling in a pool of blood. I'm so frightened I run away. As I'm running everything around me turns to a black river. That was it."

The room is quiet as Colin digests the dream.

"Why did I run away?" Marea asks.

"Perhaps reading your father's diary made you understand that there was no way you could have saved him. And maybe that understanding will allow you to let go of him now. Your father is dead—like that poor bird—and there's no way you can bring him back to life. He would want you to let go and lead your own life, Marea. He would want that because he loved you so very much."

The sobbing that erupts from deep inside her rises up without her will or consent, a sorrow from so deep down that she cannot tell herself apart from it, or from the heat enveloping her, or from the lungs that pull for breath. She cries and cries until the release becomes a dawning pleasure, a cracking chrysalis. She embraces herself, bringing her arms around her chest, and lets the agony pour out. He is gone. She will never turn a corner and find him standing there, never receive a letter telling her where to meet him, never bring him back and set the world right for him. Marea weeps for the man who lost all hope—and for herself, the girl who tried to hang on to to her hope for him for so many empty years.

She feels the closeness of breath, the weight of a hand on her own. Slowly, cautiously, she opens her eyes. Colin is crouched on the floor beside her.

"I didn't feel right leaving you to cry alone."

"Like my father did."

"Yes."

They are both quiet while Marea recovers from her wrenching tears.

At last she says, "I think you're going to make a good psychoanalyst."

He smiles. "I have something for you."

It takes a moment for his legs to uncramp when he stands. He crosses to the desk, opens a drawer, removes a leather binder, burgundy-wine-colored and stitched with green thread.

"I'm returning your father's diary. I hope you don't mind, but I bought something for you to keep it in. I know how precious it is." He walks back to the couch and holds out the binder to her. "It's my gift to you."

Marea sits up on the couch and turns it in her hands. She smells the new leather, then opens it to the first page of the diary, "Compañia Hill, July 16, 1945." The day of her birth.

Marea wakes to the sound of gurgling. Water on stones. Other than that the apartment on Hudson Street is serenely quiet. The shades are drawn on the large living room window that looks out on the river, but the morning sun is filtering through the crack between the shade and the windowsill.

She savors the lightness of the down quilt that covers her on the couch, feeling light herself, the lightness of anticipation that she is coming to trust. Andrew is back from work, asleep in the bedroom. Tim is at school teaching. Baby Rebecca is waking. Marea runs her hands down her sides and feels her own smooth skin.

The sounds from the cradle grow more insistent. Marea pads across the room wearing only her T-shirt and underpants. Rebecca is lying on her back, dressed in a red-striped stretchy, her eyes wide and scanning for something to engage her interest. They flicker at the sight of Marea, who is perhaps nothing but a blur and a possibility.

"You looking for some action?" Marea asks, bending near.

The baby screws her face into a worried pucker. She whimpers, and when Marea sees that she is about to give in to a high-pitched wail, she scoops her up. "Okay, okay. You don't have to pull out all the stops. I'm going to feed you." Marea does a rocking two-step and feels the tension of Rebecca's arching body relax against her shoulder. "It's okay. Everything's okay. You were sleeping. You woke up. Your tummy's empty. There's nothing to worry about. I'm going to get you a bottle, but it takes a few minutes. I'm not a magician, you know."

Marea moves into the galley kitchen off the living room, holding Rebecca as she opens the refrigerator and takes out a baby's bottle half-filled with milk. "Too cold," she informs Rebecca, who now seems to look back at her with intense interest. "We've got to warm it up."

Still holding the baby firmly to her, Marea moves around the kitchen, using her free hand to fill a pot with water, turn on the burner, put the pot on the flame, set the bottle into the water. While the bottle warms, Marea sits down in the kitchen chair and holds Rebecca out in front of her. "You're a beautiful piece of work."

When the bottle is ready, Marea wipes it dry and carries Rebecca back to the living room. She raises the shade and checks the clock on the mantel. Dr. Iris will be expecting her soon. She settles into the rocker by the window and tucks Rebecca into the crook of her arm. She tests the milk before offering the nipple to Rebecca, who sucks tentatively at first, and then with relish. Marea watches her cheeks pull in and push out like two little bellows. She rocks slowly in the chair, allowing herself to pretend for a moment that she is a mother and this is her daughter. Out the window, past the metallic sheen on the river, past the New Jersey ports and the oil pumps, someplace over that horizon, Marea's mother is doing the work of her own day.

Once Rebecca has finished her bottle, she looks up at Marea, eyes wide.

"What's up now?"

Rebecca's eyes go deep, and Marea imagines her question: Am I safe here? Should I stay?

"Come here, you little princess." Marea holds the baby tight to her chest as she pushes up from the rocker. She looks around the small living room, plans her path, and then fits her arms tightly around Rebecca's small body and begins to dance, slowly, carefully, moving around the room, humming the "Merry Widow Waltz." The memories flood in like the warmth of the sun, her grandpa Albert, his big hands, his flying hair, his oompah-pah, oompah-pah, and the day of the December snowstorm, his study, her tears that she could not hold back. Dance, my little princess. When the sadness comes, you dance.

Marea feels Rebecca soften against her chest as she sways with her to the music in her memories. She hears Rebecca's breath slow and then thicken with sleep. She settles her back into the cradle, covers her with the small blanket, and studies her, a little girl with her own compass to discover, someday, with the help of friends.

Marea makes a cup of tea and sits with it at the kitchen table. Her mind travels, going over where she's been, where she's come, so far, at last a beginning. She gets up and goes to the telephone on the kitchen wall. It is seven years since she's telephoned her mother on any day but July 16.

Virginia's voice is tired, dispirited.

"It's me," Marea says cautiously, apologetically.

"Marea?"

"Yes."

"I thought you'd gone away again."

"I'm not traveling anymore. I'm staying in New York."

"Oh?" Virginia allows herself only the fewest of words. She has scared her daughter off before.

"I wanted to let you know that. And I wanted to thank you again for giving me his diary to read."

"I assumed it upset you."

"It helped me."

"I thought I'd done the wrong thing."

"What you said about him losing hold of his life—that helped, too."

"Oh?"

"I think I'm ready to take hold of my own life."

"Can I do anything for you? Can I help in any way?"

"Yes, but I'm not sure how yet. I'm working things out. I promise to call again soon." Marea pauses a moment. "I'm getting better at keeping promises."

After she hangs up, she pencils a note for Andrew: *Rebecca woke—had her bottle—fell back to sleep. I'm going uptown to see Dr. Iris—be back later.*

"I wanted to tell you about my four ways of riding the subway."

Dr. Iris is intrigued.

"Each is a different prism for looking at the world."

"Yes?"

"The first is the psychological way. I study the passengers and see that they all have plays going on stage sets in their heads—and they speak each character's part, trying to put to rest the memories that are troubling them. Sometimes their lips move silently, but mostly they sit perfectly still through their long internal monologues and arguments. It comforts me to know that all passengers have histories they have to accept somehow."

"I understand. Go on."

"The second way of riding the subway I call the political way. I look and see passengers sort themselves into groups according to their clothes, their shoes, the color of their skin, a hierarchy of pigment even among black people. They sort themselves by which newspaper they read, what they carry—a briefcase or a lunch bag. Each person settles his status in relation to the person to his left, his right, opposite. Everybody is on a rung, up or down from somebody else. Each time the train stops and new passengers come in, they are immediately engaged in this sorting, looking at others and at themselves, and I study them.

"The third way of riding the subway I call the spiritual way. That's when I see the fibers that connect everyone and everything. I think of it as the pith between the peel and the meat of an orange, nothing in and of itself, but touching everything and holding all of life together. When I ride the subway and look at the world this way, I know that though this wholeness holds *you*, you can't hold *it*. The person who tries to use it for his own benefit will only harm himself and others. I saw that happen to someone a few weeks ago, another therapist of mine."

It comes out without Marea planning it, and Dr. Iris, sharp as a tack, is already on it.

"Did you say you're seeing another therapist?"

"I'm not seeing him anymore."

"But this is someone you've seen recently."

"Until he overdosed on heroin. I was the one who found him and called the ambulance. He survived, but I'm not going back there anymore."

Dr. Iris cups her hands over her knees and leans forward. "Marea, is all this true?"

"He called himself a Jungian. He said the explanation for our behavior comes from aspects of our being that we can't rationalize, and that true change requires acceptance of these forces."

"Marea, please. Stop. Stop."

Like a child reprimanded, Marea sits up straight and waits.

"Now, slowly, please. I'm trying to understand. You've been seeing another therapist at the same time as you've been coming to me?"

"Four including you."

"Four therapists? That's—extraordinary."

"Is it wrong?"

"There's no right or wrong. But it *is* quite unusual."

"Are you angry?"

"Not angry. Perplexed."

"It's like the four different ways of riding the subway. Each of you is so different from the other. Each of you has a different way of seeing the world. I stopped going to the one who said she looked at things politically. I realized that it was her way of not seeing anything at all. Like I said, I'm not going back to the Jungian, but I did learn something important from him. He helped me see that I could know myself better in relationship to other people. I still see my Freudian. He's only a student training to become a psychoanalyst, but he's sweet and very smart. I think you'd like him. And then there's you, the one who told me that change would feel like freedom."

"Yes, I did say that."

"I wasn't sure I should tell you about the others. I was afraid you'd make me choose. Or you wouldn't let me come back to you."

"And the others—do they know?"

"You were the only one I thought might understand."

"I'm curious about the fourth way."

"The fourth way?"

"Of riding the subway. You've only told me three."

"I haven't figured out what to call it, but I know what it feels like and how it's different from the others. In the fourth way, even though the subway train is speeding ahead, I'm utterly still, at rest within myself, and my mind holds all the smells, sounds, images—all the artifacts I've collected in my life—and what matters most is perception—observing what's around me in all its beauty."

"And then you write it down."

"Yes."

"As you are compelled to do."

"Why is that?"

"It's who you are. To be true to yourself, you have no choice."

"Is that the freedom you promised?"

"I would think so. Isn't that the very best definition of freedom? To know who you are and what you must do—and then to do it."

"May I still come back?"

"My dear, you are always welcome here. Always."

The trains cross on the tracks in front of me, the uptown express and the downtown express passing. I watch and wait, as I always do and probably will do forever, waiting for the moment when they line up, hoping, as always, to see through.

ACKNOWLEDGMENTS

Thanks to the following dear friends, family, and colleagues for invaluable help of all kinds: Lorraine Bodger, Erin Curler, Susan Dalsimer, Gil Eisner, Amy Entelis, Jonathan Galassi, Anne Garrels, Michael Gates Gill, Elizabeth Kaplan, Sarah McGrath, Julie Michaels, Susan Moldow, Merlyn Ruddell, Martha Saxton, and Jann Wenner.